blue valentine

Justin picks me up and holds me to him, his arms bulging with muscles as he sets me astride his rock-hard body. I work him rhythmically, sure of exactly the type of sensation that he favors. Before I start pumping, I click the automatic button on the camera, knowing that every fifteen seconds, the camera will take another shot.

X-rated. Down and dirty. The kinds of pictures that make me happy I have my own darkroom. I'd never be able to drop a roll this explicit off at the local Fotomat.

You wouldn't think it would be possible, but soon I manage to forget about the intrusion of the lens. I am too focused on staring at Justin-into his dark eyes so deep chocolate-brown they look black. His skin is burnished from hours on his surfboard, his body is sleek and lean. I suck in my breath as I push up on him, knowing exactly how to give him pleasure, but also how to take the pleasure myself. "That's the way, baby," Justin croons. "Just like that—"

alison tyler

BLUE VALENTINE

an erotic romance

First Magic Carpet Inc. edition November 2002

Published in 2002

Manufactured in th United States of America
Published by Magic Carpet Books

Magic Carpet Books
PO Box 473
New Milford, CT 06776

Library of Congress Cataloging in Publication Date

Blue Valentine by Alison Tyler
ISBN 0-9726339-0-1

cover design: stella by design contact: stellabydesign@aol.com

Dedicated to SAM

When I cast my eyes and see
That brave vibration each way free,
Oh how that glittering taketh me!
—Robert Herrick

PROLOGUE

You've heard of *The Illustrated Man*, right? Sure, you have. Most everyone at least *knows* about the classic book by Ray Bradbury, even those who never made it through the whole thing back when it was required reading in high school English class. The famous tome features a multi-tattooed man whose colorful stories come to life within the pages of the book. It's my belief that this is the original concept behind the idiom "Every picture tells a story."

I'm like that.

Not tattooed—although I do appreciate the mind-set of people who sport an artistic bit of ink on their bodies—but I'm like that with stories. Or photographs, really. My pictures are an updated form of the dark-and-twisted tattoos in the book. Fiercely animated, my photos come to life for those who take the time to get to know them. At least, they do for me. They are born when I click the shutter—captured and tamed within the hard plastic shell of my camera, but alive. Then they breathe in deeply when I silently develop them in the inky black privacy of my darkroom. Now they are howling wordlessly in public, and I'm certain that others in the crowd sense their desperation to make a difference and to be noticed.

When I look around at the gallery, I see each photo blown up to giant size and I'm startled by the effect the images have on me. These are my best photos from the last four-and-a-half years, and I think that old cliché really is true: every picture does tell a story. In this case, these aren't just anybody's stories. Not the story of some model or some pompous 'creator-slash-artiste.' They're *my* stories, the stories of my life.

But maybe I'm just drunk.

Curators always serve champagne at gallery openings, to help lubricate the wallets of those who might actually make a purchase. It's easier to spend money on frivolous, fanciful items when everyone around you is joyous and cheery. Tonight's party is no exception. The green bottles being passed by handsome waiters and lithe young waitresses hold mid-range champagne, certainly, but I can't tell the difference between this and the good stuff. Up-and-coming artists don't get a shot at high-end liquor all that often. So maybe the third glass of bubbly has gone to my head and made me wax poetic. Perhaps at this point of the evening, I'm giving more weight to old-fashioned fortune-cookie statements than I generally would. Maybe, but maybe not. Because as I look around the whitewashed walls at the giant photos that I took, my past screams to life from each picture.

Don't understand my point? It will only take a moment for me to show you exactly what I mean.

See that one? The one of the handsome man with the cigarette dangling insolently from his full, heartbreaker lips? That's Justin. From the looks of things, it appears as if he's been up all night, doesn't it? And you know what? He has, and for all intents and purposes, in that particular picture he always will. Forever, in that frame, he will have been up all night doing dirty, devious things he shouldn't have been doing with a woman he shouldn't have been doing them with. Trust me when I say that actors will demolish your heart every time. Why actors over the rest of the male population? Because you never can be totally sure that they're not acting when they're with you. Do they really love you, or is that just another line of dialogue? With the good actors, you can never be totally sure.

That's why I'm moving on. Why I've moved on. Why we should just move the f— right on to the photo next to him, a startling picture of my best-friend Kate. She's the one who pushed me to get my pictures displayed here. The one who always has faith in me, even when I no longer have faith in myself. She's the type of girl I'd like to be someday, because she doesn't care what people think of her and so she is free to say what she wants. Like now, in real time, as she slides toward me in a jade-green dress that gently caresses her dangerous curves and perfectly matches her amazing almond-shaped eyes. She comes to stand at my side and view the photo I took of her one day when she was not at all prepared to be captured on film.

"Had to get me coming out of the shower, didn't you?"

"You look like a movie star," I tell her.

"Porn star."

"Same thing," I shrug, but I'm just teasing. She looks lovely in the picture and she knows it. Her wet hair curls deliciously around her foxy face; her eyes are open and accepting of the intrusion of the lens. Unlike many of my friends and acquaintances, Kate never holds up a hand to stop me. She's one of the few people who doesn't pose, doesn't make a mocking face or crinkle up her features. With an unstudied grace, she allows me the freedom take her picture. True to the core.

Tonight she's kidding about minding being displayed up there, because I know she's proud of how good she looks in the picture. Not only stunning, but honest. That's the best thing about my photographs—I capture honesty with every single shot. My main goal is to try not to glamorize the world. Yeah, I know that some artists see whimsy wherever they go, but I don't want to. My job is not to doll up reality, not to make it surreal, or even different. I take pictures of what I see, and then I share my vision with anyone who cares to look.

Although some pictures are harder to share than others. Some mean more. And the truth is that you rarely know which one is going to win (or break) your heart when you take it. Sometimes as the shutter clicks, you have a feeling, but until you get into the darkroom and make the pictures come to life, you don't know for a fact.

Across from the photo of Kate is my prize piece—that winsome girl with the long wave of dark hair and oval-shaped eyes that look silver in the black-and-white picture. She's wearing a soft-looking black velvet turtleneck and signature silver hoop earrings, and I hear one of the patrons whisper as he walks by, "Such a pretty girl."

"Why are the eyes so sad?" Kate asks. "Hey, Alex, why such a blue Valentine?"

Simple. The woman in the picture is me. And she's finally caught on to Justin's false charms. Not by luck, though, by sheer will. Following him. Tracking him. Taking the pictures that prove what simple guesswork couldn't. Because the fact is that pictures don't lie. Everyone else might. Everything else might point you in the absolute wrong direction.

Not a photograph.

Over there, across the room, there's a picture of Connor. But it's too early for me to tell you about him. And besides, the art journalist from the Times is here to talk to me about my work. I like the sound of that. "My Work." No one better to start a buzz going then yourself, right?

So I'd better do the interview now, before I get too plastered to clearly converse. If I'm going to be quoted in a big-time newspaper, I don't want to sound like a total idiot. In fact, I'd like to sound as if I know something about something. About anything.

So enjoy the show... I'll catch you later, over by the champagne, and I'll introduce you to the rest of the pictures—I mean, people.

BOOK ONE

Snap!

CHAPTER ONE

The counter top is cool beneath me. My long coltish legs are spread wide apart, and just in case I could spread them any farther, I have my hands splayed firmly on the insides of my inner thighs, pressing out. This is almost a yoga-like move, but we aren't practicing our stretching exercises here, nor are we in the midst of some new-wave gym class or Zen-like meditation mode.

No way. Not us.

This exercise is purely carnal. A physical connection that requires two hungry people—or as kinky-minded Kate would say, two people, *minimum*—caught in a wave of the truest and most base sort of lust. Doesn't matter that Justin and I have been together for four years, or that we're supposed to be slowing down in our attraction to each other. Doesn't matter that he was up all last night at a grueling movie shoot in Pasadena's Old Town while I spent the evening taking candid photos of glamorously drunken guests at a private Tantamount Hotel party. We are hot for one another, and ready for one another, and Justin knows just what I need.

"Like that," he croons. "Right, baby? Just like that."

He hasn't showered since coming home, and I can smell the scent of his skin, a reminder of his day of hard work. Turns me on, I have to admit. The real smell of him always turns me on. Like the scent of his T-shirt at the end of the day, or the way his body smells of sand and surf and sun when he comes in from a morning spent out at the beach. There's something honest about the way that he smells, and it arouses me more than any of the fancy, high-end colognes on the market.

I feel the demanding ache at the split of my body, but it's a desirable sort of pain. I'd compare the sensation to a post-workout throb--a good, solid feeling that pulses through my entire body in waves of heat. I like being upright like this, like the fact that we're in the kitchen rather than the bedroom, where we'd most likely be sprawled out on our four-poster bed. A change of scenery has managed to alter entirely the way I feel, transforming a late afternoon's romantic romp into a completely hedonistic experience. Who'd have thought that all it would take is moving from one room to another?

I guess Justin would, because he's the one who suggested this. And maybe he truly understands the magic of a scene change, since he's an actor. He knows all about sliding into a costume, about walking onto a phony set and pretending that everything around him is real. He knows all about a lot of things, but now, the only thing that's important to me, is what he knows how to do with his tongue.

Trust me, when I say that he knows a lot.

Justin bends easily between my legs, his mouth is already busy. I can't believe how intense this feels. I'm instantly close to climax at the way his tongue makes those dreamy, loopy circles. Up and over. Around and around. Intricate ovals within diamonds take me right up to the brink in moments. He understands exactly what I like. From our years together, he has learned well, discovered my favorite ways of being pleased. And *oh* does he please me. I sigh and have to move my hands now, putting them behind me to support my weight. I lean back on my flat palms, my head tilted upwards so that I'm looking at the pale sky-blue sponge-painted ceiling, my long dark hair falling down past my shoulders. My glossy tresses tickle the naked skin of my back. How sexy is that?

I'm not entirely nude. I have on a pink-and-white checkered sundress with bra-style straps that crisscross in the back. The dress is innocent on the surface, definitely, but my Parisian white lace-edged panties are already lost in a silken puddle on the floor and my dress is bunched up forcefully at the waist. Justin slides his hands under my hips, lifting me up a bit off the counter so that he can work me even deeper. Then he continues to trick his tongue in the most decadent manner. He is a master at this—I can't believe how sweet it feels when he makes those ovals and spirals with his tongue, and then he darts away, to kiss my slender thighs and nip playfully at my skin, letting the pleasure subside for a moment until I am sighing again. Sighing and moaning and begging. Justin revels in making me beg. He likes the power behind being in charge, and he likes knowing that eventually I will actually grovel in order to get what I want. At those precarious moments when bliss is only a flicker of time away, I lose all aspects of modesty. I can't help myself. Why would I want to? I have no goal in sight except to reach the ever-so-close place called 'coming.'

"Please," I say to him. "Oh, Justin, please."

He pauses, because anticipation is his favorite power game. He knows that if he leaves me teetering on the precipice for several moments, I will climax that much harder when I finally reach the end. That sounds wonderful on paper, but in real time, I lose myself in desperation.

"Please—" I beg again. "I can't wait. I mean, don't make me—"

"So hungry," he teases, "such a hungry girl," and his fingers momentarily take over from his mouth. He strums against me, tapping and scrolling right up and over the place where I need him most. I arch and press forward, striving to gain any bit of the contact I so desperately crave. When he sees that I'm almost there, my cheeks flushed strawberry pink, my dark eyes wide and ravenous, he gives in to me.

Yes, I think. *Yes, my sweet baby. That. Do that. THAT!*

Bending again, he goes right back to work, with his lovely full lips ringing that most precious spot at the center of my body. Wetness meets wetness as his tongue touches me. He draws forth a fresh wave of my heady, steady cream, and I lift even higher off the counter. My eyes are shut tightly now as I feel myself begin to slide down the cresting slope into the purest form of desire. But Justin has other ideas. Doesn't he always? His bag of sexual tricks is never empty.

"Watch," he says. "Come on, baby doll. You watch me."

He likes when I look. He always likes to feel my eyes on him, paying attention, noticing every move. Every stroke. He knows exactly how much I can take in with a single glance. As a photographer, objects line up in my vision. I categorize every part of every image. The shapes I see. The colors. The light as it shifts and dances. Just because we're in the midst of the sexiest scenario I can remember in recent history, doesn't mean I am able to turn off my artist's eye when I gaze around the room. Even if I wanted to, I couldn't. I see the pale yellow walls of our kitchen that Justin and I spent two full days painting. I see the gray-silver metal of our stainless steel sink and the translucent shadows that move and glide on the black-and-white tiled floor.

"Watch," he insists, and I do. I take it all in. Take in every single image—

Like now, as he stands fully and lifts me off the counter, despite my desperate little coo of displeasure. I don't want him to stop.

"Not now," I beg. "Not yet!"

"Trust me," he says, flipping me around so that my hands are on the counter top and he is right behind me. My dress gets pushed again past my naked hips, and then I hear the pop of Justin's fly as he pulls open the buttons of his favorite faded jeans in a quick rush. One, two, three, four—all will be revealed. All that is necessary for this type of risqué game.

I feel his body on mine, his skin so warm against my own. My fingers grip into the counter but find no place for purchase. I think he will enter me right away, but once again, Justin has other plans. He lets me feel the rock-hardness of his sex and then he rubs it once against me. I moan so loud I'm sure we'll be found out. That our neighbors will call the super to complain about us. Again. But I can't bother myself with worries of possible future repercussions. Everything after this moment seems unimportant. I am lost in the almost unnamable yearning for release.

"Say it," Justin urges.

"Please!"

"No, baby," he laughs at my mistake, "Talk. Say what you need."

He likes when I verbally take charge of my pleasure. He likes the rich husky sound of my voice telling him exactly what I want. That takes him to a higher level, which moves me up a level with him. It turns me on to turn him on. And who am I to deny him after he has so sweetly treated me?

"I need you inside me," I tell him, and he moans to let me know that I'm going in the right direction. "I can't wait any longer for you to be inside me, Justin," I continue. And that's all that takes. That's the key that undoes the wondrous future of the rest of this sensuous session. Justin slides in deep and then seals his body to me. He's so hard and so big that I groan and arch my back at the intrusion. I am instantly filled even more firmly, and then emptied as he thrusts and pulls away, thrusts in again, even further, hands holding onto my hips to steel me for the ride.

"Again," he says.

"Do me," I insist. "Come on, Justin. Don't tease—"

"More," he says. "Keep talking." Justin so loves it when X-rated words make their way past my usually G-rated lips. My inhibitions melt away when we make love. There is no barrier, no boundary that I'm not willing to cross. At least, none that we have discovered so far.

"Just like that," I tell him. "Do me just like that. I can taste you in the back of my mouth when you ride me like that. So hard. So firm."

Is this really me talking? I hear my own voice, but don't recognize the dialogue as words that I would actually say. Yet Justin has brought me to this island in time where nothing matters but our pleasure. Where nobody will be harmed by the things we say or the actions we do.

Now, Justin brings one hand underneath my waist, searching out the split between my legs. His fingers tickle knowingly against me, taking over the remainder of the ride from where his mouth was only moments before. I am sticky and sweet on his fingertips. He tells me so as his other hand finds my mane of hair, and he holds on and uses this grip to turn my head. My heavy hair has become a set of reins, and he pulls me back just at the right moment. Just when I climax.

SNAP!

The camera resting on my tripod was set on a fifteen-minute timer, and Justin, with his uncanny internal clock knew exactly how to get the picture. This will be a striking picture of my face, my eyes open but lids heavy with the pulsing arousal within me, lips parted with a ravenous sigh so deep it echoes, hair pulled back. Nothing else will show in this photo, only my pleasure. My pleasure forever. Even if we someday dissolve as a couple, the photo will be there as a remainder and as a reminder.

*****

"That one," the journalist from the Times says, pointing. "Tell me more."

"I haven't had enough champagne yet," I smile, reaching for a fresh glass from a passing waiter. "Try me with something less seductive."

He shakes his head at me, and I can tell that he thinks I'm being arty and flirtatious. I'm not. I'm dead serious.

"All right," he says. "Self-portrait with blindfold."

"Not less seductive," I argue.

"But very interesting—"

"So...."

CHAPTER TWO

Next night, in bed, it's Justin and I playing another one of our favorite boudoir games—a guessing game complete with a sumptuous fabric blindfold and an assortment of unusual and unexpected items residing on our bedside table. I'm the one in the dark this time—literally in the dark beneath the blindfold—and I feel Justin raking different objects over my naked skin. My nerve endings are alive and crackling while my mind is busy trying to place each sensation and make sense of it.

"Come on," Justin says. "Guess."

I feel confused in the most sexy way imaginable.

"I can't," I tell him.

"Try," he insists.

Although I'm settled comfortably on the ruby-red satin sheets in the center of the bed, I am desperately off-balance. Even so, I like the darkness, and the velvet blindfold over my eyes. I like putting my faith in Justin. Not that I'd ever doubt him. I have no reason to. Yet in this case, I have to believe that he has my best interests in mind. That he won't do something disturbing while I wait blindly for the next phase of the game. Trust. It's as much an aphrodisiac to me as the way he strums and strokes different objects on my naked skin.

The rules to this sexual sensory experience are simple. Justin runs something over my body until I am able to correctly guess the name of the item in question. Then he chooses another object to try. It's a fun test to experience. With my vision taken away, I have to focus all of my attention on the stroking of the chosen article on my body. There's more to it than that. Justin doesn't let me cradle the items with my hands, or touch them with my fingers. Instead, he rubs and caresses different parts of my body with the toys and tools of his choosing, so that I have to feel with my inner thighs or the lower part of my back, or the nape of my neck and try to judge and guess from these odd tickling sensations what Justin is using.

He's very clever. Let me assure you. He always keeps me guessing.

On this night, he starts with something soft and light. Fairy-wing light of the finest material—like panties or a bra. Maybe it's a slip or a negligee. My mind tries to categorize the sensation. Not satin. Not lace. But so light, so delicate and airy. What could it possibly be? I clench my eyelids closed even tighter beneath the blindfold, as if that will somehow help me to "see" more clearly.

"You don't know yet?" Justin teases. "Are you sure, or are you just playing?" The silkiness of the fabric tantalizes the high-rise bones of my cheeks and then the soft curve under my chin. Now, he drapes whatever this piece of clothing is along my belly. Runs it all the way down over the split of my body, then dangles the mysterious object between my legs. It touches and strokes me over my nether lips, and I groan and arch my body upward, even as I picture what the item is: a pair of my stockings. I know that's what he's using, even though this feels so different from when I'm wearing the stockings under a skirt, attached to a sturdy yet feminine garter belt. The stockings have completely transformed into a sex toy, and I would be happy to have Justin tickling me with the single stocking for hours. Still, as soon as I name the item correctly, he discards it in favor of something new, because that is the rule of the game.

Next, he chooses something more substantial but slippery, and I have to focus more seriously to guess correctly. This item has an interesting hardness to it. Not a raincoat or a pair of gloves. But vinyl-feeling, and shiny. I never knew what 'shiny' felt like before. It's almost a wet feeling, even though I know the object is dry. Justin turns the item around in his hands, so that I feel different parts of the unnamed item against me. He runs it under the line of my arm, all the way to meet my body, and I squirm and giggle as he drags it over my ribs. Then suddenly the picture comes clear to me: this is one of my patent-leather high-heeled shoes. Justin has a thing for my lovely collection of sexy shoes—especially this particular pair. He likes me to wear them with a red-and-black schoolgirl skirt, and has even asked me to don a pair of knee-high socks and a sweet little black cardigan sweater. That almost innocent bit of kink can manage to push him over the edge. I don't mind. Costumes can be a fun and creative outlet in the bedroom.

I can tell that Justin is having fun being the master of my pleasure. He's gathered a collection of items to use, and he seems intent at stretching the game out as long as I'm wiling to play. The best part of this situation is how caught up I get in the guessing portion of the game, even as my body starts to grow more and more aroused by the way that Justin touches me with one item after another. The sensations are as intriguing as they are enticing, and I respond in unusual ways to each stroking touch. Who would have thought being stroked with a shoe would make my nipples so hard?

Third is a sleep mask. Fourth is a cool water glass pilfered from the end table. Although I find the different sensations enticing, Justin doesn't linger once I name the tool. But finally he chooses something that I don't want to name. Not because I'm upset by his choice, but because it feels so damn good.

Fluffy, intricate waves of lightness brush along the inside of my leg, up the entire length then down the other. The feeling is almost maddening, and I squirm, but force myself not to say, "No," and also not to tell him that I do know what he's tickling me with. As soon as I name the item, he will go on to the next, and I don't want that. Really, I don't want that. Although it's difficult to believe that tickling could be sexy, the way that Justin works this item has me creating a shimmering pool beneath me on our satin sheets. I can feel precisely how aroused I am.

"Come on, sweetheart," he urges. "You know this."

He's right. I do.

It's a feather. A long, white feather from our toy box of exotic and erotic play things. Sometimes being tickled is torturous for me. I have to be in the mood to completely give over to Justin and to his whims and wiles. But on this evening, I dive fully and willingly into the experience of surrendering to Justin with every part of my body. I grip my hands together over my head, and I set my jaw tightly and prepare to take every moment of the action. To own it. Justin sees that I am ready. Somehow he knows that I'm competing with him. Can he make me break, or will I win? Since winning means coming, I have a lot at stake here.

Justin uses the feather in the most delicious manner. He runs the very tip over my rosy nipples, then down the basin of my concave belly, and then he stops. I thrust upwards on the mattress, urgently. I am so into this moment, I can't even understand the noises I'm making. Wordless, begging sounds that mean nothing and everything, as if I'm speaking another language. But I'm sure that it's a language that Justin is fluent in, which is a relaxing thought.

The feather travels over my skin, and I feel the goose bumps rise up. The hair at the back of my neck grows prickly and wet. The muscles in my back are tight and vibrating. I'm aware of every subtle change in my body. And mostly I'm aware that what I want more than anything else is the feel of that feather between my legs. Oh, won't that be amazing! The tiny little feathery fingers fluttering over that sacred region will take me higher than anything else we've done this evening. The soft stroking texture of them, the delightful weight, so light it's almost an accidental caress—I can't wait. But I know from past experience that if I tell Justin what I want—if I spell it out clearly and precisely—he won't give it to me. At least, not right away. He's not a cruel man by any means; he's only on a deprivation kick. The longer he makes me wait, the better the end results will be. We both know that, don't we? We've done the Tantric sex thing— six hours of intense breathing followed by the most mind-blowing orgasms. We know all about postponing pleasure, of denial as an extremely erotic aphrodisiac. On a dare, we've gone a whole week without sex, telling each other in greatly detailed emails and in heated conversations over the phone line exactly what we are going to do to one another when the week is up. That was a true test of wills. When one of us threatened to cave, the other held fast.

Yet tonight I'm a selfish, ravenous creature. I'm part of the me generation, meaning that I want my pleasure, and I want it now. When I groan and arch, Justin makes a "tsk, tsk" noise with his tongue against the roof of his mouth, and I know that he's going to stop everything. He's going to make me tremble and wait, shiver and shudder. In the soft inky darkness under the blindfold, he will let me tremble until the climax is millimeters away from me and I still won't be able to reach it.

SNAP!

That's when the camera goes off. I know instinctively what I look like. The camera's intruding lens will have immortalized my hair falling over my flushed cheeks, the rippled velvet of the black blindfold, the yearning in my full, parted lips. Because it is outside of the frame, no one will know about the feather.

Just the pleasure.

*****

So I don't tell all of that to Hal, the journalist who is writing the piece about me and my photos. Not because I'm embarrassed, but because it's private. How strange is that for a concept? I've got a picture on a wall of a gallery that shows my face with blindfold on and dark hair framing my heated, yearning expression. Yet it's too personal for me to describe what I was feeling or thinking when the photo was snapped.

Instead, I say, "Plunged into darkness, yet still able to see," and Hal writes that down in his notebook before moving on, to my great relief, to a picture of Kate.

"She's a model?"

"A friend."

"She could be a model."

"I know."

"Close friend?" he asks, and I understand what he's implying, but I don't comment. "What was your goal?" he asks next. "What were you hoping to achieve?"

That's always the question, isn't it?

CHAPTER THREE

Kate and I have weekly dates. Knowing that we are going to get together every Monday gives me something to look forward to. Yes, we often end up seeing each other more than once a week, but our standing Monday-night date is sacred. Nothing gets in the way of our plans.

This evening, she has a new story to share with me. This isn't surprising. Kate always has a new story. Practically every time we get together, I can depend on her to shock me with some detailed erotic escapade. All right, so maybe in many respects I'm easily shockable. Or maybe Kate revels in telling me things that will make my eyes go big and make me say, "Really? You're kidding! You didn't!" Tonight, as we settle onto two bar stools at our favorite watering hole, she confesses that she's got one to share about her handyman, and I can't help but rib her a little, even though my interest is definitely piqued.

"Isn't that an old Alberta Hunter song?"

She tilts her head at me, obviously not able to place the name of the singer. I can tell from her expression that the name means nothing to her. Kate's more into bands like Crazy Town and The Red Hot Chili Peppers. She likes things hard and fast—from her men to her music.

"Old jazz-blues-y singer," I tell her. "You'd get a kick out of her sense of humor. She has this incredibly X-rated song about her quote-unquote handyman. He trims her lawn and he chops her meat. He gives her a nice fresh *piece* every day—"

"I don't know about any of that," Kate says, "I'm telling you about Davey."

"Davey," I repeat the name, smiling. "Sounds like a Boy Scout."

"No," she says, shaking her head. "Not at all, Alex. He's a *man* scout. All man. Trust me."

"So tell me," I say, egging her on. I like the way Kate tells stories. She draws them out with plenty of lascivious detail, as if she's penning scripts for some spicy TV movie. Living vicariously through her romantic escapades is one of my favorite activities. When you've been in a monogamous relationship for several years, sometimes just hearing about somebody else's sexual scenarios is sort of like foreplay. Later, I can go home and share my favorite parts with Justin—if he's lucky.

"You know I was having work done at my place," Kate says.

"Yeah, you complained all week. You said you couldn't get into your shower. Couldn't get into your kitchen. Couldn't bring any dates home—"

"That was just talk," Kate says, coming clean. "I liked him from the start. He was delicious. Dark hair. Dark eyes. Built. You know. *Really* built."

I nod. It's easy enough to imagine that. She's talking about a handyman, after all. They're supposed to be built. I mean, they build things for a living, right?

"And even while he was working, he watched me everywhere I went. If I came into the kitchen while he was fixing the sink, or if I wandered by him in the bathroom, I could feel his eyes on me.

And he winked at me each time, chuckled when I tried to discuss building topics with him. What do I know about dry wall, right? I was pitifully lacking when it came to engaging in small-talk about construction work."

"Sure, that's just not your thing," I say.

"But that didn't bother him at all. Because at the end of the day, he wasn't really interested in conversation."

"No?" I raise my eyebrows at her as I raise my mandarin Cosmopolitan to my lips. Kate leans closer as she gets into the dirty details that I've been waiting on the edge of my barstool to hear. "On the last day that he was going to be there, I told him that I had one more thing that I needed him to look at. And then I led him to the bedroom."

"You slut," I laugh.

Kate's not in the least bit offended. She just cocks her head at me with a serious look on her face, and then grins. "He understood immediately. He picked me up, stripped me down, spread me out on the bed. He used his own leather belt to fasten my wrists together."

"You let a stranger tie you down?"

"He wasn't really a stranger, Alex. Not someone I met on the street. He'd been working at my apartment for a week. We'd had coffee together, beers in the evening. We'd practically been dating, if you think of it that way."

"All right. So then what?"

"He fixed me."

"Were you broken?"

She giggles. "I mean, he screwed me."

"Oh, god," I sigh, guessing somehow where this is going. Still, I can't keep the pictures from my mind, and the pictures shock me as Kate continues her story for my listening pleasure.

"With a screwdriver," Kate spells it out for me, her voice hushed for once. "The handle was so smooth and rounded inside me."

"You didn't." Even as I say the words, I know that she did.

"Oh, yeah," she says, happily. And then she turns toward Van, the bartender, and asks for a Screwdriver. Just to mess with me. That's the way Kate likes to play.

"How could you do something like that?"

"He was so fine," Kate says. "Just so amazingly hot. And the tools were unbelievably sexy. I couldn't believe how it felt to have the heavy weight inside me. It was more erotic than sex toys— far more sexy because these were utilitarian items. They weren't fake contraptions, or molded plastic dildos. They were real. That's the difference."

"So what else? What else did you do?"

"*You're* the real slut," Kate smiles. "You want to know every single thing that happened, don't you? Admit it."

"Slut by osmosis," I say, waiting.

"His fingertips were all wet and I lifted my hips up off the bed, meeting him, helping him. Then he met my gaze and he saw that I wanted more. And it was just amazing. He said, 'I'm ready for you. I can fix anything you want.'"

Kate's fresh drink arrives then, and I'm glad that we are at a breaking point in the conversation, because I can just imagine what Van might say if he caught onto what Kate is talking about. But when he moves on down the bar again to help a randy-looking redhead, I decide to tell Kate about what's been going on with Justin. Rarely, do I share our bedtime secrets. I don't need validation from her, and I also don't need to hear the stories echoed back at me to make them seem real. But it's been so sexy lately, that I want to tell her. I mean, I just want to. Not to brag. Not to try to shock her, because there's no way I could. But just to share.

Kate listens carefully, and then she says, "Watch out, Alex."

It's not what I expect to hear from her. "What do you mean?" I ask.

"Just watch out."

"Just what do you mean?" I ask her again.

"When the sex heats up like it has with you two there might be a different reason."

"Different from what?" I don't precisely know where she's going with this, but I don't think I'm going to like it when she explains. I toy with the straw from my drink rather than look into the fierce heat of Kate's emerald eyes.

"From just rekindling a romance. You've read about that sort of thing, haven't you?"

I shake my head. I don't read the trashy magazines that Kate likes.

"When guys are cheating they often have even better sex with their partners."

"That's twisted," I say.

"But it's true."

"But why are you bringing it up?" I ask her. "Do you know something?"

She remains mute.

"Come on, Kate. Do you?"

I can see in her eyes that she doesn't want to tell, and for some reason I don't push her. Perhaps, I should, but I just shake my head and say, "Not Justin. I know him. He loves me."

"Maybe so," Kate agrees. "But watch your back."

*****

The truth is, when it comes right down to it, I'd far rather watch my front. Watch as Justin licks between my thighs. I mean to tell him about Kate and her handyman. It's in my head to describe exactly what she told me, because I know that Justin will enjoy hearing this deliciously decadent story. Maybe he'll break out a few tools of his own, slip one cold plastic handle inside me after another. But when Justin does what he's doing right now, all I can manage to say is, "Oh—"

Up and down he goes, his tongue caressing my inner lips, searching out my pearl, moving at just the right speed and with the perfect pressure, and I say, "Oh—"

He moves up and down, his face pressed to me, his tongue

tricking and tripping right along the seam of my body. Then he lifts up just long enough to say, "I love the way you taste," and I sigh. I can hardly take it when Justin talks like that to me. "And I love the way you get so still," he continues, "waiting to see how far I will take you."

"How far?" I beg. "Tell me. How far—"

"All the way to the final crest," he promises. "As far as you need to go. So just let it happen—"

"Oh," I say, "oh—" stretching out that single, simple word until it takes on a brand-new meaning. But what does it mean anyway? The sultry way I sound when I moan, my lips pursed, that sound emanating from my lips—what does it possibly mean except "More" and "Yes" and "Now" and "Please." I wish I could be one of those women who are aces at dirty talking. I'd love to describe in great detail everything that Kate spent the evening telling me at the bar. And yet, I go almost mute as Justin's tongue plays me. He knows how to make me squirm and blush, getting closer and closer, and I say, "Oh, yes. Oh, sweet baby. Yes."

Then he stands for a moment and presses against me, and I can feel how aroused he's become. Something about that medley of my words makes him so hard. Something about the way my voice breaks, the way my cheeks flush, the way my breathing speeds up until I can almost feel my heart beating throughout every part of my body. Something about the way I come makes him come.

He waits for it. He manages to hold control over his own raging orgasm until he senses the change within me. He waits until I am there, until I've actually sucked in one trembling breath to let him *know* that I'm there, and then he moves and slides inside me. I tighten on him, welcoming him in a series of powerful, tight squeezing contractions. And still, I moan that word, "Oh—"

That's what makes his own climax burst through from his core, wracking his body with spasm after spasm. He comes quieter than I do. He is contained in a manner. His dark shimmering eyes might glow, his lips part, but no sounds issue forth. He lets me do all the talking. If you can call it that. All the sighing is a more genuine description. All the heated moaning.

My lips pull back from my teeth, my head tilts back and my long hair falls away from my face. Then my voice, softly at first, says, "Oh...," and he swallows hard and stills himself on top of me, obviously waiting to hear it again, but this is an endless, circular game, because I won't continue if he doesn't continue, so he rocks forward, pressing into me, filling me, and I reward him, "Oh, sweet..."

And he stops again and waits, and I stop again and wait, eyes locked on his now, telling him secrets with my gaze. Can he decipher the code of my silence? He should be able to. What I want is simple. It's the simplest thing in the world. All I want is for him to keep going, but I won't tell him what to do. I'll just wait for him, and so he rocks forward and fills me and my voice grows louder and I wrap my thighs around him pulling him down.

"Oh, sweet baby. Oh..."

He draws in his breath, and he grips onto my hips, and he slides in and out, quicker now, and then he brings one hand down to touch me. Just to touch me. And I'm so hot and ready that I come again, my voice rising in pitch, "Oh. Oh, Ohhh—"

And together, together, we are transported.

*****

"That one," Hall says, pointing.

It's Justin. A hazy, gray shot of Justin right after we made love. I look at it and sigh softly, and shake my head. This interview isn't going as well as I'd hoped, because I don't really want to talk about many of these pictures. I know they're good, and I know they're real, and I do my best to explain the emotions to Hal.

"There's an innocence," I start, "sometimes, there's an innocence, even when you're doing something dirty."

*****

I take Justin's picture immediately after that. SNAP! goes the camera, sounding louder than it ever has before. The noise cuts through every emotion. It places us back in our normal roles. Justin holds up one hand, partially blocking my view. But he doesn't really mind. He looks too good, too happy, and he's really so relaxed that he can't stop me. Can't wrestle the camera out of my hands and use it on me instead, as he sometimes does.

I feel weightless being with him. No problems. No worries. And I forget Kate. Forget all about her. Forget, that is, until Justin says that he has to change our plans. With a casual shrug, he explains that he's going to surf with the boys, that he'll meet me later on in the afternoon for a snack instead of having brunch with me. And the change makes me wonder and makes me worry and makes me think of what Kate said. Because maybe she knows something—something she can't tell me. And maybe it is strange that Justin and I are once again so hot for each other. Not strange in a bad way, but odd. Unexpected.

So I do what Kate suggested. I watch my back. Or, rather, I watch Justin's back. His fine, muscled back, naked in the sterling-bright sunlight. He's got on a pair of splashy surfer shorts worn low down on his flat waist, and he cuts through the glistening turquoise-rimmed waves easily on his board. He's one of those good surfers who looks as if he could dance out there if he wanted to. His balance is effortless, and his poise makes me envious. I don't own grace like that. That's not saying that I trip over myself, or commonly fall down stairs, or anything, but cutting through the waves takes a level of confidence that I sometimes think I'm lacking. Justin has more confidence then anyone I know—except maybe Kate.

As I watch Justin, I realize that I surround myself with people who are at ease in their own skin. I take great pleasure from simply being in their company, and snapping their pictures often, as I do of Justin now, looking down on him from above. Through the lens, he grows closer. I know he can't see me way up here on the bluffs, but I shudder when he glances right in my direction. I can see him startlingly clearly, and I take the picture.

Then another.

And another.

I don't really know what I'm doing. I've never been the jealous type before. Never had the patience for that sort of all-consuming green-glazed emotion. But Kate's query raises questions within me. Why is everything hot between us right now? *So* hot. So crazy-hot that we're skipping sleep in favor of sex. Yeah, we were like that at the very beginning, falling into one another as if sex was the only thing we needed to survive. But like anything, our tempers and temperatures have changed. We strike it hot every once and awhile. But not like this. Not every time like this.

I'm not complaining—don't get me wrong. But when Justin winds up spending half of the day out at the beach, I stay out of sight and snap his photo, happily reassured to see that he's out there with two of his best friends, actors he met years ago when all were hired for a pilot that never made it on the air. Relieved to discover that no girls are present, I still follow the trio. None of the summer-time beach bunnies who flock to the Santa Monica shore wait for the boys on nearby blankets. I know all about the type. Girls who don't have to work. Who don't have to do anything but look good. That's actually a job description in L.A. If you can pull it off, there's generally somebody ready and willing to pay your way.

Of course, that's not to say there isn't fierce competition. Sugar Daddies have their pick of sun-drenched blonde cupcakes here in La-La Land. There are so many beautiful women and hungry men—made for each other. Just waiting for each other to make each other's dreams come true.

I see the girls lined up on the sand, rotating in the afternoon sun. And I see Justin out there with his gaggle of buddies, not even seeming to glance in their direction. After awhile, I pack up my gear and stroll back home again. The apartment seems to mock me.

Our clothes and our furniture surround me, and soon I flee, off to my private studio and my darkroom.

Usually, peace awaits me here. But for once, I'm embarrassed in my darkroom as I develop the roll. Embarrassed, because I know I can never show these pictures to Justin. He'd realize in an instant that I was following him, and that would make me look psycho, like a common stalker. And that's not how I want to present myself or who I want to be. So instead of processing the rest of the roll, I take a deep breath, pull open my door, and let the wild white sunshine in. Destroying the roll of film eases my guilty conscience immediately.

But can a single ray of sunlight truly cleanse my soul?

Because isn't it true that people who are suspicious often have guilty secrets of their own to hide?

*****

Hal is looking at the surfer shots. They have a clear, clean 1950s quality to them. I can tell that he like the images, the foam folding over on itself. The boards and the waves. Then he moves down to a nearby picture. This one is of Connor, and I say, "We'll get there later. We'll get there at the end."

CHAPTER FOUR

"It's almost time for your bath, dirty girl," Connor says softly.

I sit naked on the edge of the tub, watching as he adds more milk to the water. Intent on his work, Connor is unaware that I'm staring at him, memorizing him, capturing him in my mind. Dark hair against pale skin. Green eyes flecked with color, gold and purple-gray. He wears faded black jeans and no shirt. His chest is strong and finely muscled. His feet are bare.

Connor tests the temperature with one hand, adds a bit more milk from the last bottle, then nods to me. It's time. When he smiles, the skin at the corners of his eyes crinkle as if at a private joke. Then he bends close to whisper in my ear. "That's right, Alex. Get into the bath, now. I'm going to wash you."

I step in, letting the warm, white liquid surround me. Immersing myself in the creamy water. It smells light and sweet, familiar. Picking up a washcloth, soft with wear, Connor starts to bathe me. His eyes don't meet mine. They're focused on the job, washing the tips of my fingers, the ridge of my collarbones, the wings of my shoulder blades. Staying clear, for the moment, from my breasts above the water, from between my thighs below.

The cloth caresses my skin, and then Connor lets it go, and his bare hands take over the job, massaging me as he cleans me. His warm fingers linger at the crook of my arm, at the side of my ribs, now moving, finally moving, up to my firm, full breasts. His touch sends shivers through me, even though I'm warm in the steamy heat of the milk and water.

He sighs, then says, "You're beautiful," and I close my eyes, wishing it were all real. But, of course, it's not. It's just a fantasy. That's all.

It's *my* dream, *my* fantasy, but Connor doesn't behave as I'd have him. He doesn't let us finish in the tub, doesn't push me forward until my hands are resting flat on the tile wall and take me from behind. Instead, he lifts me out of the water and dries me off. Then he carries me from the bathroom to the kitchen and sets a bowl of cream on the floor. I know what he wants me to do. I don't know how I know, but I understand, and I follow the script. He watches me crawl to it, lap from it. This is the strangest fantasy I've ever had. I don't want to be a pet for him to play with. But I find myself getting wetter as I lap from the bowl of milk, feeling his eyes on me, watching.

As if he's had all he can take, Connor moves me onto my back on the floor. Quickly, he enters me and as he does, his mouth meets mine. His kiss is hard enough to bruise, but his body continues to work slowly and gently. The two sensations are confusing, thrilling, and I can't even think about what is going to happen next. It's as if someone else were writing my fantasy for me, not letting me see the next page before it happens. I am lost in it.

Totally lost.

Even so, a part of my brain knows that this is all a harmless, silly fabrication.

But you know what? My life these days is made up of a series of fantasies. Part of the time, I'm fantasizing about what Justin may or may not be doing. Part of the time, I'm lost in fantasies based on the stories that Kate tells me. And the rest of the time? It's just Connor and me in a tight clinch. So who am I to be following Justin? What nerve I have.

Wish I could talk to someone—but the only person I have is Kate, and I don't know if I could handle her type of advice.

Not now. Not yet.

*****

"I'm coming over," Kate says, when I answer the phone.

"Oh, god," I say. "Did we have plans?"

"No," she tells me, and I hear traffic noises in the background, and I realize she's already on her way to my studio. That she's calling from her sleek silver convertible to alert me of her impending arrival.

"Something wrong?" I ask. But I'm the one who should be telling—something is wrong. I have the exposed roll of film in my hands as I cradle the phone against my shoulder. What to do with it? Finally, I bury it in the bottom of the garbage bag, just as Kate tells me that she's here, waiting for me to buzz her in.

I go to the little refrigerator in the corner and pull out two beers. Then I sit in my one comfortable chair and wait for her to knock.

"Didn't get any answer at your place," she says. "So I thought you might be here."

I look at her. She's windswept and lovely, and the expression in her eyes lets me know that she has fresh secrets to share.

"All right," I say, "Spill it."

"What were you doing?"

"Developing."

"So keep working, and I'll tell you."

We go into the darkroom together. Kate sips her beer and watches me work. And as I work, she starts to spin her tale.

Kate has no boundaries. I've always known that. It's what draws me to her again and again. The way that she's willing to put herself out there—up for any experience. But when she tells me that she has a thing for a road crew, I have to stop what I'm doing and look at her.

"A whole crew, Kate?"

"No," she says, her laugh light and tinkling. "Not all of 'em. Just one of them."

"Not a convict, though, right?" I ask. I remember the time Kate picked up a seriously good-looking guy one evening in Westwood Village. She actually saw him on the street, followed him into a restaurant, and ended up having dinner with him. They had such a good time together, that they both wanted to hook up again. Which is when he told her that it would have to be several months down the line—he was about to go to jail for some sort of traffic violations.

"Not a convict," she says, nudging me. She hates that I'll never let her live that one down.

"So, tell me. Tell everything."

And she does.

The crew had been out in her neighborhood for weeks. Trimming trees. Filling potholes. "And," she says, "you know."

"What?"

"I mean, you can guess right?"

"No."

"Turning me on," she says, as if it's obvious. "Making me want to come. Not all of them. Just one of them." She says that maybe she's immune to love at first sight, but she had a bad case of lust at first sight. And second sight. And she kept on driving by the road crew to see if she could catch this one guy's eye.

"What did he look like?"

She sighs. "Truly handsome. I mean, seriously handsome. With this sleek mustache and sparkling brown eyes. He'd look at me when he was the one holding up the 'stop sign,' and I'd look back through the windshield, flush, and look away."

"Doesn't sound like you," I tease her. "You, flush?"

"Come on. I can work up a blush when I need to. I haven't lost my girlish charm."

"So how many times did you circle around?"

"Three, four, five? I don't know. Every time I went to do an errand. And I went to do more errands than usual when I knew they were at work. I put on elaborate make-up just to go to the grocery store."

I just shrug. Getting dolled up is standard procedure in Kate's book. I've never seen her look unkempt. Even when she's sick, she's glamorous, wearing a silken bed jacket and keeping her hair smooth and sleek. This is because of one of Kate's important rules: You never know which ex you'll run into when you go out somewhere, but you'll always run into one when you're looking your worst.

"So what happened?"

"After several days, I got bold. I held his eye contact and stared back at him, gazing through my cherry-flush, forcing the connection. He liked that. I could tell. He tilted his head at me and narrowed his eyes, and I could almost hear what he was thinking. 'Take me on? Is that what you think you're doing, little girl? You think you can take me?'"

"You heard him say that?"

"In my head," she says. "The men were connected to one another with walkie talkies, letting each other know when cars were waiting at either side of the work site. So today, I watched a heavy-set man radio another while the stop sign was in place. After a moment, he flipped the sign to 'slow,' and motioned me forward. As I drove around the windy roads, I spotted a golden-yellow work truck in my rear view mirror. I wondered if it was him. How was I supposed to find out?"

"You know, Kate," I tell her. "This sort of stuff only happens to you."

She doesn't stop her story. She knows she has an interested audience, so she keeps on plugging. "I kept driving, saw the truck holding steady, and finally I pulled into the lot behind one of the clubs up on Sunset. Empty at this time of day. Totally empty. And back behind the club was pretty secluded. The truck pulled in behind me, and my man got out. I knew in my head what I wanted to do, but I didn't know whether people really behaved like that outside of porno movies."

I laugh out loud. "Kate, you're playing innocent with the wrong girl, here," I remind her. "I know that you do exactly what they do in porno movies. That's your M.O."

She ignores me, continuing with her story as if she hasn't been so rudely interrupted. "Could I step from my convertible, rush over, and tell him what to do to me? Turned out I didn't have to. He knew."

"He really knew?" Up to this point, I've been thinking that he was going to ask for her number. Now, I realize that Kate's going to tell me something far more interesting.

"Yeah. With a nod of his head, he motioned for me to come toward him. I slid from my seat, slammed the door behind me, and walked to the back of his truck. As soon as I was in his range, he gripped onto my shoulders and brought me into his arms for a kiss—the kiss I'd imagined since I'd first seen him. Hot and fast, his mouth firm against mine, his teeth finding my bottom lip and then biting it hard. Then, because it had to happen, because it was right, he pushed me down on the gravel-strewn dirt and unbuttoned his deeply faded jeans. I was ready, my lips parted, mouth open, but he stopped me before I could act. Quickly, he pulled his heavy leather belt free from his jeans, and with me in the exact position he wanted, he captured my wrists tightly behind my back."

"Oh, man," I sigh, interrupting her. "Oh, my God, Kate."

"He called me a tease, and he ran his fingers roughly under my chin, tilting my head upward. I just sighed, so hungry now, so desperate, but he wasn't ready to give in. All I wanted was the taste of him in my mouth, and I wanted it more than anything I've ever craved, yet he wouldn't let me suckle from him."

I'm breathless as I listen to her, and I do my best to keep working, but I realize I've forgotten what I'm doing. I should just pause and hear her out.

"With one hand still under my chin, he ran the back of his free hand against my cheek, softly, making me tremble all over at the gentleness of his touch. I lowered my head, shuddering all over, feeling how wet my panties were growing. Feeling how much I needed this. 'Look at me, baby,' he insisted, and I raised my head.

"Now, he pushed forward, butting against my lips. Oh, God was I ready. I wanted to drink, wanted to drain, wanted to swallow him whole. But still he wouldn't let me. He plunged in, taking his pleasure, then slid back out and bent to rub my nipples forcefully through my thin white blouse. He pinched them hard, and I arched and groaned, and while my mouth was open, he slid in again. Each time he played me, he made me wetter still. I didn't know what I was doing anymore. All I knew was that I had the need—the urgency—to drink him down."

"You were behind a club?" I ask, breaking Kate from her erotic memories.

She nods.

"In the middle of the day?"

She nods again.

"Okay," I say. "I'm just working to get the picture. Go on."

"'Bad girl,'" he said, "'lost in your little games. Cruising the curves in your silver convertible. And all you want is for someone to take that sweet mouth of yours. Isn't that right?'"

"He really said all that?"

"Yeah," Kate tells me. "He really did."

"What did you do? Did you say anything back to him?"

"I think I nodded. I know I moaned. And finally, he let me have at him. I swallowed with a vengeance. I sucked and pulled, my cheeks indenting with the intensity of my hunger. He held me steady with his rough hands on my shoulders, pinned me in place in his strong grip. My eyes wide open, I saw the buildings behind him, saw his scuffed work boots below, the gravel and dirt under my knees. It was a relief to be allowed to use my mouth, to trick my tongue up and down him.

"When I could think of nothing more than draining his every drop, he pulled out again, lifted me up by my arms, and bent me over the back of the truck. My wrists were still bound behind my back, so he had to slide my skirt up for me and take my panties down. Kicking my legs wider apart, he pushed into me with the spit-slicked length of his erection. He took me so hard that his truck shook. My face pressed into the metal of the truck bed; my honeyed juices spilled down my thighs. And when we were finished, he simply unbuckled the well-worn belt and set me free."

"God," I sigh, imagining every image as if I were there, taking pictures.

"But I didn't want to be free," Kate says to me. Her voice is dead-serious, as if she really wants me to understand exactly what she's telling me. As if it's important to her that I understand.

"What happened? Did he tell you his name? Did he say anything else?"

"He said, 'You're calmer now, aren't you, girl?' I thought about the words before I answered, and then I nodded. He was right. All the nervous energy that had pulsed through me each time we'd made eye contact was now gone. I felt warm and in control. Better yet, I felt satisfied. I watched him get into the truck and drive out of the lot."

"Did you get his name?"

She shrugs and shakes her head at the same time.

"No number? No way to get in touch."

"No. That wasn't important. But you know what? When the road crew comes back to my neighborhood, I do know that I'll be ready."

I can't believe Kate. I just look at her, and I see that she's actually trembling. That telling me this story was a way for her to relive it. And then I think about something else.

"Did this just happen?"

She nods and grins.

"I bet you don't have your panties any more, do you?"

"I had a spare pair in the car," she says. Just like Kate. Always prepared.

*****

When Kate leaves, I lose myself in my own fantasies again. It's as if she's given me the freedom to daydream. Her extreme freedom pushes my own.

"Sugar?"

I shake my head.

"Cream?"

"Please."

Connor lifts the chilled silver pitcher, pours a small amount of the rich, white liquid into my coffee, watches as it makes spiraling designs against the dark, java background. I look at it and think about something else.

Then, in my fantasies, he takes the coffee cup from my hand, leans forward and meets my mouth with his. My lips are still warm from the first sip of coffee. His mouth moves from my lips down my neck. His fingers unbutton my white silk blouse and he kisses in a line down my belly, to the waistband of my slacks.

Deftly, his fingers undo the buttons, spread my white jeans open and slide my silky underpants aside. With his lips here, lips pressed to my skin, he licks me, and teases me, bringing forth the cream.

CHAPTER FIVE

"I want to talk to you about something," Justin tells me over dinner.

I look up at him, and I think of Kate—was she actually right with her off-beat advice? Is he going to tell me that he's with someone else? That he's sorry but he's leaving me. Or that he's sorry but he's cheated. In the few moments before he reveals the answer, I wonder who my rival could be—one of the starlets from the new movie he's shooting? A fellow actress from one of the many classes that he goes to? Tap? Fencing? Foreign accents? I realize my heart's racing so hard and so fast that I miss part of what Justin says.

"Excuse me?" I say, wanting him to repeat the phrase.

"Beach pictures," he says, and I flush. Does he know? How can he? "Do you want to try, baby?"

And now I realize that he's suggesting something new. Something sort of edgy for us to go do together. He doesn't know that I was tailing him, watching him cruise the waves on a sunlit day. He doesn't know anything other than the fact that he wants to take some dirty photos with me out at the beach.

I smile at him and nod, realizing with such a rush of relief how happy I am that he doesn't know. And then I'm suddenly angry with Kate. She was the one who put these nagging doubts in my head to start with. I shouldn't listen to her when she goes off on a tangent. And I should know better. Kate has a lengthy and bitter history with men, and now she manages to actually date like a man. In and out for her own pleasure, just like with the handyman and the guy from the road crew. But she knows nothing about Justin and me—not what it's like for us behind closed doors.

Or in front of closed doors.

Or out at the ocean, on a clear and crystal night.

The sky glows bright with a heavy full moon. Not yellow. Not golden like a coin. But a pure and perfect silver that reflects in the water below. And he has found the ideal place, he tells me on the ride, a spot where we can be alone. Alone together. That's a rarity in Los Angeles. Who can be alone in a city of so many busy, uptight people? People who all want to go to the same clubs and the same restaurants. Who have it in their minds to do exactly what you were thinking of doing tonight. We've done the outdoor thing before, but generally it's been spontaneous—out behind a club in the back alley. Or in the car after a sexy French movie ripe with heavy sensuality.

But this evening is different. Justin has spent some time looking, and he says that he's found us a spot out at Zuma. "Trust me," he says, "I've planned everything. Just bring your camera."

This is his only request. Simple enough. I'd have brought it anyway. I always do.

The sand sheens in the moonlight, and Justin sets a large black blanket on top of it. The ocean is right out there in front of us, the glowing lip of the waves crashing onto the sand. In moments, we're entirely naked, Justin on top of me, reaching for my wrists and capturing me instantly in his embrace. I love that feeling. Being bound by his large, warm hands. He can hold me so that I can't break free—and I adore the sensation of falling into him.

Even as he keeps me in place, he is sweet and gentle as we make love for the first time of the night. His body yields to my own needs, and he moves slowly and easily against me. We do it to the sound of the ocean, to that same mesmerizing rhythm that is older than anything I can imagine. In and out to the crash-pound-wash of the waves. I hear the music of the ocean in my head as we move together and I wonder why it took us so long to make it out to the beach. There is magic in the way the moonlight caresses our naked bodies, magic in the rough-real smell of the sand and the chill of the salt air.

Moonlight plays tricks with my vision. I see a multitude of colors in the ocean—a rainbow of light glinting in the waves. I stare out at the black water with the dazzling prism-kissed edges, and then I close my eyes.

Justin's body is so warm against mine. His heat spreads to my body, and I feel every part of him. I am in a deeply concentrating mode, like when we most recently played the touch-and-guess game. Now I am learning each different segment of his body. I feel the lines and curves of his muscles, the long flat expanse of his stomach, the hardness of his bones beneath the skin. I imagine our two bodies blending together, interlocked as we are, truly becoming one.

That's the image that brings me to the breaking point.

And when we're finished, that's when Justin gets out my camera.

These are portraits. Nude pictures of me. My hair spreads out around my body. My skin takes on the same moonlit glow as the sand. I feel otherworldly with the cool, salt-tinged breeze rippling over me. My nipples are hard and my body relaxed and at ease. Justin moves the camera and takes the picture. I stare into the eye of the lens for the whole time. Then I take the camera back and shoot pictures of my own.

*****

Hal says, "I like this one."

"Which picture?" the gallery owner asks, moving in close to see what we're discussing.

Hal nods. "The black of the night and the way your model's body seems to glow."

He's pointing to a picture of Justin on the beach—a stark contrast to the ones of him surfing.

Jane, the gallery owner, nods in approval. "That's one of my favorites, as well. So different from glowing, golden California beach scenes."

She's right. The sand looks white like snow. The water is jet black. I step back for a moment, and let Hal and Jane converse about the meanings behind my pictures. It's difficult for me to look at Justin now. To see him and remember what things were like between us when I took these shots.

CHAPTER SIX

Just because everything seems to be going well, doesn't mean that I give up on watching him. For some reason, the nagging suspicions remain real and alive in my head. They flicker with power each time I shut my eyes. So I do the only thing I know how. I tail Justin when he goes to his acting class. Tail him when he takes meetings with Judith Beck, his agent, at fancy lunch spots or in her office. I watch him pick out a pair of new sunglasses at a store on Melrose.

Taking pictures generally puts me at ease, but snooping ultimately exhausts me. Perhaps because I am so emotionally attached to my subject, I can't separate my feelings from the pictures I take. After an evening spent following my man all over the city, I sit in our apartment, staring at my camera as if it has a mind or a life of its own. Who would have thought that I'd ever get to this point? That I would doubt my own boyfriend so greatly that I'd follow him around L.A., waiting to find out something that I don't want to know.

The Yin-Yang of my feelings makes our lovemaking all the more desirable. It's crazy, I know. I worry about Justin, I think about Connor, and I lose myself in fantasies involving both of these men. I don't know what to do. Don't know how to stop.

*****

Justin surprises me at my darkroom. I am quick to hide the evidence of my obsessive picture taking, and I wonder if he can guess why my cheeks are flushed—embarrassment rather than arousal. He doesn't say anything about my appearance. He simply comes forward, takes me in his arms, and carries me into the darkroom.

In the starkly vibrant light of the red bulb, he undresses me. I feel his hands on my white T-shirt, pulling it over my head. I feel his fingers knowingly finding the clasp of my bra and snapping it open. Then he's onto my docs, bending down to undo the laces and help me kick free of those heavy boots. My jeans are next. He stands behind me, hands around my waist, as he pulls open the button fly and then slips them down my legs. Now, I'm only in my panties. My whole body is trembling. I like the quiet of the situation. He hasn't said a word. I like how I feel being naked while he's still clothed. When he runs his fingers along the edge of my waistband, I let out a low, hungry sigh. I'm sure he realizes precisely how excited I am, but still he says nothing. Offers no instruction, no way for me to guess what he's going to do next.

It's simple, really. He's going to do me.

With a rough gesture, he undoes the fly of his own jeans, then pushes me so that my hands are on the round wooden top of my stool and I'm bent at the waist, offering myself to him from behind. He slips my panties down, but doesn't have me take them off. Ready for him, I bow my head, and as he slides into me from behind, I see images in front of me. Pictures that I've taken of him. We are so different, I realize. I can always tell when something is bothering Justin, but it seems obvious now that he has no idea what sort of turmoil is bubbling through me. And it's building and growing with each passing day.

Justin kisses against the back of my neck as he thrusts within me, and I sigh again and tell myself to lose my thoughts in the moment. Doesn't matter if I've been following him. Right now, I know exactly where he is—inside of me. I should let go, shouldn't I? I should give myself over to the pleasure that is right in front of me.

Or, really, right behind me.

Gripping onto my hips, Justin works me at a steady, sexy pace. The groove of his body against mine is like a dance. I think of times when we've gotten all worked up together on the dance floor. Grinding against each other at a club, so excited by the way our bodies move that we can hardly wait to get back home again. I recall an evening when Justin made love to me against his bike in the back of a music venue with the cold metal beneath me, and the cool night air all around us.

What was I thinking at that moment? Was I worrying about what he did when he wasn't with me? Was I secure with him?

His fingers cradle me and stroke between my legs, and suddenly my questions disappear and I am with him. Coming with him. Melting with him. I see no pictures in my head as the warmth rocks through me.

What do I feel now? Nothing but bliss. However fleeting it may be.

*****

It's probably my fault. All my fault. I was the one to bring photographs into our bedroom. I was the one who introduced Justin to the world of pictures coming to life, of images frozen in time. I taught him every stage of the process, from the set-up through the development. He understands the rush of waiting in the darkroom for the pictures to slowly emerge. Or re-emerge, really. Will they match the images that we have captured in our minds? Or will they expand what we believed to be true, pushing our fantasies and our boundaries even farther.

Now he likes taking photographs as much as I do. He's not quite as arty, perhaps, not as finicky or precise, but he brings a joyful naiveté to the photos that he takes. He is all about staging. He wants a picture that he sees in his head. He visualizes it first, and then works to make it happen. I'm the opposite—I have a free-wheeling attitude when it comes to my portraits. Especially my self-portraits. I'm not being bold here. That's what a reviewer once said about my work. I capture life for a second, an instant, in exactly the way it happens.

Question: How can you own that pleasure forever?

Answer: Simple, you take a picture.

Which is what I'm known for—even outside of the bedroom, if you would believe it. But, yes, I do like the boudoir shots. I must admit that. There's something interesting to me about exposing secrets, about letting viewers into a world they wouldn't ever get a chance to see. Behind closed doors. Inside my mind and my libido. Secrets intrigue me, and photographs hold the key to secrets.

*****

Kate sees the beach shots, and she likes them. She'd have to be blind not to. They're good. Then she looks around my darkroom, at the many rolls of film I have yet to expose all lined up in a row. She can't believe how far behind I am. Rarely do I let myself get this overwhelmed. But I have been working on choosing pictures for my show, and it's been difficult to keep up to speed.

I know that Kate would go nuts if she lived in my skin for even a moment. She is so totally organized. She likes everything in its place, while I am about chaos—that's the artist in me. This is why my darkroom isn't in our apartment. Justin couldn't stand the mess, either. But the randomness doesn't bother me in the slightest. I know where everything is. That's the most important thing.

"You look glorious," Kate says, pointing to one of the pictures with me on my stomach on the blackness of the blanket. The sand is like white gold around me. It's as if I'm floating on a tiny midnight island in the middle of a salt sea.

"Justin took it," I tell her, not the slightest bit shy about the fact that this is a nude. I have lots of different hang-ups, but nudity isn't one of them. Many of the pictures that are in my show will be nudes. Bodies are bodies. Pictures—photographs, that is—are equalizers. Curves and lines and shadows become art. Everything to a camera lens can be art. Doesn't matter if a model is heavy or slim, round or angular. Cameras can make all people beautiful.

"Will he come to the show?" Kate wants to know. Justin is notorious about blowing off my exhibits. He always claims a rehearsal or an early call in the morning.

"Think so," I tell her, but I don't meet her eyes.

CHAPTER SEVEN

"Don't forget," I tell Justin in the morning.

"Forget that you love me?"

I shake my head.

"Forget how much you like to ride my great, big c—"

"Forget about the show tonight," I say, but I can't help but laugh. Justin has a filthy mind.

I have a small showing at a cafe in West Hollywood. It's not a big deal for anyone except me. Justin's promised to meet me at my favorite bar. We'll leave together from there. That's the plan, anyway.

"Sure," he says, nodding. "Of course, I'll be there, baby. Wouldn't miss it."

*****

But he doesn't come to the bar. Even though I'd believed he would, was certain that he wouldn't let me down this time, he doesn't come.

At five thirty, I hit the pay phone to check my messages. None from Justin. One from Kate. Connor watches me look at the clock, look at the phone at the front of the bar, look at the clock again. Christine, the manager, feels my eyes on her and turns to give me a winning smile. I smile back, but only with my mouth. In the mirror over the bar I can tell that my eyes remain sad.

How could he?

"You need a ride?" Connor asks, leaning across the bar and saying it softly.

"I'll call a cab."

"You *need* a ride," he says, not asking this time.

I look at him, but don't answer. Kate dropped me here, went home to change, and is planning on meeting me at the cafe later. She can only stay for a short while because she has a business engagement after, but she'll show up for as long as she can to show her support. That's how Kate is. And this is also how Justin is.

How could he do this?

Connor walks over to Van, whispers something I can't hear. Van looks over at me, shrugs, and then looks around the bar. "Sure, we're slow," he says, then adds with obvious satisfaction, "But you'll owe me." I wonder what that statement means in "Van Speak." What will Connor owe him? A night watching the bar, or something else entirely? Something much darker, much more sinister. The comment doesn't bother Connor at all, and I watch as he takes off his white apron, sets it behind the counter, undoes his tie, and motions to me with one hand.

"Are we going, Alex?"

"You're serious."

He mimics me in an exaggerated manner: looks at the clock, looks at the phone, looks at the clock. Then he walks around the bar, reaches for my hand, and holds it. "You're going to miss your own opening if we don't leave now."

I stand up, but still I hesitate. Connor calls out to Christine, "If Justin calls, just tell him to meet her at The Dark Light, okay?"

Christine nods.

"Ready?" Connor asks. This time when he motions for me, I follow him, through the restaurant, out the back door, across the marble lobby to the elevator to the garage. He hums something familiar as we walk, and I try to place the song. As the elevator doors open and we step inside, I recognize Bob Dylan's masterpiece, "Lay, Lady, Lay." Connor raises his eyebrows seductively at me, and the he presses the button for the garage.

The thing of it is that I like him and he knows it. Yet I've always gotten by on pretending that we're just buddies--acquaintances more than friends. Usually, he plays the same game. I wonder if he fantasizes about me sometimes, the way I fantasize about him.

"Did you hear about the rebel who attempted a seduction on the way to a fancy opening?" he asks casually.

"I missed that one," I tell him, following after him through the rows of cars until we reach his red pick-up truck.

"It was in all the papers," Connor assures me, opening the passenger door and waiting as I settle myself inside. "Front page headlines."

He shuts the door, and I watch in the rear view mirror as he walks around to the other side of the truck. When he opens his door, he looks over at me. I can tell that he sees worry in my eyes, and he instantly stops joking, leans forward and says, "Justin's just late at the studio. He meant to be here. He probably couldn't call because he's on the set."

It's the nicest thing Connor's ever said.

*****

The drive takes only several minutes. We are silent on the way. Connor parks the old Ford a few storefronts down from the cafe. Then he gallantly walks to my side of the car and opens the door for me.

"You know," he says, "you look amazing." I do know, but I don't say so. I took extra time with my appearance tonight, and I have on a fabulous black dress that's cut perfectly. To add to the feminine look of the outfit, I've chosen a black fringed shawl to wear over my shoulders. The shawl is woven through with tiny silver threads. It's arty and different from something I'd usually wear. I feel glamorous in the outfit. At least, I would have if my boyfriend hadn't blown me off. Now, I have to say, that I feel like a loser. No matter how gentlemanly Connor behaves, how graciously he acts toward me.

"Thanks," I say, aware of how close together we are. Connor is the leading man in my fantasies. He's my number-one crush. But he's also a buddy who teases me, who shoots me and Kate free drinks every third round. Now Connor offers his arm, which I take, and then he lets me set the pace of our walk to The Dark Lady. I'm silent as we walk, thinking of Justin and thinking of Kate and thinking of Connor, himself, and the way that he so gently holds my hand.

"I don't think he's coming," I say, hearing the sadness in my voice. But I continue to glance around, just the same. It would be like Justin to suddenly appear, running through the crowd, calling out to me at the last possible minute.

Connor holds the door to the gallery for me, continuing in his role as the very proper date. I stride ahead of him into the casually decorated cafe, into the welcoming arms of the owner. When I turn back toward Connor to introduce him, he gives me a thumbs up sign. I know immediately what he's referring to—the cafe is packed. My photos appear everywhere on the brightly colored walls. It's amazing for an artist be surrounded by her work. Even more amazing to see the way other people react to your most personal creations. Connor's seen small pictures from my portfolio in the past, but he's never seen an exhibit before. I get the feeling that he's impressed. He makes his way around the room, and even though I'm talking to other people and accepting congratulations, and keeping an eye out for my late boyfriend, I pay attention to where Connor is and what photo he's looking at.

"Genius," a bald-headed man says as he walks passed Connor. "Pure genius."

Connor nods in his agreement. Standing in front of a portrait of Justin, Connor takes his time observing the photo, sipping from his glass of cheap champagne.

"Nice," he says, when I make my way to his side.

"You don't really think so."

"The picture's great, but if I ran into Justin tonight, in person rather than on the wall, I might have to punch him out. Sorry but that's the truth. Someone should do it."

"Come on—"

"It's disgusting that he treats you like this," Connor says, and I feel myself flush because Connor is my friend. Sort of. He works two jobs—tends the counter at my favorite bar and works at the grocery store. One of the scrounging artists who does what he can to pay the rent until he manages to make enough money doing what he loves.

And then, the sound of a motorcycle can be heard out on the street. I turn my head, recognizing the engine of a Harley, and the smile on my face as Justin walks through the door makes Connor look away. I'm not dense. I know that he likes me. But I understand Justin. We're two of a kind. I hear Connor say something softly as he moves a few feet away.

"Sorry I'm late," Justin murmurs into my ear, kissing my cheek. "Got caught up." Justin lifts two glasses from a waiter with a passing tray. "To you—" he says, but before he's even finished with the toast, I'm spirited away to a far corner, asked to describe my work by the cafe owner for an interested party who wants to buy three of the pieces.

Yet I still keep my eye on the boys. I feel the electricity in the air, and I wonder whether Justin will get it. Then suddenly he does. Moving into a corner, away from me, Justin looks over at Connor. He shakes his head and hurries to my side.

"What's the bartender doing here?"

"I'm talking," I tell him.

"*We'll* be talking," Justin says to me. "Later—"

"Justin," I say in a calm tone, trying to placate him.

"I'm serious," he says, eyes wide. "You took your bartender to this thing instead of me?"

"You weren't anywhere. He offered me a ride."

"A ride," he nods. "I know all about those sort of rides, baby."

He's the one challenging me, now, and I feel the guilt flood through me. Heat shows in my cheeks, and I know that Justin takes the flush to mean something other than what it truly does. I can't say anything in my defense, because anything I try to say will sound like a confession. I know this. Still, I try to think of some way to explain, but Justin wants none of it. He leaves in a huff, followed by the scream of his Harley engine revving. Idiot, I think to myself. Maybe he's caught onto an attraction between Connor and me, but I would never act on it. Now, Justin's put himself in the position to be on the high ground, making me ask for forgiveness. Doesn't make any sense, does it? Not really.

When Kate arrives moments later, I try to explain what has happened, and she gives me her famous look that lets me know exactly what she thinks of Justin—which is not much. He takes all the time, she says. Expects but doesn't return. Kate has no patience for long-term relationships and I know she'd rather see me single so that I could party with her.

"But Connor came?" she asks, and I can tell from her expression that she knows I like him.

I shrug. "Connor's nothing more than a friend."

She shakes her head. She doesn't believe my lies.

"A good friend who actually stays all evening," I tell her when she kisses my cheek and says she has to go to an industry party at the Tantamount. But I'm just messing with Kate. I'm pleased that she was able to make it at all. Now, we're down to Connor and me. When I'm ready to leave, Connor grabs my hand and squeezes it.

"You didn't have to stay," I say.

"It was your special opening," Connor says matter-of-factly. "You want to go somewhere and have a drink. I can tell." We walk together down Melrose, toward the magazine stand on Gardner. I stop in front of it.

"I can just get a magazine and entertain myself."

He raises his eyebrows.

"The fall issues are out. The fashion magazines are four-inches thick this month." I hold my fingers apart, indicating the size. It makes Connor grin, lecherously.

"That's all it takes to keep you interested?" He doesn't wait for my response. "I've got to be better company than *Elle*," Connor continues, "And if I'm not, lie to me and tell me I am." I just stare at him, "Come on, let's get that drink."

We walk the six blocks to Angelica Crowne and sit at the counter. Connor orders for the two of us, impressively naming the best tequila on the market, and then telling the bartender exactly how to serve it.

When the bartender finally sets out the order, Connor lifts his glass and clinks it against mine. I suddenly realize that it's the first time we've ever had a drink together. First time we've ever really been in a situation outside either of his work places.

"You really didn't have to stay," I tell him again.

"That's not a very good toast," he says, but he clinks my glass again anyway, and we both take that first, delicious swallow. I look outside the windows at the bustling activity along Melrose, where groups of college students are heading to the Groundlings Theater to see the improvisation troupe when Connor asks, "What kind of a guy is Justin?"

I wish that I were good at improv right now. Wish I were able to think of clever answers at the spur of the moment. Although I can tell that he's staring at me, I keep looking out the window instead of meeting his gaze, finding that it's always easier to talk about Justin when I'm not eye to eye with the interrogator.

"An actor," I say to my reflection in the glass. I look tired. Exhausted, really.

"That's his occupation. What kind of a guy is he?"

"Tall—"

"Alex," he says seriously, putting his hand on mine and patting gently to get my attention. "You know that's not what I'm asking."

"You didn't have to wait," I say, as if it makes sense to keep repeating the statement. As if the more times I say the words, the more sense it will make. It's my new mantra.

"So you mentioned," Connor smiles at me. But the smile leaves his face as he asks, "Why do you stay with him?"

I open my mouth. He quickly interrupts. "And don't say that idiotic thing about rocks and holes again. I'm serious." He's talking about my favorite statement: the rocks in my head fit the holes in Justin. But Connor's not buying it.

I shrug. "We're well-suited to each other."

"He treats you like—" a Harley engine revs down the street just as Connor says an expletive that gets drowned out.

"When he's with me," I say, "it's perfect." I think about the way we've been acting together lately, and then I think about the fact that I've followed him all over this city. Rocks and holes? Sounds plausible enough.

Connor tilts his head in that familiar way, takes another, larger swallow of his tequila, emptying the glass, and then says, "If you say it's so, I'll trust you." He motions to the bartender that he's ready for another, then kindly switches subjects in his casually abrupt manner. "You hear about the car-jacker who couldn't drive?"

"I know this joke," the bartender says, coming over with a fresh napkin and another Bud.

I smile, thinking we're clear from the Justin conversation until Connor adds, "Why?"

"You said you'd trust me."

"I lied." He pauses for a moment, then says, "You're in this co-dependent thing—"

"No psycho-babble."

"I mean it. I've been there. You're always covering for him. That's part of it. That goes with the territory." He pauses. "Like tonight. He showed up obviously under the influence of something, and you're still covering. You seem resigned to it."

"It's not important. Times like these aren't important." I pause, then turn on the seat to look at Connor and ask, "Did you know that people who like vanilla ice cream are gregarious, but basically very private?"

"Really?" he asks, right on cue. He and I play games like this at the bar all the time, regaling each other with bits of useless information. For some reason, we both like to collect tidbits of trivia that nobody else seems to care about.

Now I wait.

"And you're going to tell me next that you like vanilla? That it's been your favorite flavor since you were a tiny, little child. That vanilla ice cream is the only thing you've ever asked for in a sundae."

I nod.

"So I should enjoy the part of you that comes out to play, and let the rest alone? Trust you when you say you know what you're doing and stop pressing issues that don't concern me. Basically, stay the f— out of business that's not mine?"

I nod again.

"What did it say about people who like chocolate chip?"

"You're competitive and can't stand losing."

"You know what?"

"What?"

"We really can't."

I'm the one who smiles at Connor now, and then I reach into my leather bag—one that's far too big for this outfit, but necessary to hold my camera—and I pull out my Nikon and take his picture. The look on his face is classic. Resigned yet at ease, as if he knows something I don't. As if he can see the future.

*****

"Tell me his story," Hal asks, pointing to the shot of Connor with the alcohol bottles lined up in the background behind him, the empty shot glass on the counter. Hal is impatient. He won't wait for me to get to the whole story in my own time. He wants me to explain out of order. I want to stay on target.

"Tell me what you see," I say, testing him.

"He looks serious, but not drunk," Hal says. "I like the black-and-white here, because there is something so old-fashioned about the set-up. Especially with his vest and loose tie.

"What else?"

"You can see that he wants something, but I don't think it's just another drink."

CHAPTER EIGHT

The next night finds Justin and me playing together as if nothing stressful has entered our relationship at all. We have our moments like that all the time. Then we back off into our own private corners, regroup, and come out again—not ready to fight. Ready for something else entirely.

Tonight, we're playing a costume game...one that's brand-new to us. I like that quality of the occasion--the fact that this is something we've never done before. And I like that Justin is able to pull this off without collapsing in a fit of giggles. Some men would look silly in this outfit—but not Justin. I mean, he just looks hot and ready and ripe. When he emerges from the bedroom in the matte black corset that I bought for him this afternoon, the garter-less fishnets, spiky high heels, all I can think is how much I want to do him. It's a completely unexpected reaction. I'd have thought the look would make me laugh. In reality, I'm more turned on than I can remember. But I make myself back off, try to force myself to go slowly.

Mentally, I picture each frame. I see myself pressing my body to his. Feeling the glossy softness of the expensive material against my skin. Feeling his skin between the laces, above the garters, under the silk. I want to drive my fingers beneath the boundaries of the fabric and touch him. Just touch him. Then I want to bend him over, show him that I'm packing a toy on my harness, and let him know what it's really like to be taken.

All right. Not really. Not all the way. Because on some level, all of this is an illusion, of course. We are acting for ourselves, an audience of two. Outside, in the real world, we would never show this play to anyone. It's something I'd never even tell Kate. But right now, on our private stage, we let everything go.

With one hand, he cautiously motions for me to come forward, and I follow him into the bedroom and sit on the edge of the mattress, trying to drink him in. But I'm having a difficult time. I don't know where to look first.

His hair is that birch-blonde that looks white in direct sunlight and pale like a cloud in our dimly lit room. And with his tanned skin, blue eyes, sweet pout of a mouth, I just want to eat him up.

"This is really strange—" Justin says, indicating his reflection in the full-length mirror that hangs on the back of the closest door. He looks at himself yet doesn't seem to recognize his reflection. I understand what he's thinking. He has transformed. Every once in awhile, this sort of thing happens with a model I'm shooting. I'll take some gorgeous young actress, one who is sweet and clean and pure. And I'll use oils and lotions and get her dirty and messy, as if she's drenched in sweat, or as if she's been up all night drinking. The make-up artist will use kohl around her eyes, and the costume designer will search out something appropriately ripped and tight and black. When the photos come back, the proof sheets, nobody will recognize her, even the actress herself. This has happened more than once for me. Changing someone so drastically in pictures that the end result is almost unrecognizable from the start.

And the funny thing is that I still believe that pictures don't lie. Even when I see for myself how they can trick the eye. Because I believe that the images I've brought forth from my models actually exist within them. The way that this side of Justin lived and breathed within his skin long before I went out costume shopping and brought the ensemble home to him.

Maybe he's never seen himself look quite so pretty before, and he doesn't know how to deal with the image. Maybe he thinks that dressing up like this somehow reflects poorly on his masculine side. I don't agree. I think one of the sexiest images of all time is Tim Curry emerging from the elevator in *The Rocky Horror Picture Show*. I think both men and women can appreciate how erotic Curry looks in that shot. How ripe for sex and untamed. Seeing Justin dressed in a similar fashion brings out the same feelings in me. Somewhat confused, slightly conflicted, but very, very aroused.

Tonight we're actually playing out more than just a fantasy. I don't think either of us would ever have come up with this situation on our own. Justin has a role as a cross-dresser in a new TV movie. This evening is actually research. The fact that it is turning us on at the same time is simply a bonus. We've explored situations like this in the past. Once, Justin played a villain who handcuffed women to a wrought-iron railing on the balcony of his apartment. He wasn't a sadist, precisely. He exerted his power over females in unusual ways. But prior to the role, Justin went out and bought a set of fur-lined cuffs, and that started us on our occasional journey into mild bondage games.

What's funny to me about that is how all our friends thought it was so subversive. They watched Justin in the role, and they couldn't believe he was so easily able to blend into the part. All of our associates pretended that they'd never played that way. Tying someone up or being tied down. But I know through Kate that lots of men like it like that. Why it's taboo, I don't really know.

Bondage doesn't have to mean ropes or chains. The props can be as simple as scarves. Even serious sessions, with cuffs, can be playful and lighthearted. Yet I don't think Justin and I would ever have gone that route if he hadn't won the role.

As I come forward now, standing behind him, touching him, I can tell that he's as excited as I am. How can I tell? Because I see the bulge under those tight black satin panties. I wouldn't have thought those two concepts would go together: bulge and panties. But they do. Oh, do they ever. Justin clad in those sweet panties is one of the sexiest sights I've ever seen. He strains dramatically against the soft shiny fabric, demanding attention.

Now, I know exactly what I want to do—what I have to do—and I'm fairly certain that he's not going to stop me. I don't even bother to ask. Instead, while he watches, I go down on my knees on the floor, and I run my hands up and up and up his fishnet-clad legs. The patterned stockings feel delightful under my palms. I've been on the inside of fishnets often enough—when we go out fancy, I favor wearing colored fishnets over plain sheer hose—but I've never on the outside before, and now I can understand what a turn-on they are. I can see his legs, and touch his skin, but there is that deviant barrier between us. I continue to stroke him until my hands press against the crotch of those panties.

If he were a girl, the panties would be all dreamy wet in the center. The cream of his arousal would be thick enough for me to taste. As it is, his erection makes a dangerous outline beneath the fabric. Christ, he's hard. I press my lips against him through the silk, and then I use my tongue to stroke up and down.

"That's right," he moans, and he sounds exactly like the same person I know. The same person I live with and sleep with and curl up in bed with. The same man I bend over for, or ride astride, or lick and lap and suck. But when I look at him, see him in this X-rated costume, this sexy disguise, I can tell that he's turned into someone else. That's all part of the fun, isn't it? There's the illusion that an outfit can transform a person into someone else. Slip into this costume and leave your worries behind. Nothing more freeing than that, is there?

The change in him brings out a change in me. I am in charge. I am in power. I want to swallow him down, and I also want to press him down flat onto the bed and take him. No image has ever been so clear in my mind before. Even though we've never played like this, somehow, I know exactly how it will feel. Is that because Kate has regaled me over the years with her sexy stories of seducing cross-dressers? Of sharing her nighties and her knickers with a femme creature for one night only?

"You should try it," she always tells me. "Dress him up and be the guy for a change."

"Why would that be sexy?" I ask her every time. "I like being a girl."

"It's just amazing," she says. "Trust me."

"Tell me more," I insist. "Make me understand."

She's done her best. She's described the sight of a man picking up her discarded panties and sliding them into his pocket. And the next time they were together, she discovered that he was wearing them beneath his neatly pressed khakis. Such a surprise, she told me, floored her.

So it turns out that Kate was right. But I don't know why. Is it because the whole experience seems so strikingly taboo? As if we are crossing a brand-new barrier, and that once we knock it down, all hell will break loose.

The fact is, I don't know what has us so aroused. All I know is that for this evening, I'll be in charge, and Justin will come because of my power. But although I'd like nothing else than to go racing toward the finish line, I force myself to start slowly, to stretch this evening out. This is a present for me. *He* is a present for me. All wrapped up in the glittering packaging of my choosing. So now I need to take my time. I carefully lick him through the panties, getting the fabric wet where he can't get it wet. He sighs hard, and that urges me onward. I make my lips open and sloppy and draw as much of his satin-clad sex as I can into my mouth. He immediately arches to help me, pushing his hips forward in a greedy, hungry way, demanding with his body that I give him more of the contact that he so desperately craves.

But I always like the feeling of being hidden at the beginning. When it's me on the receiving end of a little tongue-pleasure, I love the moments before Justin reveals me. When he eats me through my panties, pressing his mouth against the satin or lace or silk, I think I'll go crazy if I can't feel his tongue on my naked flesh. Now, I treat him to this same sensation, until I sense he is on the verge.

Only then do I reach up and grab hold of the waistband and slide those panties down. As I do, I think about what it feels like when he ultimately takes my panties down. When he moves over me on the bed and glides my underpants off and down my thighs. I tremble with the knowledge of what is about to happen. He's the one trembling now. I am extremely aware of the fact that I have a harness on under my jeans and that my newly purchased sex toy is packed in there, getting warm from the heat of my body. It's as if that sexy toy is actually growing larger. I know this is all in my head, but I feel myself expand, as if the synthetic sex really is a part of myself.

Gingerly, he steps out of the pretty panties, and then he stands there, and he waits.

"Aren't you behaving well for me?" I ask.

Justin doesn't say a word.

"I know that you want to toss me onto the mattress and take me hard. I know that. But this is my night, my call."

Still, he's silent.

I have read the script that he will be acting in. I know that there is no actual sex, there is only the allusion to what this character likes when the lights are out. But we are pushing the limits, aren't we? We're going deep into our research now, so that later, when he's playing the part, he'll have this evening to draw from. The truth is, of course, that he doesn't need us to do this. He's an actor, after all. He knows how to play make-believe. Otherwise, would he have to kill someone when playing the part of a murderer? Would he have to cheat on me if cast in the role of an adulterer? No. Not at all. But this sort of sidetrack into another world is fun for the two of us. If it makes him a better actor, that's an added bonus. If it makes him a better lover, that's something I get to enjoy.

The wanting urges throb in his eyes, yet to make me happy he waits. Good boy, I think as I lead him to the mattress. Sweet boy, I think as I help him to lie down on the bed. I make my way down his body, licking from the curve of his neck to the top of his corset, touching him wherever the skin is exposed.

When I can't be patient any longer, I mean, I just can't wait, I part my slacks and reveal my toy. But that's as far as we can go on that route, because I can't really take charge of Justin in that way. Yes, he looks sweet and subdued in his newly purchased outfit. And yes I have gotten turned on by playing the role of the aggressor, but now I need Justin to take over, and he knows it. Going the other route just wouldn't be right for us. Now, I need my man back.

He can't do it while he's wearing the girly corset. That would be too much. While I watch, he rips his way out of it, and only then does he take charge, plunging into me so hard that I scream. I don't know what it is about tonight that's made us into these two wild creatures, and I don't have the time to ponder it. I simply revel in the fact that we're let loose, out of control as we come together, and then collapse in a heap in each other's arms.

Naked on the bed, he looks up at me with a glazed happy expression; the well-satisfied expression of a perfectly worn-out lover. It's an echo of the look on my own face, I'm sure.

"Smile for the camera," he says, and then reaches over to press the button, capturing the discarded corset in the corner, the fishnets still on his well-toned legs.

*****

Taking pictures of Justin as I follow him on his normal, everyday routines does more than make me feel guilty. In some dark, dangerous way, it excites me. I find myself deeply turned on by following him, and I can't fathom why this is. Maybe the illicitness of the act is what I find appealing. Or perhaps it's just the fact that I'm really and truly giving in to being a voyeur. Every photographer is one at heart. That's a fact that almost goes without saying. Now I'm wallowing in the experience. I take pictures of Justin on his Harley, and photos of him as he goes into his agent's office building.

Truthfully, I would have thought that following someone was harder than it turns out to be. But Justin has no reason to suspect that he's being followed. He's lost in his own world as he makes his way through his day-to-day life. He simply never looks in my direction as I snap pictures of him through diner windows when he's hanging out with his friends, or entering his favorite bar.

Rolls upon rolls gather on my shelves—the evidence of my growing addiction. So when Kate invites me to go shopping with her, I immediately say 'yes.' It's a way for me to be sure that I won't go out following Justin again; at least, not this afternoon.

"Where are you going?" Justin asks on the phone.

"Shopping."

"Where?"

"You know. Probably the mall with Kate." I name our favorite stores, and he laughs to himself.

"Don't go crazy," he says.

"No," I promise. But I can't tell him the rest. Can't tell him the truth.

I've already gone a little crazy, haven't I?

*****

At the end of the afternoon, when we've chosen and paid for far too many items—Kate and I take a cab down the street to Dinnah's Diner for an early supper. Kate has decided to wear a gorgeous new red dress to dinner. She looks amazing, and she knows it.

After folding herself into the cab she starts to tell me a new story. "A salon story," she says. It's comforting, as always, to listen to Kate tell one of her tawdry tales. This fact is what has tied our relationship together for so many years.

She keeps her voice low at first, to capture my attention. "You know I'm particular about my hair." She pats the blonde bouffant that has managed to stay in place even after all her outfit changes, and I nod. "And someone at work recommend this new place, Menage, saying to ask for Darren. The girl who recommended the salon has fabulous hair, so I decided to try him out."

"Literally and figuratively," I guess.

"Don't rush me. I'm getting there," Kate says, giving me a sly smile. "The place is in West Hollywood, and it's really high fashion. The girls behind the desk are identical to the ones at Stingers Bar & Grill. Tall, thin, model types. I could have knocked one over with my pinky." Kate sighs. "I got changed and was led by one twiglet to Darren's station, and he just, well, he seemed very taken with me."

"What's he like?" I ask, wanting a mental picture to go with the sexy story.

"French. Extremely French. All around the mirror were pictures of him with famous people. Huge celebrities. Most of the photos featured his arms around the most stunning starlets, and from the way he looked in each picture, I decided that he was straight. That and the way that he kept staring at my chest. I'd draped the robe around myself, of course, but the neckline was slightly open, so..."

I feel sure that the cabby is listening to the conversation, too. Kate must have noticed, but she doesn't stop talking. In fact, Kate seems to actually raise her voice, obviously enjoying her audience. Kate rarely stops when she has people listening.

"So...," I prompt.

"So he was exquisite with my hair. You know it's blonder now than it used to be, and that's all Darren's doing. He's a master at color, and he doesn't usually do anything but color. He has other people who cut and shampoo and blow dry, but he did it all for me."

I poke her and she pokes me back.

"I mean, he washed my hair, he dyed it, cut it, and then styled it for me. But the blow dry was the most sensational part." She pauses dramatically. "It was like sex."

"What do you mean? Like sex how?"

"He had my head tilted back against the flat of his stomach, and he worked over my hair with the brush and the blow dryer, smoothing and fixing and crooning in French to me the whole time. I sort of rubbed the back of my head against him, and he lowered the chair slightly, so my head was leaning lower. Leaning you know where. And I could tell he was as turned on by me as I was by him."

"You're kidding. That's got to be customer harassment, or something."

"Not when I was the one initiating it, silly. Or, if not totally initiating it, then responding to it. Moving with him, each and every step of the way. Pretty soon my hair was done, but he didn't stop stroking it with his fingertips for several minutes. When he was through, he led me to the back room to get changed. And that's when things got really interesting—"

"More so than fondling him with your head in public?"

"Much more. He led me back to the changing room, and I went in and then left the curtain partly open. Only a crack, but I could tell he was standing there, waiting. Was I going to put on a show for him through the opening, or was I going to invite him in with me? That was the question."

"I know the answer," I say in a sing-song voice, and Kate play-punches me. "Finally, I put my hand out between the slit in the curtains and drew him into the room with me. He stayed with his back pressed against the wall, watching as I took the robe off, stopping me before I could put my dress back on. He was so gentle, his hands on my breasts, his mouth on my neck."

I am extremely grateful when Kate finally lowers her voice. "And I know that it sounds cliché, but he could definitely French kiss. I mean it was as if he had taken lessons. The things he did with his mouth were unbelievable, and then, what he did with his you know what—and my was he big—"

"You did it in the dressing room?" I pause before backing up to her previous statement. "How big?"

"Big. You know," Kate gestures with her hands and I suck in my breath at the length she's describing. "We did it right against the mirror. There were other mirrors in the room, so we could see ourselves from all these different angles. It was like being in a hotel room in Vegas, I guess, but not sleazy. There was this totally erotic effect of seeing us reflected so many ways. He had his clothes off, too, and I could see his back even as he was in front of me. The whole scenario was sort of disorienting, but very arousing."

We arrive at the restaurant, and Kate pulls me from the cab. The driver seemed so sad to see us go. "Of course," Kate says in a hushed tone as we enter the building. "I left out the best part."

"Best?"

"He was totally kinky."

"Kinky how?"

"He still had the hairbrush with him, and when we finished doing it the first time—" I look at her, wondering how many times they managed to have sex in one evening, but not stopping her to ask, "—he told me what a naughty girl I was, seducing him at the salon, having my way with him."

I sense exactly where she's going with this. I know from Kate's tales in the past just how much she likes to have a man take charge of her. Kate has no fear when it comes to exploring her sensuality and sexuality. If she wants to be tied down, she says it clearly to the man she's with. And if she wants to do the tying, she is just as up front about her desires. So the fact that she is about to tell me that this new lover gave her a sexy spanking, should not shock me at all. That said, it shocks me anyway when she says, "and he pulled me over his lap and used the back of the brush against my bottom."

"How do you find these guys who like to do stuff like that?" I can't stop myself from asking.

"I don't know. It's as if like minds are drawn to each other. Like fate, or something. Besides," she says, "spanking is hardly taboo anymore. You just don't get out enough."

"What do you mean?"

"Did you see that issue of the latest Entertainment magazine? The one with all those celebrity portraits?"

I shake my head.

"Geez, you should pay attention. They were pictures like you take. Odd, off-the-wall photos of big-time celebs. And there was this one of Ben Stiller in a suit with this pretty girl over his lap. He had his hand raised to spank her, and she was just getting a huge thrill out of the whole thing. The photographer claimed to be going for an old-fashioned porno look, and Stiller went with it."

"Wasn't it loud?" I ask Kate, bringing her back around to her own story. "Couldn't other people hear?"

"I was his last client of the day, and he'd let the other people go before following me into the changing room."

"Didn't it hurt? I mean, a hairbrush?" I swallow hard. I can't picture it. Can't visualize any part of what Kate's describing. I mean, I can see it in my head, but I can't imagine it actually happening. Not to her. Not to me.

Kate shrugs. "I've got a bit of padding back there," she says matter-of-factly. "And it's supposed to hurt a little, if you know what I mean."

It's obvious from my expression that I don't.

"The slight sting makes the sex that much sweeter afterward.

Or during. Because he even slapped my ass while we were doing it, and I could see his flushed red handprints on my pale skin in the mirror. It just drove me wild to be marked by him."

I shudder again. It sounds intensely daring. Maybe that's why it's making me so wet. I feel lucky that Kate could be so open about her desires when she talks to me, and I wish I could be more open about mine. Of course, that's why I've always liked hanging out with Kate—her total and heartfelt honesty. The upshot of her honesty, of her need to talk about her deeds, is that her endless supply of stories serves as fuel for my fantasies. What would Justin say if I confessed that I wanted to try some of the things that Kate talks endlessly about? And if Justin wouldn't be into it, then what about Connor?

CHAPTER NINE

I finally work my way through some of the rolls of film that have been waiting impatiently on my shelf. Impatiently, how? Inanimate objects are generally fairly patient, right? They don't complain or argue or whine if you leave them alone. But I do get stressed when film backs up on the shelves in my darkroom. My memory goes slightly hazy about which pictures are the most important to get to. I plan a marathon session because Justin is at another night shoot. I crank Pink Floyd's *Dark Side of the Moon* and I work slowly and steadily through the evening.

Sometimes when I work alone, I drink. Not a lot. Just a little. By one in the morning, I'm slightly lubricated, but still going strong. The momentum pushes me forward. Yet it still takes me a minute to realize that some of the pictures I'm developing aren't shots that I recognize. This is strange, because I keep good track—at least, good mental track—of my work. I know what I take—if not each individual photo, then at least each scenario. And I know that these pictures aren't mine.

The last twelve on the roll are photos that I took at the Tantamount Hotel's private party. I did it as a favor for Kate, taking three and half rolls of candids for her own personal use. But the rest of the photos are new to me. There's a picture that's over-exposed, followed by several photos of a woman. Close-up photos so that I don't recognize the woman's body as someone I know. But I do know that the model is definitely female.

This isn't a roll of someone else's film that I accidentally picked up. The final pictures are mine. And even though this is a back-up camera that I used, I don't leave my camera anywhere that anyone could get to it. Nobody at the party had access to my camera for even a moment. In fact, nobody but Justin could ever get a hold of my bag without me knowing.

Justin.

Watch my back.

That's what Kate said, and as I look at the pictures, I can't get her words out of my mind because Justin and I have a rocky history. We've been together for the roller-coaster ride of four years in our early twenties, when drama is queen and turmoil seems somehow sexy. And now we've settled down into a comfort zone—or at least, we had. So why the sudden heat again?

Kate said watch my back.

But that doesn't make any sense, does it? I should be watching my heart. I should be building up strong towering walls and protecting myself from the inside out, making sure that I don't get hurt. Yet I can't make myself do that. I can't be hard and cold on the surface the way Kate is. I can't melt for a new man one night, then turn back to ice only to melt for another the next. That's not the way I am. And that's not the way I'm supposed to be, right?

No, not when it comes to love. With love, you're supposed to glide on without worries. Supposed to, I say, because nothing really works like that, does it? Not outside of a Danielle Steele novel, anyway.

So maybe Kate is right. That's what I start to wonder. Sure there could be a logical explanation to why there are naked pictures on my roll of film. But none come immediately to mind.

Maybe Kate knows something that I don't know. Kate knows a lot. That's for sure. She's been around the block several times, and I mean that only in the nicest sense of the phrase. She's lived her own wild, turbulent lifestyle, and she has seen the proof of others. As the manager of the ritzy Tantamount Hotel, she has watched temper tantrums in the lobby, has seen lovers stalk in and out in throws of anger and fits of passion. She has the experience in order to offer advice.

I'm not a lunatic, though. I'm not overly protective of Justin. I don't quiz him about where he goes or what he does. But after another exceptionally dirty night together, I decide to follow him once again. The day at the beach was just that: a day at the beach. The other times I followed him, well, I can write those off as taking candid shots of the man I love. But does he always go where he says he does? Are there times when he takes shortcuts, or side streets, or back alleys?

Thinking like this is crazy, right? Crazy, maybe, but so what. I can't help myself. So I take my camera and I stake out his Harley where it's parked at the studio. I wait, planning on following him when he returns from the shoot. After several hours, I curl up in my car and I watch. And the thing of it is, I don't learn anything. Not anything hard and cold that I can use. All I learn is that he doesn't come back to get his bike. Not all night long. Which is what I expected, anyway, because he told me he had a night shoot. Night shoots generally last all night long. Sometimes they last longer than that if the cast goes out drinking afterwards. People get all wound up from the experience of working; they need to go out, to drink a little, to talk a little. No harm in that. Never thought so, anyway.

But in my car, waiting, I start to see the potential harm.

Because when I close my eyes, all I see in my head are pictures of that woman—her curves and her lines, and the secrets of her body. I own her now. Without every having met her, I own her—and I shake my head and try to clear an image there that will never go away.

And in the morning, Justin strolls up the sidewalk and I see him, cigarette dangling from his heartbreaker lips. Maybe I know right then. Maybe I know everything.

But the thing of it is, maybe I don't want to believe.

*****

Of course, I have to admit here that I'm no innocent myself. Is it easier for me to distrust Justin because I have flaws of my own? That said, is anyone perfect? Can you trust anyone all the time?

Not to say that Justin should be tailing me, but I will confess that just like the majority of the population I have my weaker moments. I think for the first two years that Justin and I were together I didn't see another man. I don't mean 'see' as a euphemism for dating or screwing. I mean I actually didn't see any other man. Males of the species simply didn't exist for me. I was wrapped up in my world with Justin, pleased to have blinders on.

Then one day when Kate and I were out together at one of our favorite cafes, she pointed to a guy she thought was attractive. Or to use Kate's exact words— "Man, is he hella fine."

I looked up, saw the guy in question, and nodded. Yeah, he was good-looking. Really, good-looking. Not my type, precisely, but definitely hot. Chiseled and picture perfect. And then I realized that I hadn't really looked at a man for years. So I started. It was as if that one glimpse reminded me that men were out there. Not that I looked a lot, and not dangerously, but I watched. I saw cute men when Kate and I went drinking, and I paid attention sometimes when they flirted.

Sure, when I take pictures, I see guys. But that's different. That's solely on a professional basis—and my eyes are always focused on unique situations. Not handsome. Not pretty. Not comely or fine. I just see lines and curves, planes and shapes.

And then I saw Connor.

Look, I don't know how to describe what that meant—that I saw him. But I did. We didn't act on it. Not then, anyway. We simply made the non-verbal acknowledgement that we liked each other. That was good enough for the moment. Good enough to know that we'd made the agreement not to act, but that we were each interested in the other. Anyone could see that. Attraction that strong is hard to hide. Didn't mean I'd ever give up Justin for him, or that I'd ever cheat on Justin with him. But are fantasies really cheating? Do we all believe the Jimmy Carter rule—I've sinned many times in my heart?

*****

The automatic doors of the grocery store whisk silently open. There, off to one corner, is my crush. And, God is he cute. I mean, really amazing looking. Rock stars have nothing on Connor. He's just one of those people who makes anything look good-- even a white t-shirt, jeans, heavy black work boots, and a green apron. There's nothing model-like or phony about him; simply his fine, strong arms, his hard body, his boyish grin. The way his hair falls into his eyes and he tosses it away with an impatient flick of his head. The way his eyes widen when he sees me, and he ducks his chin in a wordless greeting.

Yep, there's my crush. Number-one crush.

Doesn't everyone have one? Someone who you think about sometimes even when you're in a relationship. A solid relationship. Even when you're not supposed to fantasize about someone else. Don't tell me I'm the only one, because I know I'm not. Eighty percent of women fantasize about cheating—and I don't want to even get started on how many actually go through with the dirty deed. The number is far too depressing.

Today, Connor is working in the produce department, busy with the green plastic containers of deeply ripe, black cherries. When he sees me staring at him, he smiles and we engage in our standard flirtatious glances. But this time is different. This time I walk over and push forward with the small talk. Connor gives me a smile, but his eyes change when I pull out my camera.

"What?" he asks.

"Humor me," I tell him. "I'm always like this—"

It's not like this is anything new. He knows all about me. He knows that I take his picture at the bar, and at the grocery store and that I like to catch him when he's not looking and I don't mind taking his picture when he is looking. Still, he teases me.

"Always taking pictures of people when they're playing with cherries?" Why is that sentence so erotic? I gloss over it as I answer.

"Always taking pictures," I tell him, and then SNAP! I've caught him forever in my lens.

For some reason, seeing Justin come home so late changes the way I look at Connor. Not that I'd trade Justin tit-for-tat. Not that I'd give up all we have for one sweet fling. But today I don't make any effort to hide the fact that I like Connor. I actually flirt with him, almost as if I'm trying the concept on for size. And the thing of it that surprises me is that this makes me feel almost more miserable than I was before.

Almost, I say, because I have to admit that when Connor smiles at me and says my name as I leave, I feel a fluttering in my chest that warms me all the way home.

*****

I don't tell anyone what I've got myself into. I don't even tell Kate, and usually I tell her everything. But I stake Justin out again. In fact, I start to stake him out almost daily. Because I'm a photographer, I don't have the type of regular job that would make this an interference. I can't imagine being on a full-time stakeout if I were a manager of a hotel the way Kate is. Yeah, I do have occasional deadlines—I take pictures for a few different weekly 'zines, and I've landed a few cool gigs, as well. CD covers. Posters. But mostly I take pictures. So taking pictures of Justin doesn't slow me down any.

I catch him at all angles, in all sorts of situations. And I know he doesn't know. That he doesn't have any idea. Why should he? Why would he ever think I'd do something as loony as this? Nothing in my personality suggests that I would crack so quickly, that I would skulk around and try to find out facts. I'm the type of person who is as honest as my pictures. In the past, if I've had a problem with something he's done or something he's said I've come out immediately and told him how I feel. Given it a name and waited for him to give it a solution. We've been adults in our relationship for the most part. I'm behaving immaturely now, and I'm in too deep to stop myself because all I see are pictures in my head—pictures of a naked girl who I don't know, who I can't place. I can't let it go. I can't ask him. I have to follow. That's all there is to it. I have to watch. When I know for a fact, then I'll be able to make my decisions, to make my confrontations. When I know, then I can be sure. Until then, I'm in limbo.

But I am changed by my snooping. I have to hide the rolls of film that I take. He can never see the pictures of him surfing out at the beach, or drinking beer at the James Beach Cafe with his buddies because there's no reason for me to own these images. I have to catch myself, force myself from slipping up, from letting on that I know more than I know. I have to let him tell me things in his own time, and when he omits facts that I know, then I start to wonder.

Kate said, watch your back.

So I'm watching.

*****

SNAP!

Justin hears the camera and he turns to look at me. I see his eyes focused on mine through the viewfinder, and I lower the camera. I've followed him out to a club, and I've gotten closer than I generally would have dared to. But he was busy chatting with his buddies so I didn't think he'd notice. I was wrong.

"Hey, Alex," he says, smiling at me. "Hey, baby, didn't think you could come out tonight." He's pleased to see me. I can tell that it doesn't occur to him that I've been up to anything indiscrete. He thinks it just me, his photographer girlfriend. Same as always. Taking the pictures wherever I go.

I shrug, as if I've planned this, even though my breathing is too quick. My cheeks flushed.

"Do you wanna go in?" he asks knowing that I don't do the club scene too often anymore. Way back when, I hung out at the places people go. Coconut Teasers. The Whiskey. The Viper Room. Now, it's just a lot of noise to me. Unless I'm there in a professional capacity, taking candid shots for one of the Weekly papers, I generally avoid the raucous scene. So I shrug again, to see what else he might be offering. And what he's offering is the back alley behind the club.

"You game?" he asks, nodding his head in the direction that he wants to go.

I follow him immediately, to the happy, boisterous catcalls of his friends. We don't care, though. We have no problems. No worries. But as we make our way behind the building, a whole different wave of emotions crests through me. I am on fire, once again, for Justin. And I am so guilty... My conflicting emotions make me behave in a strange manner. But I can tell that Justin doesn't mind. In fact, my odd behavior seems to excite him.

"What's gotten into you, Alex?" he wants to know as I aim the camera at him, catching the harsh sulfur-yellow light from the windows of the apartment building next door and the vermillion neon from a back-alley bar down the way. He looks vibrantly tough and rebellious, like some hoodlum straight out of a 1950s movie, and I come in close and take another picture. My heart is racing, and I know that when he gets close enough to me, he'll know just how turned on I really am.

"Come on," he says. "Put down the camera for once."

Immediately, I let it dangle from the strap around my neck and let Justin wheel me around so that my hands are on the cold brick wall, and my body is in the proper and ready position for him. I hear him whistle under his breath as he presses his body up against mine. He can tell that I'm hot, and he can tell that I want him, and he doesn't tease me this time. He doesn't take it slow or easy, but goes forward with a quick, hearty motion.

Why do I feel as if I'm spinning? Why are my thoughts racing so quickly in my head? Don't know. Can't answer that.

I think that perhaps it's the bricks that get to me. The hard, chipped dirt-red wall of bricks. My hands are flat against that wall, and from this close-up vantage point I can see every crack, every crevice. I know that Justin's far more interested in an entirely different crevice, the slippery wet one between my thighs. Yet I see what a camera would see. I see the manmade building right in front of my face, and the earthly natural action of what we're doing, juxtaposed with the city smells and gritty surroundings.

Now he's pushing up against me, sliding me into the wall with each thrust. First one hard, firm thrust, and I catch my breath, dragging in the night air, filling my lungs with the smell of the alley behind the dance club.

Tonight, I dressed to blend with the crowd, dressed sexy just in case I got caught. Is it possible that I wanted him to catch me? Maybe, because I don't usually wear outfits this risqué. I chose silver—a T-shirt style, over black fishnet stockings that stay up without a garter belt. Justin slides the dress up, high, revealing my secret weapon—no panties. And then he says, "Oh, man," and I look over my shoulder at him.

No panties is what gets to Justin. It's what makes him harder than hard. Harder than steel. It's what makes him bend down on his knees on the asphalt and press his face to the split of my body from behind. Licking me there. Drawing forth the slippery sex juices with the heady wet heat of his mouth.

That's what gets to Justin

But it's the bricks that get to me. The hardness in front of my face while his own hardness slides between my thighs. There's no resistance with the bricks. I can push as hard as I want to with the palms of my hands, and I will get exactly nowhere. The wall is set. My body is the only thing here that's going to give. Sweetly. Easily. His sex slips back and forth, driving hard inside me. I groan, lowering my head for a moment to stare down at my deep red-painted toenails visible in the open-toed sandals, the fishnet stockings crisscrossing over the nails. I need to steel myself, need to catch my balance, but I can't.

Everything feels too good this evening. Too right.

The way he pushes in, and then pulls back out again, leaving me empty and craving. The way he reaches one hand in front of my body to stroke against me, to strum his fingers against it in the exact rhythm as the beat emanating from the bar band. We can hear it all—the music, the laughter, the partying. But we're not a part of it. We are on our own—an island of two, and that's fine.

Two is all we need.

The feel of his dark denim jeans against my thighs makes me moan again. The fact that we're both mostly dressed while we do this. I love how hard he wants to do it, and yet how slow he's taking this. Even though we're out in public. Even though we could be caught, spotted and forced to stop, at any moment. He doesn't rush. He just glides in and out, teasing me all the while with his knowledgeable fingers. And then he moves in even closer, so that he can use both hands between my legs. Parting my nether lips wide, as he slides in deep again. I can't believe how sexy it feels to be opened like that with the night air on me, the rush of it on that wettest of skin. Then his thumb tricks over my split again, and I know I'm mere moments from coming—sheer sweet, desperate moments.

And when he grips my waist and pulls me hard down on him, I hear him sigh again, because he realizes exactly what he's come up against—just like my hands on the brick wall—no resistance.

*****

"Why is that one called 'No Resistance'?" Hal wants to know.

He's pointing to the picture I shot of Justin right before he did me against the back wall in the alley.

"Tough quality," Hal nods to himself. "Same guy out there on the surfboard and the beach, huh? Pretty versatile."

Now I'm the one to nod.

"Like the lighting," Hal says. "Maybe we'll use that picture in the paper."

"Oh, no," I shake my head. "Not that one. How about one of these?" And off we go to another corner, where I can point out a few of my favorites. Pictures that don't immediately make me wet when we look at them. Because reliving moments like that is dangerous. Flirting with fire, that's what the picture should be called. Flirting with explosives.

CHAPTER TEN

When it happens again, a set of pictures that I don't remember taking appeari on a roll in my camera, I start to feel kind of strange inside. Am I living some sort of double life that even I don't remember? Could I be taking pictures without recalling that I've done so? Doesn't seem probable, plausible, or even possible. Not unless I've developed some sort of wildly unusual case of amnesia, and none of my friends or acquaintances have the heart or desire to clue me into this disturbing fact.

I look at the naked woman in the pictures, and I try to figure out who she is. Her body type reminds me of someone. Not a movie star's. Not a friend's. At least, I don't think so. She's pretty. At least, her body is. But the angles make it difficult to learn much about her. I can't tell whether she's tall or short. I know her curves and I know the clear expanse of her silk-like skin. No matter how hard I stare at the pictures, I can't figure out who she is.

Finally, I decide to ask Justin. At least, I think I decide to. But when he comes home, I just look down and tell him that I'm going out with Kate tonight. Facing Justin means coming clean about what I've been up to. Staking him out. Flirting with Connor. Being bad when I should have been good.

For some unexplainable reason, I can't do that yet.

So maybe I'll tell Kate first and see what she has to say. Maybe. Big maybe.

*****

Although nobody walks in L.A.—it's like an unwritten rule, or something—Kate and I decide to, just so that we won't have to worry about the ride home. If the bar were farther away, we'd take a cab. Since it's only several blocks, we hoof it. It's nice to be able to drink freely every once in awhile. Plus, the walk is good for me. It gives me the ability to lose myself in the feelings of the night: the jack-o'-lanterns in the windows of several houses in the neighborhood, the way the air in Los Angeles sometimes smells of orange blossoms if the wind is blowing right from the valley. I'm not being poetic. It's true.

Halloween season in Los Angeles is an event in and of itself. People are so freaky anyway, that given a holiday to be extra bizarre is like courting disaster. Lola's, like The Tantamount, takes this pagan holiday seriously. Miniature glowing skeletons dangle in the windows, blinking off and on every couple of seconds. A carved pumpkin with a comically menacing face sits in the window to the right of the sign that reads, 'If you're not twenty-one, go to McDonalds.' Several candles burn inside the shell, their flickering light making the wicked face look truly evil.

When we walk through the front door, ducking under thick strands of cobwebs, I can't help but smile. Van's tending bar. Or not tending bar, as usual, but leaning over it and talking to two extremely attractive female customers. Van has a way of hosting a conversation, turning it almost into a one-man show, mesmerizing his clientele. He only mixes drinks when he truly likes the person he is serving. In general, Van serves shots and beers. Once, I witnessed a girl asking for a Convertible. She described it enthusiastically to Van as a new cherry and almond liqueur drink she'd read about in a European fashion magazine.

"Never heard of it," Van said, dismissively.

"It's new," the girl said, eyes wide with expectations. Here she was, a customer, wasn't Van supposed to mix her what she asked for? But Van had his own idea. "How about a shot and a beer?" he said with a wink.

Now, seeing us approaching, Van straightens up and turns toward the shelf of liquor. From the rear view, he looks amazing, muscles bulging, arms huge in a white ribbed tank top, hat cocked impishly on the back of his head. I catch sight of his reflection in the blue-tinted mirror behind the bar. His face is decorated with black ink tattoos from a youthful brush with gang life. The ebony tears permanently etched beneath the corners of his eyes go dramatically with his weightlifter's body. One of my very best candid pictures is of Van at the end of the night, locking up the bar. It's a quiet shot—subdued and even slightly graceful. The black and white captures an essence in Van, an almost gentlemanly quality that people sometimes miss. The tattoos make him look more than slightly menacing, but the facial decorations don't keep him from getting women. He's a charmer.

Van knows what we drink, and he has the martinis ready for us by the time we grab our favorite barstools off to one side of the bar, across from the jukebox. We take this gesture for what it was—a genuine compliment—and tip accordingly. Van graciously sweeps the money off the counter and then slides back to chatting up the two women, who I now notice are twins. Their bright red hair is swept off their faces in identical ponytails. Their clothes, emerald green slip dresses, show more skin than I generally reveal on the beach. It doesn't seem to me that Van is favoring one twin over the other. He's like a porn movie come to life. I can easily imagine him in a redheaded twin sandwich, Van the filling, the two girls the skinny pieces of white bread.

The image excites me. I mentally see myself taking pictures of such an erotic act, and when Van turns toward me for a moment, he shoots me a quizzical stare. What kind of expression is on my face? I can only wonder.

Kate and I sip the drinks appreciatively for a moment, and then my friend turns her eyes on me.

"So?" she asks. "You want to tell now, or wait until you're drunk."

She can sense something is wrong. We've known each other long enough for that. She can sniff out my troubles, even if I haven't given her any sort of clues. No hard and fast ones. But the truth is that I don't want to tell her, or anyone. I don't want to admit to the fact that I've been following Justin. And I especially don't want to tell Kate that she's probably right about him—don't want to tell her about the pictures, have her guess what they might mean, put my suspicions into words. So I just shake my head.

"Maybe later," I tell her. "Right now, just talk to me about anything; literally, anything. I don't want to think about me for awhile."

Kate smiles as if she's been waiting for the opening. "I most definitely have something juicy to share," she grins. I lean in closer to hear. Kate's stories are the best. They're like some decadent dessert that you dream about weeks ahead of time, something you remember wistfully long after it's finished. Maybe someday I'll share my own stories with Kate with the same amount of relish that she gives to each and every tantalizing tale.

"I was off yesterday," Kate begins, "my first day of freedom since I started training Maggie as assistant manager." She rolls her eyes to let me know how that endeavor is going. Obviously, it's not going well. Not many people are born with Kate's grace, her ability to handle difficult situations with ease. Training someone to fill in for her when she's unreachable is something that Kate doesn't enjoy.

"Sorry," I say. "I know how much you hate that."

Kate shrugs. "Has to be done by someone," she says, "so to celebrate, I spent the morning puttering in my apartment. I fed the cat, took a shower, and sat on my bed in my robe reading the *Los Angeles Times.*"

I visualize the picture. I accompanied Kate on the shopping trip when she bought the risqué robe. It was a Kitten's Top Drawer purchase—a short blue satin number that has matching open-toed, high-heeled slippers. The type of slippers that send most men into fits of instant ferocious fantasy. The shoes are almost too delicious to wear, and the robe itself is like some incendiary device. You can't look at it without thinking s-e-x.

I easily imagine Kate dressed in her goodies, even though she says she was by herself at the time. I'd never wear frivolous items like the ones she has if a man were not involved in the scenario. I'd feel silly parading around in my apartment all dolled up if I didn't have someone to view my fancy dress. But Kate is a firm believer in self-pampering. Whether she's seeing someone or not—and she generally is—she takes care of herself, getting pleasure from dressing sexy even when she is alone. You read about how healthy this is in ladies' magazines, but I don't know anyone else who actually does it. Whenever Justin's out and I'm home alone, I wear my oldest, rattiest gray sweats that I've had since college. This is a glitch in my wiring, something Kate is constantly after me to change.

"At some point, I looked out the window and saw a man."

"On the street?"

"On the roof, across from my building."

"What was he doing on the roof?" I picture some thickly muscled cable worker in a stained shirt and ripped jeans-- just Kate's type, of course. She's an equal opportunity seducer.

"Smoking," Kate pauses. "I know I shouldn't say this, since you just quit, but he was so sexy. You know how some men can really do a cigarette justice? The way they inhale and let the smoke just leisurely curl out of their mouths. This guy didn't know I was watching him, didn't think anyone was watching him, and he was deeply really enjoying his first cigarette of the day. He had finesse."

I take another sip of my drink, waiting. Kate is a master story-teller. She gives each story a strong edge of suspense, drawing you in slowly, saving the very best details for when you're salivating and ready like I am right now.

"I moved closer to my window, sitting right on the edge of the sill, so I could see him better. He was tall with straight blonde hair. He was wearing a white tank top, and there was a band tattoo around his right arm."

"What kind of tattoo?" I ask. I like tattoos. They seem dangerous in an intriguing way, regardless of the fact that they fade in and out of fashion in the rest of mainstream society. In L.A., they always seem the appropriate accessory, whether you're wearing a t-shirt or an evening gown.

"I couldn't see from my apartment."

"Well, what was his body like?" I ask, wanting to keep up with the mental picture. I love Kate's stories. And tonight I'm dying to hear one of her fantastic tales—anything to keep my mind off my own various troubles.

"Fine," Kate says, shaking her head appreciatively. Her dangling silver-and-turquoise earrings sway back and forth, sparkling even in the dim light of the bar. "Fine," she says again, smiling at the memory. I can tell that she doesn't mean fine as in adequate. She means fine as in fabulous. "It was obvious that he worked out. His tank top was tight and thin, and he had the kind of stomach that has ripples of muscles in it. Washboard, right? But his body wasn't overly pumped, not the way Van's is."

Van turns in our direction when he hears his name, and I realize that he's been eavesdropping even as he's flirting over in the corner. In answer to Kate's comment, he flexes his biceps at us and smiles.

"He was tan," Kate continues, "probably from sitting out on top of the roof, and he had Wayfarer style sunglasses on, which are my absolute favorite." She pauses, thinking, ready to reconstruct. Kate's always willing to give detailed information, to make her tales really come to life for her listeners." He was wearing faded jeans slung low on his hips, and all in all he looked like one of those guys in *Playgirl Magazine*. Just with more clothes on."

"So you watched him smoking all morning?" Now, I smile at the thought. I know Kate is capable of spending hours staring at a man. I've been with her at cafes when she won't let us leave because she has her sights on some handsome stud. We've spent whole afternoons lingering over cups of coffee while Kate plays her 'look, look away, look back' games with her prey. She has this way of getting a man to think that he's the one who's spotted her, when really, she is the one in charge the whole time. While I sit at her side, growing jittery from too much caffeine, Kate makes romantic movie plots come to life.

"You think I just watched him smoke?" she asks me. "Does that sound like something I'd waste my time doing?"

"You're such a voyeur."

"And you're so sheltered," Kate replies casually, "I'm only at the beginning."

"Then tell me," I say, and my voice borders on begging. "Stop teasing."

"Never," Kate smirks, finishing her drink and waving to Van that she's ready for another. But she doesn't make me wait long. Telling me the story is obviously one way that she can relive it herself. "First, I started brushing my hair, not looking at the guy directly, but able to see him out of the corner of my eye. I wanted to catch him right when he noticed me." Kate's white-blonde hair is an eye-catcher. Men always glance up at her when she comes into a room.

"You know," I say, pleased, "this sounds just like the beginning of one of those dirty letters you read in *Penthouse Forum*. The kind that start, 'You're not going to believe this, but just the other day I was sitting on my window sill, brushing my long blonde hair when I saw the most amazing man...'"

"How would you know about those letters?" Kate asks, "Those dirty letters," she adds, emphasizing the word *dirty*. She drinks a bit more of her martini and watches me blush, but she doesn't push me. "You're right, though. It could be," Kate agrees, "and it gets better.

When I knew he was looking, I stood up and undid my robe."

"You did not!"

"I behaved as if I were just getting dressed for the day," Kate says, "but my shades happened to be open. I mean I acted entirely innocent. You know, like, I'll take the robe off, and then—*Oh, golly! What am I going to wear? I just can't decide. Oh, innocent and naked me!* —I wandered around my room in the buff for a while, knowing that he could see me, all of me, and then I grabbed a thong, one of my white lace ones, and slid into it, slowly. I stared at my reflection for a moment, then took off those panties and put on a pair of sheer pink ones. I stared at these for a moment, as if I just wasn't sure whether they were the ones for me. I wanted to be sure that he'd seen me naked, that he'd caught sight of the new design I'm sporting down there."

I held up a hand to stop her. "Excuse me?"

"You know, after I got you to try out the latest Sphinx look, I decided on something else."

"Which is?"

"You know mine's really light. So I had Gizelle etch a pink heart right where it matters most."

I try to imagine asking someone for a request like this, and I can't. I would never have had the nerve to do even what I've done down there if Kate hadn't given me the treat as a present. She starts talking again, now, assured that both Van and me are picturing her pink-tinted private parts.

"Finally, I pulled my jeans on and added a silk tee-shirt. When I came back to the window, he was staring right at me."

"Of course he was, after a show like that. He must have burned himself on the cigarette butt."

Kate ignores me. "When I looked back at him, he waved."

"Waved like 'hi, there'?" I wave my hand back and forth and Van, seeing me, waves back but doesn't come over. It looks as if he's about to seal the deal with the redheads. I forget Kate for a moment, as I think about what that might possibly mean, what it must be like to live in Van's world—where every customer is a potential bedmate, and every bedmate is a potential twin. Who lives their life like that? Apparently, the two redheads do. And Kate. And Justin—

No, I don't want to think that right now. Blinking quickly, I turn my attention back to Kate.

"Or waved like this?" I use my hand to motion, fingers crooked in a "come here" gesture. Now Van starts toward us, but I shake my head quickly, indicating that I am not quite ready for another drink.

"The second one," Kate says, "so I kicked on my mules and walked across the street to his building. I wasn't even thinking clearly. I mean, how was I going to get in, right? He was out on the roof. I was down below on the ground. But it must have been fate... "—Kate is a big believer in fate—" ...because some guy was coming out of the apartment building, and he held the door open for me, which is absolutely unheard of on my block, but I didn't question it. I walked right in, as if I had every right to be there, and I literally ran up the stairs until I found the door that said, 'roof.' Good thing I've taken all those step classes, or I would have been totally out of breath. That would have been a total turn-off." Kate's a curvy girl, but she's toned.

"And he was waiting for you?"

"There wouldn't be much of a story if he'd left, right?"

I nod in agreement as Kate takes a sip of her drink. "He was exactly where I'd last seen him. Sitting on the edge of the roof, still smoking, but now he was facing the doorway instead of my window."

"He knew you had come up to see him?" I prompt.

"Of course, he knew. He'd watched me walk across the street and everything. But when I saw him, I stopped at the doorway, staring. His tattoo, which I could see more clearly, was some sort of tribal design done in that blue-black ink. It looked awesome around his big, hard bicep. I stayed where I was, quiet, not sure what to say."

"That doesn't sound like you."

"All right," Kate admits, "I said, 'Hey there, I saw you sitting out here all by yourself, and I was wondering...?' And he said, 'Yes?'

and he had this deep sexy voice, like a radio announcer, or like the deejay at Club Starstruck on Sunset. You know?"

"Yeah," I tell her. "I know." Voices can be really important. I remember how excited I was when Justin first left messages on my answering machine. I'd save them, listening again and again to the replay of his dark, whiskey-soft voice.

"I really had no plan, so I just said, 'I was wondering if you had a light.'"

"Smooth," I say, trying to imagine what I would have said in a similar situation. But since I've never really been in that sort of situation, since I don't let myself *get* into those types of situations, I can't picture it. What would I have done? The only thing I can think is that I'd have taken his picture. That's what I always do. It's how I met Justin. It's how I met Kate. I take people's pictures everywhere I go.

Kate continues with her story. "He said that he did have a light, but I didn't have a cigarette since, as you know, I don't smoke. It didn't matter, though. By the time I'd walked over to him, he'd crushed out the cigarette and was just waiting there for me, this extremely patient, very interested look on his face." Kate mimics the look for me, making me laugh out loud. It isn't merely "interested." The expression on her face is incredibly hungry, eyelids half closed, lips curved into a half-smile. The look is pure sex in motion.

"What did you do?" I finally ask, and then I shake my head in disbelief, "You're not actually going to tell me that you made love to him." Except, I know that is precisely what Kate is going to tell me. By this point in our relationship, is there anything that should shock me about Kate? No. Not really. Yet she manages to surprise me every time we meet. It's what makes us such good friends. I'm the straight man for her. I respond exactly how she needs her audience to react.

But now Kate shakes her head, and for a moment I am taken aback. Will this story have a surprise ending? "Of course not, silly. I never make love to a man on the first date."

"Date?" I challenge.

"On the first whatever—the first chance rooftop meeting, the first window-striptease. You call it what you want." Kate sips her nearly empty drink, then motions to Van that she's ready for another. Kate can put them away. She doesn't speak until I kick her, lightly, under the bar, and then she says, "I didn't make love to him, Alex. He made love to me. Screwed the living daylights out of me, to be precise."

The woman on the bar stool next to Kate turns to look at her when she says these words. Kate ignores the girl, but thankfully, she lowers her voice when she adds, "He was an incredible lay." Even though she speaks in a stage whisper, I can tell that our bar-neighbor has heard the words from the little laugh that escapes her.

I look over at the girl and when she smiles at me, I see a flash of silver in her mouth—she must have a pierced tongue. Although that isn't a new type of adornment, the concept always floors me. I'd like to stare at her longer, piercings captivate the photographer in me, but Kate puts one hand on mine and squeezes it, wanting my attention.

"Did he have protection?" I ask, staying with Kate's story.

"Yeah," Kate laughs. "I guess he usually has something on him, because there was no way he could have had an idea that I was going to come over and seduce him."

"Or that he was going to seduce you—"

"Right," Kate says, before admitting, "You know, the rooftop wasn't exactly prime romping material. A gravel roof doesn't mimic a mattress in any way, shape, or form. Remember that for future use." She smiles kindly, obviously thinking that even in my wildest dreams I would never find myself having sex on a rooftop. "We started up against the edge of the concrete railing, but then we slid down onto the roof, and it was not the softest thing I've ever used for sexual romping purposes. He pulled my jeans down, and my knees and palms got all scratched up on the gravel." Kate turns her hands upward to show her wickedly acquired war wounds.

Again I try to put myself into the situation, but can't immediately wrap my mind around it. Then, in a mental flash, I understand what she's saying. "You did it doggy-style? For the first time?"

"Sure. Why not?"

"I don't know," I shake my head. I really *don't* know, but in the mirror over the bar, my face holds a look of shocked wonderment. "It's just always seemed sort of impersonal that way. When you're face-to-face, you can at least look into each other's eyes." Justin always likes it from behind—and I do, as well—but I hadn't let him do me like that until we'd been dating for several months. Solidly dating.

"I'm surprised *you* even keep your eyes open," Kate teases. She's the one friend I let get away with statements like that. "You know, Alex, sometimes face-to-face just isn't all that important. Hips to ass is nice. And when you're head to tail you have an entirely different perspective."

Kate gets off on trying to shock me. I get off on trying not to let her know when she succeeds. She's far better at this game than I am.

"So despite not looking into each other's eyes, we were pretty personal," Kate continues. "I can assure you that he got to know me very, very personally in only a few minutes."

"How long were you up there?"

"Well, we went at it for awhile on the roof, with the sun beating down on us and the noises from the street rising up to us. It was intense. His hands were all over my body, on my breasts, on my ass. I had put sunscreen before going out on the roof, and my hands were still a little slick with it. When I touched him, the oil rubbed from my skin into his, and I could smell the summery fragrance of it, and that just turned me on more. The whole situation had a vacation feel to it. Strangers connecting on a beach, or something like that."

Kate closes her eyes for a second, remembering. When she speaks again, she lowers her voice dramatically, "And just before he came, he dug his hands under me, searching out that hot gem between my legs. And then he leaned his head way back, and he just groaned in this really loud, animalistic way that made me come, too."

I sigh. The whole story sounds amazing to me, doing it like

animals in broad daylight on the roof of an apartment building.

"Then what?" I ask, my voice hoarse.

"We fixed our clothes in silence. We weren't really naked, just in disarray. Then he took my hand and led me to his apartment, and we did it again there, first on his futon, still a bit gravely and sweaty from being outside, and then in the shower. It was only a tiny shower, just like the one in my apartment, but he had me pressed up against the cool, blue-tiled wall, and he talked dirty to me the whole time."

"Dirty, how?"

"What do you mean, 'dirty, how?' Dirty like dirty. Like, filthy. Like, he said, 'You're such a bad girl. You're such a little slut. That game you played getting dressed today, standing almost naked where I could see you. I've seen you in your window before, naughty girl, and I know you like people watching you. I knew every bit of your body before you stepped onto the roof. I had it memorized. The curve of your ass...' and then he spanked it. " Kate's voice is a true whisper, but still I'm aware that the woman to her left is listening in again, and I have to lean closer to hear her.

"Really?" I ask. "Did you like that?"

"It just made this remarkable sound since we were all wet beneath the shower. I mean there was an echo or something. Totally sexy."

"But you let this man do *that* to you? Someone you didn't even know?"

"You're so funny." Kate gives me a look of absolute fondness, as if I were a naive student and she my willing teacher. "You're okay with the fact that I had roof sex with a total stranger, but not okay that we did it doggy-style or that we sixty-nined or that I let him spank me? You draw lines in odd places, Alex."

"Maybe I do," I admit. "But tell me more." I have to say, her story makes me more than a little hot, and I cross my legs and hope that Kate doesn't notice, or that if she does notice, she won't tease me about it. I can't tell how successful I am. She eyes me carefully, then smiles. I stare at her as she orders another drink for each of us, and when I take my first sip, the taste of gin instantly relaxes me.

"He was just my perfect kind of guy," Kate grins, "and I don't mean only because he had me bent against the wall of his shower while he slapped my ass until it was bright red. I mean he was my dream man because he had class."

Kate drains her nearly empty martini glass, then takes a sip of the new one Van had set down before continuing with her story. "And I scoped out his place while I was there. He definitely lives alone. His apartment is a studio, and he had really cool toiletries in the bathroom. So he is obviously the kind of man who spoils himself. You know I can appreciate that."

"What kind of toiletries?" I ask, still trying to sound normal. I look at the girl seated next to Kate, the one who has been surreptitiously listening to our conversation. This girl now sticks her tongue out at her friend, and I can see that I'd been right—she's showing off her piercing. A round silver ball shines against the pink of her tongue, and just this spark of glinting metal makes me suddenly dizzy, as if everything around me, every statement, every motion, is drenched in sex.

"Nice-smelling soap and a shaving brush made of real bristles," Kate replies, apparently unaware of my discomfort, "like they sell at The Soap Factory. They're absolutely decadent. And fluffy towels. The really good kind, Alex," she says, "Not ones that he'd stolen from a hotel or ratty old things that he'd had since college."

I realize that Kate, unconsciously or not, is comparing the man to her last real flame, a cheapskate named George who stole toilet paper from the hotel whenever he visited Kate at work. What I most remembered about George was his predilection for stupid rhymes. We'd be having a drink in The Stinger Bar & Grill, and George would turn to Kate and say, "I love you, I love you, I love you so well. If I had a peanut, I'd give you the shell." Once, on a double date with Justin, George had recited over appetizers, "I love you, I love you, I love you, I do. But don't get excited, I love monkeys, too." Justin had looked as if he were about to get sick all over the fajitas.

The habit of telling silly poems alone should have made Kate dump the guy, in my estimation, but Kate went on and on about the way the man could screw. She overlooked the nursery rhyme nonsense because George was talented between the sheets. It took someone even more proficient to make Kate forget George.

"We had sex three times," Kate says now, pulling me back to her tale, "and then sat in his apartment wrapped in towels, talking and drinking coffee that he made. Fresh from beans, not from instant." Kate is a coffee purist. "He had rocks of sugar like you get in Europe, in a sugar bowl. It was totally sweet."

"What does he do?" I ask, "aside from making killer coffee and smoking on rooftops and watching you through windows. Or is that his occupation?"

"He's a set designer at the little theater on La Cienega, right down the street, which is why his place was decked out so well. He has awesome wooden bookshelves and built-in cabinets. He did the whole thing himself. Plus, when I stood up to get myself more coffee, I could tell that he hadn't lied to me."

"About what?"

"You could absolutely see into my window from his place, so I knew he honestly *had* been watching me before. I don't know why I'd never seen him. I must be getting blind in my old age."

"What's his name?"

There's a long pause. Then Kate blushes—a rare occurrence for her— and says, "That's the funniest part," she grins sheepishly. I get the feeling that this is a question she hoped I wouldn't ask. "I never found out. Even when we were talking, it just didn't come up."

I put on my most shocked expression. I have a good one.

"Think about it," Kate says, trying for a suitable defense. "We didn't introduce ourselves on the roof when we first met. It would have sounded insane: 'Hi, my name's Kate and I'd like you to screw me against the side of your roof until I collapse in a puddle of liquid pleasure.' When we went inside, on his sofa, my mouth was pretty busy, so even if I had introduced myself, the words would have been all slurred against his skin. Kind of sexy, sure, but not that much of a help for actually learning someone's name. And it's not the kind of thing you say in a shower. 'Spank me harder please. I like it really hard, and, by the way, you can call me Kate.'

"When I realized, at some point during the after-conversation, that I didn't know, it was just too awkward to ask. Way too awkward. What I did, though, was write *my* name and number on a pad of paper and leave it for him. When he calls—and he *has* to call—I'm hoping I'll be able to look through the window and see him on the phone. Then I'll know for sure it's him."

"Good idea," I say, "I guess."

Van arrives with a fresh shaker full of martinis just as Kate says, "But I am thinking of writing to *Penthouse Variations*. Like you said, it's one f— of a good story, isn't it, Alex?" And Van smiles winningly at us and says, "Language, ladies, language. We're not all truckers here, you know."

I smile back at Van, reach into my purse, and bring out my camera. He gives me a look but doesn't turn away.

*****

Hal says, "That one's a little disturbing." He's looking at Van, who is facing the camera with a menacing snarl.

"He's a pussycat," I say. "Really. You have to remember. You can't judge a person by their photo."

I watch, mildly amused, as Hal writes that down.

*****

Back home I try to keep the room from spinning. At first, I don't have much luck. I squint my eyes as I attempt to tally the drinks I had with Kate. Several at the bar with Van sending over a free one as a compliment after I took his picture and then a nightcap with Kate at her place,

Kate's cat Mona running back and forth over my feet, so happy to have company that she acted as if she were a trained animal in a circus.

Kate had made a new drink, a Razzmatazz: raspberry vodka, Chambord, and 7-Up. Kate always has ingredients for mixed drinks, and she likes to try unusual ones: infusions, Vulcan Mindblowers, Flirtinis. She even has the right kind of glasses for each drink, martini style ones for Hemingway, slender shot glasses for rose-colored grappa. It's one of her favorite past-times—learning new cocktails—and since Van doesn't like to make them for us, we do it ourselves.

We'd sipped the drinks while Kate played back her phone messages to see if her new man had called. He hadn't, which made Kate frown, but two other dates had left detailed messages, both hoping Kate would call them as soon as she got in. Kate made faces as we listened to the men talk. "Boring," she'd said about the first one. "This guy talked about his dogs all night long. How he'd had them operated on so they couldn't bark any more. How one was on Prozac." Kate grimaced at the memory. "Incredibly selfish screw," she'd said about the second.

"How would you know?" I asked, teasing. I take every opportunity to tease Kate.

"Don't get me started," Kate said, collapsing on her bed and groaning. "Just a selfish, uncaring bedmate. After he came, he went right to sleep, without even unlocking me from the cuffs. Lovers like that are the absolute worst!"

"How'd you get out?"

"I kicked him until he woke up."

Drunk off our butts, we decided to get the kitty high, too, or "happy," as Kate calls it. Kate took a container of catnip from a secrete hiding place, and we spread a handful on the rug, then giggled helplessly as Mona ate every leaf, licked the rug with her rough tongue, then lay on her back with her paws in the air, purring contentedly.

Thinking about the events of the evening now, I sit upright in bed with my back firmly against the wall. Justin is out tonight.

Out filming some made-for-TV movie in the Valley. It has a high budget for a television flick, because the rights have already been sold internationally. This means that for the next few months, Justin won't have to worry about cash. It also means that tonight I'm on my own. He isn't due back home until dawn— but dawn's not really that far away now.

The digital clock on the nightstand reads 3:03. I look at the numbers, consider watching TV, but it doesn't appeal to me. There won't be anything on this late except public access shows and infomercials. And I've seen the one with the mop that can clean your ceiling way too many times. So I drink a ginger ale and stare out the window and into the Los Angeles night. This is my favorite part about living in La-La Land. At night, the lights make the city come alive in the most magical of ways. They glitter like multicolored jewels against a black velvet backdrop. For some reason, they always make me think that good things are going to happen—even in L.A.

The room is only half-dark. Lights from the city give it a hazy, dreamlike quality. I think of Kate's story, visualizing myself now in the starring role. Quickly, I slip my skirt off and kick it toward the foot of the bed. Then I bring my hands to the split of my body, stroking myself lightly through my knickers.

Because Kate is such a good storyteller, I easily visualize the man on the rooftop as Kate described him; see myself in a blue satin robe and tall slippers with marabou fluff on the toes. Working like a director, I place myself in the window, brushing my deep brown hair until it shines in the sunlight. I can feel each stroke of the brush, and my body tingles at the thought of someone observing me. There is something about being watched that is intensely arousing. Even when I'm only down at Santa Monica beach, wearing my modest tangerine-colored one-piece bathing suit and baking in the sun, I adore the feeling of eyes on me. I've never really experienced the role as an exhibitionist, but I am starting to see the positive aspects. Maybe Justin and I will start leaving the shades up.

Maybe Kate's tale will have a real and positive effect on my life. Right now, it has an effect on my solo sex life.

In this fantasy, when I look at the roof across the way, the man waves toward me. I take total control of the encounter. Slowly, I shake my head and crook my finger, motioning for him to come to my place. I do this consciously because of what Kate said about the gravel. I want to float. I want dream sex, but on a soft bed of pillows and satin blankets not rocks and pebbles. Even in a make-believe world, I am not ready to experience the raw edge that Kate lives for.

While I watch, the handsome man disappears through the door on the rooftop. I see him reappear down on the street below then I stand and walk to the door and unlatch it, leaving it partially open. Envisioning each frame of the X-rated movie in my head, I continue to stroke myself in real time, moving slowly to bring the climax closer. Sometimes, slower is better. Sometimes a long, drawn out orgasm—one that you wait for, straining, yearning—is the most satisfying.

In my imagination, I peel off the robe and sprawl out on the bed, facing the open doorway. Within moments, the man rounds the top of the stairs. He pauses in the doorway to look at me then quickly walks into the apartment.

Who is he?

I squint my eyes closed even tighter. This is important for some reason. Am I going to get off on a picture of Kate's own handsome stranger? Or will I use someone from my own casting call of characters. I work to see the man's face.

Not Justin.

Not some stranger that Kate described.

Connor.

Oh, Connor. Guilt doesn't stop me from continuing the fantasy. I want to live this out; at least I can do so in my mind. Once he has joined me in the room, he strips off his own clothes. Kate had described a single armband tattoo. I don't know if Connor has any ink, but I give him a tiger on his lower back, and an old-fashioned heart-and-dagger on his forearm like something a sailor would have from the 1940s.

Finished adorning him, I allow my dream lover to climb on the bed next to me. His skin is soft and warm from sitting outside on the roof. His fingers play up and down my body. Pulses of heat radiate through me from his touch.

Since I'm not myself, since I have assumed Kate's role, I don't have to act like myself. But that doesn't make much difference. Because I am me—starring in a fantasy doesn't change that. Even in my daydream, I reach for the camera that resides in its proper place on my bedside table, cock and aim the lens and— SNAP!—I take the picture.

I take it as I come and at that very same instant I bring myself off. And then, so quickly, so fiercely, I fall asleep.

But it isn't too long at all before I wake up again. There's someone in my bed. Someone long and hard and well-muscled; someone with strong, knowing fingers that play over my body with the precision of a concert pianist. Although I understand that I'm not alone in the bed, the feeling I have as I wake is almost surreal. For a moment I think that I am dreaming—I have to be dreaming. Who wakes up to a sensation like this? Then the fingers find the split between my legs, and they start to make sensuous circles over my delta of Venus. When the fingers are replaced by a warm, wet mouth, I sigh out loud.

In my dream, this would be Connor. Of course, it would be. He would know what to do because we would be perfectly in tune. But this isn't a dream. I remind myself twice in order to shake the cobwebs from my mind. I am not asleep.

In real life, I reach out my hand and meet naked skin, run my fingers up the back of my lover's neck to find short, thick hair. Justin. He lifts his head from my body, pulls the blankets back, and smiles up at me.

"You sure were out of it," he says fondly, his lips already coated with my honeyed juices. "I was able to take a shower, to climb into bed, to snuggle up against you, and you still didn't wake up."

Snuggle. That's a perfectly good euphemism for what he's doing. I wonder if he'll introduce me to new definitions for 'cuddle' and 'hug.'

"Kate and I had a few cocktails," I murmur, by way of explanation.

"Cocktails," he repeats. "While I was working, you were playing. How many did you have?"

Since I'd actually lost count of how many I'd had—which is rare for me—I can't give Justin an actual number. I try to tally them up in my head, but he calls me on the fact that I have no clue. This makes him laugh.

"My little partier," he says. "What's gotten into you?"

I don't know how to answer that. What's gotten into me? My desperation to know what's gotten into him. Now, I look at the clock on the bedside table. It's a quarter 'til five. So I hadn't actually been asleep that long, but oh had I been out of it.

I close my eyes as my blond-haired partner moves up my body to lock lips with me. I taste myself on his tongue, and the seductiveness of that sensation is overwhelming. Then, as I watch, he slides out of bed and walks toward the windows. His ass is divine, and I am lost in the movement, wishing he would bring it back into the bed with me, so that I could make love to him for hours.

But Justin has other plans. It's as if he was inside my head while I fantasized about making love outdoors or with open windows. With ease, he swings back the curtains and then opens the glass doors to the patio. He steps outside, totally nude, and then looks over his shoulder at me, issuing the challenge.

I still feel the alcohol buzzing through my system, but that simply makes it easier for me to get totally naked myself and walk onto the balcony to greet him. Justin hoists himself up so that he is sitting on the cold concrete wall that rims the tiny area. That makes me nervous, but he doesn't seem frightened at all. Behind him, the sky is beginning to lighten, still a deep blue, but no longer cobalt. Toward the east it gradually turns a faded denim color, like worn jeans.

"Alex," Justin says softly, bringing my attention from the sky back to his dazzling face. I take my time drinking in his features. Then I pull him down off the railing and go to work with my tongue.

Of course, it isn't really work. The feel of his soft skin under my fingertips, under my tongue, is the ultimate pleasure. I press my lips to the back of his neck and lick him. Then bite him. He shivers against me, and makes a soft sighing noise to let me know he likes what I'm doing. He should. I've become a hungry lioness, and he is my prey.

I play him, sliding my hands up his arms as I bite the nape of his neck the way a mama cat does when it lifts a kitten. Justin moans softly and I bite harder now and work my way down his body, kissing along the ridge of his spine before maneuvering him so that I can take him down my throat.

As the sky continues to lighten, I work him with my tongue and fingers. When I sense he's close to coming, I slow down, taking my time, which is always important, and I bring him repeatedly to the edge of climax without letting him reach it.

You never want your lover to get there too soon. Yes, it will feel good. In the history of the world, it's my belief that nobody has ever had a "bad" orgasm. But the best ones are those that you can almost taste in your mouth before they wash through your body. This is the kind I bring to Justin, finally sealing my mouth to his body and varying the intensity of my sucks until he grips onto my shoulders and moans. The pleasure rages through him, slamming through him and leaving him both satisfied and drained, staring down at me with a look of total satisfaction in his lovely eyes.

I don't have to ask him how it was, and he doesn't have to tell me. But he whispers one word, "Perfect," and smiles.

"Why perfect?" I ask him.

"No camera," he says next, as if surprised by the fact that we have managed to have sex without it.

I spread my hands wide to show that they are empty.

"No," I say softly. No camera.

CHAPTER ELEVEN

The truth is, I take pictures of everything. It's not a hobby and it's not my job. It's my life. So when Justin and I make love over the weekend, there I am once again, taking pictures. My expensive tripod stands in the corner. The camera rests on top, poised to immortalize every frame. From the bed I can reach down and press the red button, capturing the mess of the white sheets, the tangle of our sun-glazed bodies in the pale light of dawn.

This is the perfect light for pictures. It gives everything that glowing tone, makes each shot look as if it were a still from some French movie. One of those art-house features in which everything goes wrong for everybody, but it doesn't matter so much because, well, because it's French. And in French films people don't seem to mind being depressed, being married to the wrong person while loving the other. Just think of a few of my favorites *Too Beautiful for You, Going Places, Menage, Betty Blue....*

Justin doesn't mind me chronicling our love life. In fact, he likes taking pictures as much as I do. The film allows us to be voyeurs into our own bedroom. Later, when we look at the photographs, we stare at ourselves as if we are looking at strangers.

And in a way we are.

Strangers who have been together for four solid years. Strangers whose lives are as tangled and jumbled as the sheets on the California King-sized mattress. Because what does Justin really know about me when it comes down to it? He knows what I look like, what I smell like, what type of lipstick I favor. (Hot Nature by Chanel.) He knows how I wear my hair when I'm in the mood to feel extra-glamorous. (Up on my head with a few tendrils hanging free.) And he knows that every so often I'll go out on a date with him and leave my panties in my knickers drawer. (That's about as risqué as I can manage.) But what does he really know about me?

And more importantly, from my standpoint, what do I know about him? I know that he says that he loves me, and that he is definitely turned on by being with me. I know that he wraps me in his strong arms when we sleep, and that he spoons his firm body against mine almost automatically. But I also know that half the times he tells me he's going to be one place, he ends up somewhere else entirely.

Truth is, we're simply strangers who have chosen to stick together for several years. We've had blissful times, and we've had fights that have echoed through the hall of our apartment building. Generally, these have been followed by fierce attempts at make-up sex that have been just as raucous. Are we yelling because we're angry or because we're ready to romp?

Justin picks me up and holds me to him, his arms bulging with muscles as he sets me astride his rock-hard body. I work him rhythmically, sure of exactly the type of sensation that he favors. Before I start pumping, I click the automatic button on the camera, knowing that every fifteen seconds, the camera will take another shot.

X-rated. Down and dirty. The kinds of pictures that make me happy I have my own darkroom. I wouldn't want to drop this roll off at the local Photomat.

You wouldn't think it would be possible, but soon I manage to forget about the intrusion of the lens. I am too focused on staring at Justin, into his dark eyes, so deep chocolate-brown they look black. His skin is burnished from hours on his surf board, his body is sleek and lean. I suck in my breath as I push up on him, knowing exactly how to give him pleasure, but also how to take the pleasure myself.

"That's the way, baby," Justin croons. "Just like that."

He rings my waist with his hands, intent on helping now, but with a quick headshake, I tell him no. Let me. I want to be in control. He gives me a sly half-smile, and settles himself onto the mattress, yet he doesn't obey my request. With each upward thrust of his hips, he gets back in the game, taking me higher, physically and emotionally, each time he pushes forward.

Again, I shake my head. I want to ride this ride, and I want to do it all by myself. Leaning forward, I pin him down to the bed by his shoulders, and I use the whole force of my weight to slam into him. I like the feeling of being in control, even when I know it's only an illusion. He could topple me in an instant if he so desired, but he doesn't desire that. He's giving me what I want right now. I like being on top, too, because of the way I can swivel my body. If I lean forward, I connect with him so that the hot little button of pleasure between my thighs gains the contact that it so desperately craves. Waves of pure heat flush through me, and I feel that familiar tingling sensation begin to warm me from the inside.

"You like it like that, don't you, sweetheart?" he murmurs. "You like to ride—"

I swallow hard and lean even more firmly against him, connecting our bodies so that we are truly one. My chest to his chest. My legs to his legs. We fit so sweetly together when we make love. We fit perfectly.

The camera clicks as I arch up again, tossing my hair away from my face. Justin is in mid-motion, his fine body moving, and I know in my most professional sense that the picture will blur. I can see it in my head—the motion changing the quality of the picture from crystal clear to out of focus. But I know that I'm going to treasure this one, as well. Life is motion, after all. Blurry vision isn't always a bad thing. I've been living with blinders on for months now, haven't I? If I cared to look at my life through a magnifying glass I might not be able to live with what I saw.

As he moves, positioning himself on top now and me beneath him, I sigh with true pleasure. His powerful body slides against mine, and I bite my lip as he thrusts forward. Justin closes his eyes as he loses himself in the moment. I keep mine open to watch him. He has the strong symmetrical features of a high-end razor model, which he's been in the past. I loved to watch him on television, spreading the fluffy foam along his jaw line and then preparing to zip away each bit of whipped-cream like lather with the number-one selling razor.

He thought I was teasing him when I played that advertisement endlessly on my VCR, but I just adored how serious he looked in every part of the ad--as if it were his life's mission to make people by this particular type of razor.

"That's acting for you," he grinned when I told him how much I liked to watch. "That's my job."

But it's the same look that's on his face now. Not selling razors, but selling something. Selling my pleasure to me, and making me glad to buy it. He slips his hips forward, and then rotates them in a steady circle, and then, when I think things can't possibly feel any better, he brings his thumb to the split of my body and traces it up and down in a diamond.

"Oh," I sigh. Just that one syllable. Not even a word, really. "Oh."

He gives me the motions I crave, alternating harder and softer as he times his own peak. We are going to reach the finish line together. I sense it. And I realize that I want to pay attention. I want to memorize every part of this sexy samba because this dance will be one of our last.

Of course, I don't know it yet. That's the strange thing about fate.

I don't know that after we do it, all hell will break loose. I don't know that for a fact, it's simply a feeling I get in the pit of my stomach. It's a deja vu feeling--that odd shivery sensation of fear and excitement and trepidation. I don't know anything for sure, until the camera takes the last picture, and Justin makes the last thrust, and I collapse beneath him, sweaty and wet, and completely unprepared somehow—yet at the same time very prepared—for what happens next.

"Oh, wow," Justin sighs, pulling out and lying at my side. "I mean that's all I can really say. Wow—"

"I know," I whisper back, cuddling into him.

"That was brilliant," he says, turning his head to grin at me, his eyes still glazed with post-orgasm high. His eyelids flutter shut and his fingertips skim my breasts, tweaking my erect nipples as he continues, "Brilliant, Judith," and I flinch and pull away as if he's slapped me hard.

"My name's Alex," I say, as if we are strangers. And then I see it all too clearly. I see Justin going to his agent's office more often than need be. How many times a week does he need to visit her? I think about his agent, Judith Lioni, and about her long blonde hair and her lovely lean body and the fact that she has the Zone diet delivered to her office in fancy blue coolers.

I think about the pictures on the roll. So many rolls. The pretty woman. The close-up shots. Judith? Why the f— not?

*****

The journalist from the Times points to another picture and wants to know the history. That's why I'm here, at this fantastic shindig--to explain my work., or at least, to offer any explanations that I can. But sometimes, there aren't any. Sometimes, a photo is simply a photo. I don't know what it means, or why it's any good, I only know that I took it. That sounds strange, I guess. Aren't artists always supposed to know what's going on in their world? Or, to revert to a cliché, shouldn't every picture really tell a story? Every good picture, at least.

Yeah. In the best possible world.

But look at that one, the one right next to the gallery door. That was a fluke. It's a picture of Connor that I took through the window at the grocery store. Shouldn't even have come out. The glare from the sunlight outside and the fluorescents inside should have turned that photo into an opaque wash, a picture of nothing. Instead, you can see clearly through the doors and into the produce section, where Connor stands stacking fresh navel oranges. He doesn't know about the camera's intruding lens. He's off in his own world. Maybe he's thinking about me.

There's something pure about black-and-white pictures. Old-fashioned. The light can gleam, can create halos and shadows and pure sophistication even in an ordinary scene. That's why this picture is so good. It could be anyone. Anywhere. But the roundness of the oranges and the way Connor's face seems chiseled, the harsh strong features of his jaw, the lines of his muscles visible where the t-shirt ends. Everything comes together in that shot.

No plans. No stories. No secrets to share.

But the journalist from the Times wants secrets so he can write an interesting piece. Kate hovers nearby, pushing her way into my realm of consciousness and trying to jar me with a clever bon mot. Kate is my guardian angel. She takes care of me.

I look at her, where she stands, nodding and winking, prompting me. I look at the journalist. Then I look through the front door of the gallery, where I see Justin getting off his motorcycle and heading towards me.

Every picture tells a story?

How about every boyfriend. Every ex. Everyone you've ever known, or dated or slept with. Mine are all around me in this room, on these walls. And here comes one of them. Is he here to offer me his congratulations or to tell me to go screw myself. I don't know. I'll have to wait and see.

"What about that one?" the journalist asks. He's pointing to a picture of a stunning blonde woman coming out of the ocean. It's like

a movie still from that Bo Derek classic, 10, except that Judith would never go in for cornrows. Christina Aguilera, she is not.

The waves are gray blankets behind her. Folding over with crocheted lace. The sun is a bauble suspended in the silver-white sky. She is gorgeous and she knows it. Her hair wet. Her body is glistening.

"Who's she?" Hal asks. "What's her story?"

*****

My head is spinning. I'm not in the right frame of mind. Really, those are the best explanations I can offer. Justin says 'Judith,' and rather than flip out at him, I do my best to joke it off. I shake his hand as I reintroduce myself. "You know," I say. "Alexandra. Your girlfriend. Love of your life. Fire of your loins." He shakes his head quickly, as if to get rid of a bad dream. Then just as quickly he reaches for me, cradles me in his arms and says, "Sorry, baby. Must have been thinking of this audition I've got coming up."

That's it. The best excuse he can give: He was thinking about work.

I try to be supportive and pretend that nothing has happened. That he didn't just call out another woman's name while we made love. But my mind takes a trip of its own into a darker area—a world of tawdry sex and fetish-drenched fantasies in which Judith does things for him that I do not. In which Judith is part goddess and part whore and she makes Justin come like he's never come before.

But what magical things would she do for him? I'll do anything. At least, I've always done anything that Justin's suggested. So these are simply fantasies. That's all they are. Stupid, juvenile fantasies.

And I know exactly how to get rid of them.

I have to admit, I grow sick to my stomach when I think about what I am going to do. That I'm going back out there, that I'll be following him around town again. I thought I'd gotten it out of my system. Now, it's right back there, alive and kicking.

Why can't I just confront Justin in all seriousness? Why do I have to keep skulking around? Peeking through windows. Spying around corners. Why am I always so drawn to watching?

Every photographer is a bit of a voyeur, right? That shouldn't come as any big surprise. But what does surprise me is how good I am at it. I got my shots every time. Nobody seems the wiser.

CHAPTER TWELVE

I've always enjoyed the short commute from my apartment to my darkroom. The palm trees bending over the boulevards remind me of why I moved to Los Angeles in the first place. Most of my photographer friends live in New York, London, and San Francisco. L.A. seems too bright to them. And too dirty. They don't see what I see. If you know where to look, Los Angeles still possesses a remnant of the glamour that I'm sure was prevalent in the twenties and thirties. The mystical quality surrounds a town devoted to cinema. Wherever you go, traces of the movies are evident. But today, my mind is on Justin, and I don't notice any of the pretty atmosphere around me. Can't focus on anything except what he is (or is not) doing and who he is (or is not) doing those things with.

When I drive by the grocery store, I see that Connor's truck is in its usual place. Immediately, my mind takes off in a new and much more desirable direction. And for a moment, I reconsider my feelings about Justin and Judith. Who on Earth am I to judge Justin for calling out someone else's name? I have lost myself in countless fantasies featuring my favorite bartender/grocery store worker.

Obviously, he's working the day shift today, and I find myself pulling in beside his truck and parking my car. A shiny, mint-condition, lipstick red Ford, his truck is like a homing beacon to me. As if I don't have any cares or worries, I wander over, run my fingers along the metal, imagine what Connor would look like on the day he washes his vehicle. I make a guess that he's not one of those who would trust the machine to a car wash. I believe that he would instead strip down to a pair of old Levis and a tank top, putting his muscles into the motion of buffing the metallic surface to a highly polished shine.

My mind takes another turn, and I imagine Connor, still dressed the same way, polishing me with a buffer instead of his truck. Or, to use that beautiful Ford as a prop, I visualize us in the bed in back, limbs entwined, parked on one of the curves in the Hollywood Hills. The lights of the city twinkling unseen before us, Connor's bright eyes focused directly on mine. His lips warm and soft and....

All right, perhaps I still have sex on the brain. But I force myself to shake off the fantasies, and I get back in my car before Connor notices me through the windows. I don't have it in me to converse with him now. I'm too confused, too totally drained. I make it the rest of the way to my darkroom without getting lost in daydreams, and I enter quickly and get right to work.

With one hand, I wrap my hair into a tight twist and capture it in a ponytail holder. That's all it takes to send me off to fantasyland once again. I think of Kate and her story of visiting Menage and Darren. I think of what it might be like for something so unreal to happen in a very real setting.

Again, my mind turns to Connor, and I imagine him brushing my hair for me, sitting on the edge of my stool and playing with it. Oh, and since I've put a brush in his hand, he might have even more fun with that, pulling me over his sturdy lap, sliding my skirt up to my waist....

Okay, I'm nuts. I have to admit it. Staying up late and following Justin is wrong, wrong, wrong. And my anger at him, or concern or confusion or whatever, has obviously turned me into some fantasy junkie. I just can't make my mind stay focused on the matters at hand.

I do know why I'm daydreaming about Connor. He's always been nice to me, always caring and looking out for my best interest. Yet when I tell this to Kate, she always just grins and says, "Crush. You have a crush."

And I do.

So maybe I'm just as bad as Justin. Whatever he's doing, he's acting on some impulse that he has. What would happen if I acted on mine?

CHAPTER THIRTEEN

Connor leans over the counter when I go in the next day and drink my coffee in the bar. He says, "You're making me crazy."

I don't answer.

"Alex, I'm going out of my head."

I start to respond, to say something, anything, but I stop. What can I tell him? How can I respond to that?

"I have to see you."

"I shouldn't," I say, instead of "I can't."

"You think about me." He leaves it there—the truth vibrating between us.

"Yes."

"I think about you, too. All the time."

He puts his hand over the counter, rests it on top of mine. Just for an instant. A split second. Heat rushes through me. It clarifies everything for that moment of contact. Then he takes his hand back, leaving me as confused as always.

"Come away with me," he says, "Just to the movies, Alex.

Please?" Then he stares at me for a moment, and he says, "I'm not asking you to leave Justin. I'm not asking you to lie to him. I'm just asking you to go to the movies with me."

I nod and shrug at the same time. My face turns crimson. I think I say "yes," but I don't know.

*****

It's our first date, if that's what you're supposed to call it when you're cheating. Our first rendezvous. Our first foray into the wrong place, into the dark side of love.

Connor suggests that we meet at the mall in Century City. With all of the alleys and walkways, we'll blend in and become an inconspicuous part of the crowd.

In order for us to quickly find each other, he gives me directions to meet him at a particular place, an escalator near the rear of the mall. He beats me to it, and I'm happily surprised to see him wearing black jeans, a white shirt, and a beat-up leather jacket. He's always in his uniform at either of his places of work—crisp slacks, white shirt, tie and vest at the bar, or chinos, workshirt, apron and boots at the grocery store. Dressed in street clothes, he's more attractive than ever. From a distance he appears at ease, although as I approach I sense that he's as nervous as I am.

"Thanks for coming," he says softly. I wonder if he'll kiss me, but he doesn't. He doesn't even hold my hand. Instead, we walk to the theater, keeping a safety zone between us, setting the mood for the evening. I am more aware of the six inches that separate us than I have been of any other distance in my life.

Standing in line to buy tickets, I catch our reflection in a store window. We look like a normal couple, and this gives me an inordinate amount of pleasure. I think of holding his hand, slipping mine into his, but I can't. What if someone sees us? Someone who knows Justin? Someone who knows me? I keep my hands to myself, thrust them deep into my coat pockets as if I can't trust them to behave on their own.

Up the escalator, through the doors, we forego snacks, both of us high on nervous energy. We walk down the carpeted hallway to the final theater, the smallest one in the place, and sit in the back row.

The film is something stupid. Something neither of us would normally pick. It doesn't matter. What matters is not touching him in the darkened theater. He sits still. I sit still. He has the armrest. I keep my hands in my lap, fingers interlaced as an added precaution. Despite all our efforts, his elbow brushes mine when he moves in his seat to get more comfortable. For the rest of the movie, all I can think is this: *His elbow touched mine. His elbow touched mine. Maybe if I move slightly I can touch him back.* It's as if I know that his hand in mine will make everything all right—change the world and turn it upside down. But that doesn't make any sense at all. I'm smart enough to know it, and I keep my hands to myself.

After the film, we go downstairs to have a beer at a Mexican restaurant situated at the far edge of the mall. Connor says, "Alex, tell me what we're doing." I look out the window at the bookstore across the way. The display features bestsellers, murder mysteries, thrillers, romances. If I were to design a book jacket for us, a glossy photo cover, would it be torrid? A muscled man in an open shirt, a woman with her alabaster bosoms heaving? Or would it be a hazy bedroom seen through a partially opened door? Just one push and all will be revealed.

"What are we doing?" he asks again.

"We're having a beer." Innocent. That's what it is. Innocent. Until his foot brushes my foot. Accident? On purpose? Accidentally on purpose? It happens again.

"Are you sure you want to do this?" he asks. "What if someone sees us?"

Seems strange that he's asking these questions, even though he's the one who invited me out with him. Maybe he didn't think I would go. But I had to go. That's the truth. As soon as he asked, I had to.

"We're friends having a drink," I say. Is that believable? Not really. Since friends don't behave this way when they go to the movies or have a beer. Friends don't tell their boyfriends they're out with their girlfriend Kate. Friends don't tell people like Kate not to call their apartments for fear they'll blow their cover.

We pay for the drinks. Then Connor walks me through the underground parking lot to find my car, as if he's simply accompanying me for protection, as if he's not going to kiss me when we get to the car. Through the maze of concrete pillars, of fancy sports cars and SUVs, he walks next to me, not holding my hand, not even coming close.

At the car, he leans his back against the driver's side door, facing me. One push and all will be revealed.

"Are you ready for this, Alex?"

I shake my head, hypnotized by those eyes, mesmerized by the way he stares at me. Connor puts his hand against my cheek, slides two fingers under my chin, tilts my head upward. There is something almost indecent in the full shape of his lips. I want to feel them against mine. I think, kiss me. My mind screams the words: kiss me. Now. Here. Before I can back out. Before I get smart and call this whole thing off. I am bound and gagged with responsibilities. It's up to him to make the first move.

Kiss me, I think again, and he does. His lips meet mine. His hands come around my body, wrapping me up. His faded leather jacket is soft against my skin. His arms surround me, taking me into him and making me one with him.

Just like my fantasies. Better than my fantasies. This is real. Hard and raw and real, with all of the magic that comes with things that are real. The way he smells. The way he tastes. The way I want more of him, want us to strip off our clothes in the underground garage and make love on the hood of my car.

He kisses me deeply. I don't change my mind. I don't say "no." I don't tell him to leave. I lean into him, those lovely lips against mine, his eyes closed, dark lashes, dark hair, warm bodies pressed together.

He pulls back. He looks down on me. "Let's stop," he says.

I'm breathless. I don't want to stop. I haven't felt this alive for a long time. How strange is that? How crazy is it that being with Connor makes me feel normal when simply being with him is the most abnormal thing I've ever done.

"You need to think about what's going on," he says. "I don't want you to be with me for the excitement. I don't want you to feel bad afterward. Think about it. Then tell me what you want."

I open my car door and climb inside, looking at him. He stands a few feet away, leaning against a concrete pillar, watching me.

And here's the thing—even though I have my camera with me, and even though I know what the photograph of Connor would look like, I don't take the picture.

*****

In the middle of the night, I jerk myself awake. It feels as if I have been physically pulled from a dream, wrenched from it. My body is wet with sweat. The place between my legs feels swollen and used. I cannot think of another time that I have masturbated in my sleep. Justin would have told me if I had, would have teased me mercilessly if he had caught me.

I bring my fingers to my face, smelling then, catching the scent of my pleasure. I must have pushed four fingers inside me, must have rocked my hand in and out, pushing in deep, curving the tips of my fingers to stroke the inner walls. This is so unlike me. I assure myself that I am behaving oddly simply because I am wracked with guilt. But even I can tell that I'm lying to myself. My mind is filled with images of Connor and me together. Images that drip with sex, and these visions keep me awake, my heart pounding in my chest, and though I will myself to go back to sleep, my mind will not let me.

I take a deep breath and try all the tricks I use whenever I am plagued by insomnia. I close my eyes and count backwards from one hundred, first in English, then in Spanish, which I manage to recall from my high school days. I imagine myself tucked into a hammock, swinging back and forth between two palm trees, the sun beating down on me, the waves folding over to kiss the sand just below the woven hammock. I create a mental paradise where I relax sublimely naked under the sun.

But every time I close my eyes, I am consumed by thoughts of Connor, by images of him. I can see him at close range, leaning in to kiss me. I can feel the warmth of his body at the Mexican restaurant, sliding closer to me, his hands probing under the table, finding the edge of my skirt and pushing it up. Revealing me inch by inch, playing teasing games with her fingertips until he found the ridge of my panties.

What would he have done if we hadn't left?

What had I wanted him to do?

My mind spells it out. I am in the restaurant once again, and this time we play a question and answer game. He says, "Tell me about yourself," and I say, "I want to be bad. I'm tired of being good all the time. More than anything, I want to be bad." It's a simple statement, but the only words I have power over are these: I want to be bad. He understands and he nods, and his fingers push forward, and there, wet and hot and ready, he discovers my center, plunges my core.

Why didn't I give in tonight? Why didn't I tell him that I was ready?

Sleep will not come for me. I climb out of the bed and walk to the window. It's almost two a.m. If I'd gone to Connor's, what would we be doing? Would we be asleep yet? Or would we be on the floor, or on the bed, or on his fire escape. Yes, the fire escape. I think I'd have a strong desire to do just that, to make love where people might see me. To do it where the wind and air could flow over my naked body. I can visualize doing this with Connor. I can imagine having his strong arms around my body, his head leaning in toward the back of my neck to lick me, to kiss me, his hips pressing against my backside, thrusting, teasing.

There had been a promise in Connor's eyes.

I want to see exactly what that promise means. And I mentally beat myself up for not going home with him, for not being daring enough to explore the unknown. Why do I have to process every situation? Why can't I simply give myself up to a new situation?

I contemplate this, coming quickly to the answer: It's my nature. Focus the lens. Work slowly, steadily, methodically. Don't rush it or you might get it wrong. It's hard to live spontaneously when you're always questioning yourself, checking the aperture, the light and the shadows. Besides, why try to live in the moment when you can live vicariously through your best friend's exploits. Isn't that easier than letting yourself be free enough to try something new, something that might possibly get you hurt? Or allow you to hurt the people you love.

But maybe with the right person, maybe with Connor, I could give in to new things without a fight. There are so many things to explore, and Connor might be the perfect partner to join me in my quest for knowledge.

I climb back into bed and pull up the covers. The street noises fade, the honks and sounds of car engines meld together, become a lullaby that I hear but can no longer recognize. When I dream this time, I'm at a Christmas party nine months earlier, one held at Connor's bar. The tiny strands of white lights glimmer about the bar, the warmth from many bodies move on the makeshift dance floor, t he throbbing music of a jazz band hired to play for the evening lilts over everyone and everything.

It's crazy that I'm dreaming this, but I know I am for a reason. This was the first time I noticed Connor. The first time I really saw him. Kate and I were there alone. Justin was off at some industry shindig. I dream the night again, as if I am there, reliving it.

Connor has his strong arms around me under the mistletoe. And this time, my voice does not interfere, does not stutter or stammer. Connor's suede jacket is deliciously soft to the touch. His lips on mine make me feel drunk, as if I've downed glass after glass of the champagne being served by dapper looking actors in tuxes and tails.

I dream about the kiss. For the rest of the night, I dream about the kiss. Every moment of it, every nuance—SNAP! goes the camera in my head. Taking the picture.

*****

Now is the time for me to come clean. I haven't broken any boundaries yet. Real boundaries. I haven't made the decisions that will damage us forever. But the problem is, I don't come clean with Justin. I only come clean with Kate. She doesn't judge me. I knew she wouldn't. She listens carefully, and then she offers her advice. And I'm surprised by what she tells me.

Kate says, "So you kissed him. You got it out of your system, now move on."

"What are you talking about?"

"You were testing the waters, finding out whether you would feel guilty or not. You do. That proves you love Justin. If you didn't feel bad, you'd have a problem."

I'm shocked that she's telling me to stay with Justin, after all her negative remarks about him. She seems to be pushing for me to work things through. "This is a problem," I insist. "He's the one who stopped us. I would have kept going. I would have made love to him in the back seat of my car."

"Your little convertible?" Kate laughs. She's focusing on the wrong issues.

"I'm serious," I tell her. "I would have."

"Talk to him," Kate says. She takes a sip of her espresso, swallows it, then rips open one of those paper packages of cream. Watching the white liquid swirl against the coffee makes me feel dizzy. It makes me think of Connor, of my fantasies. It makes me wonder what he'd say if I confessed it to him, if I leaned over the counter and said, "Forget that cream. Take care of me—"

I come back into focus as she says again, "Just talk to Justin. It can't hurt, Alex. It can only help."

She's right. Once I talk to Justin, he'll make things better. It won't come as a surprise to him. He must know something is wrong. Something is really, very wrong.

*****

"Nothing's wrong," Justin says over dinner.

"No, really," I tell him.

"What do you want from me, Alex?" he asks now. He looks genuinely perplexed.

The thing is, I can't put it into words. I want to know whether he's cheating on me with Judith, whether things are so hot between us because he has something else, or several somethings on the side. I want to know why he doesn't come to my openings. Why he's always late, or blowing me off.

When Justin and I first met, he snuck into my dorm with a bouquet of white roses, left them in a heart shape outside my door. He waited outside my last class at the end of the day, and when I came into his arms, he would tremble as he kissed me. Holding onto his hand while we walked through the campus made me feel a bit steadier, just for having his body near mine. I remember the way he said my name on the phone, the way he seemed to taste it, as if it meant something sweet.

"Talk to me," I say. "Let me know why you called out her name."

He shrugs. "Can't tell you that," he says.

And the girls? I wonder. The women on the film. Or the woman. Who are they? Why can't I ask? I bite my lip. It's easier than biting my tongue.

CHAPTER FOURTEEN

The windows are open. The blinds are up. Judith is home, and she has a guest. Bingo. Striking in rich with the very first turn of the wheel. I take picture after picture. And then, as Justin leaves the apartment, I stand there by his Harley, not moving. Not caring if he sees me. As soon as he catches onto who I am and why I must be there, I turn away. Now, for some reason, I need to flee. Need to run from him.

"Alex!" Justin yells out to me, coming forward. "What are you doing here?" He closes the distance between us quickly, grabbing onto my arm and spinning me around to face him. He gets it. I can tell. I don't have anything to explain to him. He has everything to explain to me. But I don't want to hear it.

I click the shutter in his face—knowing the flash will momentarily blind him.

SNAP!

That picture is on display right across the way. Justin, features marred by anger, lunging forward. I don't have any ego about pictures like that. I mean I know it's good, but when I see it, all I think is how angry he was—and then I wonder how he could possibly be angry at all. Really.

The journalist from the Times wants to know how I staged the shot.

"Staged?" I ask, and I recognize I'm tipsy and wonder if he does, as well. Can strangers tell when you're drunk? What if you look the same? What if you act the same, you only tell more than you mean to. Or, more honestly, more than you should.

"I mean, what was going through your mind when you took the picture."

Fear. Anger. Sadness.

"Is that why the show is called 'Blue Valentine'?"

Maybe it 'tis and maybe it 'tisn't. This is what I want to say. Instead, I snag another glass of champagne from a passing waiter, and I give a flirty little wink to the writer and put a spin on his question.

"You tell me," I say. "Artists always want to know what the public thinks of their work. So you tell me. What was I thinking when I took the shot?"

He just looks at me for a moment. He can't tell if I'm being hard-to-deal with or functionally artistic. "So, how about that one?" he asks, pointing to a picture of Connor and me in a tight clinch, and I drain the glass of champagne in a swallow and decide to tell him. And as I say the words, I see the pictures in motion, moving in my head.

BOOK TWO

Crackle!

CHAPTER FIFTEEN

People who live in L.A. claim that you can get anywhere in the city in twenty minutes. That's the golden rule. Climb into your car and check the clock on your dashboard. You'll arrive at your chosen destination in twenty minutes or less. This is the L.A. promise.

But believe me, I know this from experience: L.A. lies.

The drive from the beach to Hollywood takes over an hour. According to the newscaster on the radio, this drastically unexpected delay is due to an injury accident on the Ten Freeway. I remind myself that I shouldn't be upset. However bad my day is going can't be as bad as the poor person—or people—involved in the accident. Other commuters tend to forget that out here. They moan and complain when their schedule is adjusted by fate—but they have no compassion for the victims who are having a much worse go at it than they are.

Want proof of that? There's an awful story I heard on the news about a deranged woman who held up traffic in L.A. by standing on a freeway overpass and threatening to dive off it onto the cracked black asphalt below. Police shut down traffic and attempted to talk her down to safety. But after hours caught in the glazing sun of the auto jam, drivers started yelling at the woman to go ahead and jump. I think that story sums up the impatience of people in Los Angeles.

This evening I could have taken surface streets, but I am not in a hurry. The red taillights in front of me give me something to fixate on while I picture Judith and Justin going at it. I can't help myself. In my mind, I imagine Judith bent over the edge of the sofa—*my* sofa—her long hair spread out around her like a golden fan, her body slender and supple. I can easily picture Justin's thicker body pressing into her from behind. I know how much Justin likes to do it doggy-style, likes to slide in from behind because it gives him the deepest access possible. I try not to think of things like this, but I can't help it. Basically, I spend the commute wallowing.

As the traffic slows, I recall the final words Justin said to me. *Wait. Don't go. Let me explain.* With each slow roll forward on the freeway, I can hear my own voice, at a louder decibel than usual. Then I can hear Justin, sounding hollow, like an echo in a cave. How could I have been so wrong about him? How could I have spent so many years at his side?

But that's not fair, is it? We were both playing our own little cheating games. I simply caught onto his before he caught onto mine. And I didn't take mine quite as far.

When the accident finally clears, I shoot the rest of the way toward Hollywood without a hitch, getting off at the La Cienega exit and taking it straight up the hill to Sunset. I hit the stoplight at the top of the hill, as usual. My car suspended by the break, I dial Kate on my car phone. I'm not special. Everyone has a phone in L.A. Kate's direct line is busy, and instead of leaving voice mail, I pull up in front of the Tantamount Hotel, let a uniformed man unload my suitcase, and valet-park the car.

Orange and black Halloween ribbons decorate the white-veined marble pillars in the front of the hotel. Inside the entryway, two giant orange blown-glass pumpkins stand on either side of the revolving door. The Tantamount is the type of place that welcomes any holiday. And although it's difficult to tell by the nearly tropical weather, fall has arrived, and Halloween is less than a week away.

A strong, captivating young man, dressed impeccably in a dark charcoal suit, helps me inside with my luggage, bringing it into the lobby and standing with it as if he were my own private guard while I go to the front desk. Other extremely handsome young people mill around the lobby, all dressed in similar suits. The Tantamount is known for hiring the most attractive and friendly staff. Each time I make eye contact with one of the help, I am rewarded with a dazzling, pearly-white smile. My personal guess is that ninety-nine percent of those who work here hope to break into the movie business. When you live in L.A., you get accustomed to being surrounded by the best-looking people all the time. Your busboys are gorgeous, the man at the gas station is stunning and the woman serving double-large non-fat lattes could be on the cover of a magazine. L.A. has a magnetic pull. It draws the best and most beautiful from around the globe into its barriers. Once you've been here for a while, you forget that the rest of the country's population doesn't always appear to have just emerged from the gym, or a tanning bed, or a hair salon.

"Is Kate Derrick here?" I ask. My best friend is the hotel manager. I don't usually bother her at work, but I can't help myself right now. The short-haired woman behind the front desk, another beauty with bee-stung lips in a permanent pout, stares at me for a moment. She obviously wants to know whether I'm important enough to be a valid disturbance to Kate. I meet her gaze, wondering whether she can sense my mood. Just as I am about to ask her what the heck she's looking at, she nods to herself and dials a number into the house phone.

"Have a seat," she says, indicating a velour-covered Dalmatian print chair in the lobby. "She'll be right out."

I wander over to the chair, setting my camera bag on the floor at my side. I suddenly feel ill at ease in the ultra chic environment, especially with my puffy eyes and disheveled clothes. Self-conscious, I brush off my skirt, smooth my dark hair out of my face, then twist the length of it several times around my fingers and tie it in a knot low on the nape of my neck.

A recognizable rock star, complete with entourage, makes his way into the hotel in a flurry of activity. The Tantamount is quite the hangout for the hipsters of the entertainment world. It's why Kate fits in so well. She looks the part, even if she's simply a hotel manager. As I turn toward the office door, it opens, and she emerges. Even the rock star stops for a moment to watch. Kate's difficult not to stare at. A tall, voluptuous platinum blonde who knows how to walk across a room, Kate moves in the manner of a 1940s screen siren. She glides. This evening, her dangerous curves are becomingly draped in a stunning black suit. Her zebra-striped, four-inch heels make clicking sounds on the tile floor. The rhinestone butterfly pin on her lapel is poised for twinkling flight. At all times, Kate likes to sparkle.

I stand, and when Kate arrives at my side, I open my mouth to tell her. At first, the words come out in a rush. "I'm sorry to bother you, but—" Then I stop. I simply can't explain about Justin and me. And Judith. Not yet. Not standing in the center of a hotel lobby, looking like a victim in the war of love. As usual, Kate knows just what to do. She strides away from to me whisper something to the pretty lady behind the counter, speaks quietly for a moment to the man with my luggage, and then leads me up the purple-lit stairs to the restaurant on the second floor. Kate's ability to take control of a situation is what makes her such a good hotel manager. In any sort of crisis, she knows what to do. Now, her firm grip on my hand is warm and comforting, and she squeezes my fingers gently as we walk up the stairs.

The tables for two at The Balcony restaurant are positioned

against the railing for lobby viewing. Tables for four, complete with matching red velvet loveseats instead of chairs, are further back, nestled against the wall for more private tête-à-têtes. After a few more hushed words to the maitre d', we are safely ensconced at the farthest table in the corner, two chilled martinis positioned directly in front of us. I sink back into the loveseat and sigh, then say, "Fact is, I didn't know what to do."

And, of course, at this moment I hear a familiar sound—SNAP!—and I stand and look over the railing to see that a journalist has taken a picture of the rock star. This is a posed shot, with the musician and his harem of beautiful girls sprawled on one of the lobby's decadent sofas. The image is ripe with sexuality. One can easily picture the musician making love to the six women at once—his hands, and arms, and body all involved with the business of pleasure.

The familiar noise of the camera continues, and when I sit again the SNAP! SNAP! SNAP! makes me cross my legs tight under the table, makes me sigh and relive mentally the moment of being with Justin only several hours before. Of being with him before he was with—

"You know, I slept with him," Kate says, breaking me from my memories.

"No," I say, "I don't know that. You slept with Justin?" there's ice in my voice, and my fingers tighten around the fragile stem of my martini glass.

"Right, dummy. That's just like me." Kate glowers, waiting.

"You mean the rock star?"

Now she nods.

"Oh, man—" I say.

"He was good," she grins. "Exceptional. Usually they're so into their own inflated egos that they can't give you any pleasure at all. Sometimes they spend the whole evening watching their own reflections in the mirror. But he was different. Caring, I guess."

"A caring rock star?"

"Just sweet."

"Oh, God, Kate—"

Kate shakes her head, silencing me. She is a fabulous mood reader, and always seems to know exactly what I need and when I need it. Perhaps it's the fact that we've been close friends since high school, but I think it has more to do with Kate's stellar personality. She just always seems to know what's going on.

"I didn't know where else to go," I try again to explain. Sighing, I run my hands through my hair again, in one of my recognizable nervous and distraught gestures.

I've moved my hand from the glass, and now Kate nudges one of the drinks closer to me, and I lift it and take a sip. The way I feel about martinis goes deep into my soul. It's not because they are once again the drink of the moment, the way steaks are the food and cigars the hip smoke. I have *always* loved martinis—they make me feel both adult and in control—probably two very false things at this moment. Yet the very first sip of one puts me instantly at ease.

Watch out, I warn myself, but I brush the thought aside. This day, of all days, is not the time to question the feeling of peace—faux or not.

"You can stay with me," Kate says, still not knowing exactly what's wrong, but guessing with the fairly blatant clue of my suitcase and unexpected arrival at her hotel. "You know my place is small, but you also know I can fit you in," she pauses for emphasis, "for as long as you want."

"Thanks," I tell her, meaning it. "Really, thank you. But maybe I'll stay at the hotel—at least for tonight. I think a little space of my own would do me good."

Kate nods, indicating 'your wish is my command,' still in her managerial role. Then she adds, "Once you've had both of those," she nods to the drinks, "we'll talk about what's going on."

I lean back against the cherry-red sofa and lift the drink. The bartender, another serious stunner with a face purely crafted for the silver screen, has mixed it perfectly. I hardly taste it as I drain the first martini, and I let Kate put the second one in my hand without a word of protest. Why would I bother? Who do I need to impress? When I finish half of this one, I look directly into my friend's green eyes and whisper, "Judith."

"Oh, Jesus," Kate groans. She must have simply been imagining a fight between Justin and me—news in itself because I'm always known for giving in, for attempting to keep the peace above all else—but this is obviously worse than even she'd thought. Kate's met Judith on several occasions: at parties at our house, movie screenings, or at chi-chi industry events. Just from those few connections, she has obviously been able to recognize Judith's type. The girl is like walking dynamite. Adding her into any situation has the potential to create explosions.

"It's over," I say, my lips numb to the sting of the alcohol. I don't feel angry any more. I feel as drained as the second empty martini glass as I set it back down on the table. Kate doesn't argue. She doesn't say that things will look different in the light of day. She just nods, then asks, "Where's the rest of your stuff? Jasmine said she was checking your one bag."

"That's all I brought." I shrug. "And I don't even know what I packed. I tossed things together pretty randomly. I had to get out of there."

"We can go back together and get the rest whenever you want. Sometimes simply having another party present can do wonders for diffusing a situation. I know that when George and I broke up, it made all the difference to have you there, packing my boxes up with me."

"I'm not going back."

Again, Kate doesn't press me, although I can tell that she has more to say on the subject. I appreciate the fact that she knows when to talk and when to be silent. Instead, she checks her watch, then looks over at the bartender and holds up two fingers.

"I can't do two more of those," I cringe.

"One's for me. I'm officially off now, and anyway, too much of a good thing can be wonderful." Kate has always enjoyed quoting her favorite sex symbol, Mae West. In fact, she makes a point of working such bon mots into any and every conversation. I think that in her head, she imagines herself to be a modernized version of W.C. Field's luscious leading lady.

When the drinks come, I start to tell Kate. I don't explain how I know the things I know. I don't even tell her about the original photos that I found on my old camera. I only tell her that I learned that he was cheating and that I know it for a fact. I tell her I don't want to go into the dirty details because I can't stomach reliving them. She's indignant for me, as a best friend should be, and she wants to rehash it all in hopes that exorcising the situation will make me feel better, but I'm done.

"You're sure he was doing Judith?"

I nod.

"Factually sure?"

I nod again.

After we finish our drinks, Kate tells me to go up to one of the hotel's fancier rooms, instructing me to clean myself and then change into "boozy bar attire." She wants to make everything better, as if a shower and a few drinks can erase what I've gone through. Although Kate can be convincing when she wants to, I still try to dissuade her.

"I don't want to," I say. "It's been a long enough day. All I can picture myself doing is taking a bath. A long, hot bath with plenty of bubbles." It's true. I can see it in my mind. My body submerged in a tub, candles lit on the porcelain edge with their light flickering over me. I want to have my own version of the Phoenix's rebirth—not from a pyre of ashes, but from water.

"I didn't get you a room with a bath," Kate announces matter-of-factly and erasing my mental image. "You don't need to sit and wallow in a tub of tepid water. I put you in one of our rooms with a waterfall shower. You know, with boulders on the walls. It makes you feel as if you're outside in the wilderness, which in my estimation is better than actually being outside. No bugs. No animals bothering you. Just fresh water and fake rocks."

"A shower, then."

Kate shakes her head. Her perfectly coiffed platinum hair is sprayed into strict obedience and does not move with her gesture. "I'm not letting you sit alone in your hotel room and cry. That will make me cry, and you know I hate when my mascara runs." She does her eyelash bat at me again. She ought to patent the look.

"I don't think I can put on a brave face and pretend to act normal."

Kate brushes my reservations aside, as if she doesn't hear me, or as if English isn't her native tongue. "What are you going to do instead? Sit in your room and suffer? Take a shower. Then we'll go to Lola's and have a few drinks."

Reluctantly, I follow her orders, climbing into one of The Tantamount's incredibly cool elevators and riding to the top floor. Each elevator is lit with a different color light—green, red, purple, or orange. I manage to snag the red one, and I watch my reflection in the mirror on the back of the doors. The light gives me a slightly evil air, as if I'm consumed with dangerous thoughts. I have to admit, I sort of like the look.

Reaching into my bag, I pull out my camera and take a picture. With the mirrors and the lighting, I know it will be an artsy shot. But I think that it will work.

Now that I am free from Justin—and I have decided to think of it that way—I can recreate myself. Do I want to be evil? I've never tried it before. I stare at my red-tinted reflection until the elevator reaches my floor, and then I walk to my room, feeling as if the ride up ten floors has actually changed me.

Of course, it hasn't. I know that.

But it's a start.

*****

Los Angeles is a magic city. Despite what naysayers have to complain about the city, I believe it to be one of the most unusual in the world. In the light of day, it can appear gritty and dried up, angry, even, with the sun beating down harshly through the thick brownish smog. Unless you're out at one of the beautiful spots, by the ocean, or up in the hills, L.A. can honestly be the ugliest place on earth. It has no ability to complete with San Francisco's lush curves and beautiful bay. It fades in comparison to New York's striking skyline and glamorous architecture, or London's history, or Paris' monuments. But at night, Los Angeles changes. Mystically, magically, it transforms into a new creature. A heart beats in the center of Hollywood. The lights are expensive, borrowed jewels that it wears casually and comfortably. It knows it's beautiful—that's all part of the charm.

The journalist from the Times wants to know where I was when I took the picture of Sunset Boulevard, all dolled up with lights--glistening and ready to party. Because more than any other city I've been to, L.A. is a girl who knows how to party.

"In a hotel." I say it simply. Say it like I spend most of my nights in hotels. The L.A. Marmont. The Mondrian. The Argyle. Why not? Why shouldn't I be the type to flit from one penthouse suite to another? Why? Because, plain-and-simple, I'm not. Anyone can look at me, look at my weathered black, bootcut jeans, my black-and-white cowboy boots, my kohl-rimmed eyes, silver hoops, and long dark hair and know—flat out know—that I'm not the type to fiesta with the starlets.

"Which hotel?" he wants to know.

I shrug as I say the word, and I see Kate look at me, because I'm naming her place— "The Tantamount."

"Oh," the man smiles. "Rock-star heaven. That makes sense."

So now I'm the one to ask him what he means. "Why would that make sense?"

"You take good pictures of rock stars. I saw the one you did of

Ian Langer for the cover of Rolling Stone."

As soon as he says Langer's name, I blush. Can't help it. Can't stop it. And I see Kate's face, as her lips curve into a smile. Nobody knows, is what her smile tells me. Just you and me and Ian. But I can't help but glance at the photo of the two people entwined on a sheet-strewn bed. No way to identify them. Just limbs wrapped around each other. But I know.

I nod to Kate. I know.

CHAPTER SIXTEEN

When I get out of the shower, the phone is ringing. Kate tells me to hurry up and get dressed, she has a new set of plans for us—far better, she assures me, than an evening at Lola's—and I shake my head back and forth even though I know she can't see me over the phone. No way. No how.

"Come on," she insists. "Trust me. I know what you need."

"Look," I say in my most serious tone of voice. "I really do think I want to be alone—"

"Maybe that worked for Marlene Dietrich—"

"Garbo," I say, automatically. "Garbo."

"Fine, Garbo," I understand from her snarl that she's glaring at me, even over the phone line. Kate doesn't like to be corrected. Especially, when someone can figure out the gist of her statements regardless of how factually correct they are. Now, she pushes forward. "Get dressed, Alex, and come downstairs now."

"No," I say, even though I'm sure that I sound like a spoiled kid. No, I don't wanna. You can't make me.

"Listen to me, Alex," she insists. "This isn't a request."

Muttering to myself, I hang up the phone. She can't tell me what to do, I promise myself. Yet even while I'm lying to myself, I do what she says. I don't know why. But I do. Maybe I'm predictable. Maybe I just don't give a flying f—.

When I arrive in the lobby, Kate is still on her Garbo kick. "The 'alone thing' doesn't work for you, Alex. You don't have the same impact when you say it. And, anyway, you really don't need to be alone."

"How do you know what I need?"

"I know—" she says. "Haven't I gone through enough break-ups of my own to know?"

"Your relationships aren't long enough to warrant break-ups. They just end when the date ends." I'm not being mean. I'm being honest. Kate has no patience when it comes to romance. She likes to get in and out, without dirtying her pretty, well-manicured hands. Occasionally, a man will stick with her for a while. But most are on a near drive-through basis. Now, she doesn't seem to even hear me. She's busy glancing over at the rock star, whose eyebrows bend in a silent question. Apparently, he's hip to the fact that we're talking about him.

"So," she says, "He's interested."

"Interested?"

"You know," she continues. "What we've talked about in the past. He's on for it."

"I'm not going to do a ménage," I tell her, understanding her intentions immediately. "If I didn't want to do one with Justin, why would I do one now?"

"Because you're not with him. Show him how crazy you can be."

"That's not right. He won't ever know."

"Of course, he will," she smiles. "You take pictures of everything. You can upload and email the most amazing scenario—"

"For strange men to download on their computers and mail to all their kinky buddies. And I'm sure that he—" I motion to the musician, "will be really super-keen on me taking candid photos of him in bed."

"You can invite Justin over, make him think you want a reunion, and then show him the shots," Kate says, ignoring my arguments. "It will drive him out of his head. What you need is a little revenge in order to get yourself back in control."

"No," I shake my head. "Not today."

"Take your mind of things," she assures me.

"And give me all sorts of other things to freak me out."

She smiles kindly, as if to say it' my loss, but she understands. Then she heads back to the rock star and his entourage. I wait for her for a minute before I realize she's busy there. She's not coming back. Then I think about going up to the room, of going to sleep all by myself, and that seems far too pitiful to consider.

*****

I've always been the type of person who learns from doing. Having a hands-on experience makes a more lasting impression on me than spending hours reading about subjects in dryly written books. This is why I tend to pay such close attention to Kate—to her experiences and her attitude. To the way she dresses herself and the way she flirts to get the things that she wants. I have always had the feeling that she likes having someone look up to her, and I like having someone so breathtakingly confident to learn from. Maybe our relationship isn't entirely even, but think about it— whose is?

So now, after being left alone for a moment with my thoughts, I walk over to where Kate is perched on the arm of the rock star's chair. She's so beautiful and confident. She fits right in, talking to this man who plays concerts for millions of people all around the world. I grab onto Kate's hand and pull her away from the group. She shoots me a curious look.

"Give me one good reason," I tell her. I need her to woo me just a little bit more. Yet I know even as she's talking that I'm going to give in. My head feels light and my thoughts are shaking around, bubbling up as if carbonated inside my skull. Who am I? I don't know. I used to be able to answer that question easily: a photographer, a girlfriend, a best friend, a caffeine addict, an artist? Maybe. Maybe someday.

Breaking up with Justin shouldn't revamp my list. But he's shaken my level of confidence. And it's not as if I'm vanilla. I know that's difficult to believe, but really, I'm not. Although Kate does manage to shock me on a daily basis, I'm actually a pretty evolved creature when it comes to sexual habits. I guess I should be more clear about my definitions, though. "Vanilla" to me means someone who won't cross the line. The definition transcends the subject of sex—although sex remains a definite aspect of it. People who are satisfied to stay in the bedroom and do things in a "normal style" are missing out on a great deal of satisfaction. Who could ever return to the missionary position once girl-on-top has been introduced? Who could stay in the center of a bed after reveling in an outrageous outdoor experience? Who could deny the pleasure of being blindfolded after experiencing the seduction of deprivation?

Not me. That's obvious enough by now, isn't it?

But to my way of thinking, "vanilla" goes far beyond the sexual realm. The term equals bland, and bland means someone who avoids the risks that make life so enjoyable. Why play by the posted rules when breaking them can be so much fun? Kate taught me that concept way back in high school, figuring out in a brainwave that as the darlings of the class, nobody would dare hold us back and keep us from graduating. We were too smart to challenge and too cocky to be called on our indiscrete and inappropriate behavior.

And once we had that knowledge, well, nobody could stop us. We started cutting, skipping out on boring lectures to go get stoned with our boyfriends by the beach. Showing up late in the morning rather than sit through some talk about life after high school called

"The Best Years of Your Life...So Far." Who were these people kidding? Or, more honestly, what were *they* smoking?

Pressing limits served me well on my college campus, too. Rather than join a sorority, I'd gone it solo. "You'll have no friends," a fellow student predicted early on, shaking her head at my refusal to pledge at her sorority house. "UCLA is all about the Greek system. All of the parties. All of the fun. You're going to be by yourself every Friday night. And you'll have no chance to do one of the Bruins."

But it wasn't the end of my social life in the slightest. I quickly managed to create my own network, my own circle of buddies whose philosophy on the ancient Greeks was much more in tune with the hedonistic lifestyle of those living on Lesbos than those tailgating a football game.

Now, I watch other women around me in Los Angeles, and I understand immediately simply from reading the expressions on their faces, which ones play dangerously. Which ones keep things neat and clean. It's a game I play with myself to see if I can read a stranger before being introduced. My goal is to see whether or not I can sum someone up in a glance or two—or, more honestly, in a single picture.

Sure, I know that you can never really judge a person from exterior appearances. I've learned that over the years. (You can't judge a person by the photograph on their ID, right? So how can you judge someone on a first impression?) In college, I'd immediately pegged my roommate for a good girl. She seemed the part. It only took me a few weeks to learn that Melanie liked to sneak into movie theaters without paying. That she rarely went to class, but got As by cheating. That she used pot as a method of relaxing even when her stress level was non-existent. And that she love-love-loved it when her boyfriend spanked her. Especially, when others could hear.

My first beau also fit the "can't judge a book by its cover" rule.

He wore leather jackets and drove motorcycles, and yet he was the most law-abiding creature I'd ever seen. He refused to go places that I wanted to. Refused to do things to me that I truly needed to have done.

And look at me. Here again I'm a perfect example of the rule. I appear to be one way on the surface, but deep inside, I'm someone else entirely. Yet I've always believed that if a person were to look hard enough, I mean, that if someone truly were interested enough to stare deeply into my eyes rather than be satisfied by my exterior, that person would see how I like to play.

Which is *this* way—the stark opposite of vanilla—as multi-flavored, textured, and colored as you can possibly get. So maybe it's time to go for something new with Kate. Why am I holding back now?

Who am I trying to prove something to?

*****

"It's partly because of the taboo," Kate explains, her voice low in a sultry, soft croon. "And partly because there are all those extra body parts to play with—extra sets of hands, fingers, an extra tongue..." She lets the sentence trail off, leaving the rest of the sizzling scenario to my imagination. But, honestly, I can't really imagine anything at all. I can't get a clear crisp picture. I've gotten mentally lost at the possibility of simply *being* with Ian Langer. Not only being in a room with him but being in a bed with him, on a mattress, in his arms.

Justin and I occasionally used to play the "freebie" game. Each one of us would list five people we fantasized about making love to. Because the possibilities of being with a rock god or movie star are so desperately slim, it was a fun game to play. Who really ever would get to sleep with Harrison Ford or Gabriel Byrne or, in Justin's case, Julia Roberts and Shirley Manson.

Now, it's as if someone has offered up the celebrity of my

dreams for one night only because Ian was number three on my list. The man is more than handsome, more than confident. His ability to play beautiful music is transcended by the way he makes you think he's singing each song just for you.

From my expression, I think Kate senses that I'm in over my head.

"So Alex," she starts, lowering her long lashes over her dark green eyes in that coy fashion of hers. "Would you be interested?"

"Interested—" I stammer, as if confused, even though I know what she's offering. All right, so I'm not vanilla. That doesn't mean acting like this comes easily. Maybe to Kate, but not to me.

"In joining me and Ian?"

"Joining," I repeat, and I think of what that word implies. Joining as in a bridge made of three different people.

"He's a friend," she continues. "You know that from stories I've told you in the past. We've done this sort of thing before." And I know that's true, because she did tell me. Kate tells me everything. And I remember thinking that I was happy to be in a serious relationship, so I wouldn't have to consider whether or not I felt that my life was missing something—illusive excitement. Sex appeal. The dangerous eroticism of doing things that others consider naughty and taboo.

Then I think about Justin and Judith—the two J's. They were doing something naughty, too, weren't they? Did he go to her because he thought she was more exciting than I am? That thought hurts inside. When did I ever turn him down? Blinking those questions away, I find that I nod in the affirmative and that my lips form the word 'yes.' But really I'm still lost in a daze. All I know is that Kate understands, quickly purring to me that everything is going to be fine, just fine, and then leading me to the bank of elevators. She's ready to start now. It's obvious.

"I need a minute," I tell her. And I do. Honestly, I do. I need to get my head together. Need to make my heart slow down and my breathing return to a normal, healthy pace. That's the truth.

Kate looks me over with an unreadable smile on her face, and then tells me the suite number, hands over a key, and disappears into the elevator. I pace around for a minute, then go to my room and grab my bag. I'm not leaving, though. I just feel better if I have my camera with me. It's my all-grown-up security blanket. When my camera's nearby, I feel as if nothing can harm me. Sure, it's a fallacy, but at least it works the magic on me that I need. Immediately, when I stroke my hands over my camera case I feel at ease.

When I get to the suite, I find Kate waiting for me in a king-sized bed in the middle of the dimly lit bedroom. This hotel room is even more sumptuous than mine. Tapestries drape the walls, creating a cozy feel even in such a spacious environment. A mammoth gold brocade sofa faces a giant black-veined marble fireplace. The fire is lit, and the flames crackle invitingly, although I can't tell from where I stand whether this is a real fireplace or a gas one. The effect is the same. A romantic glow fills the room, further enhanced by several lit candles. Kate looks lovely in this ethereal light. As soon as I see her, I pull out my camera and take her picture. Can't help myself. At the click, she gives me a semi-stern look and says, "Put that thing away, baby. You're not a photographer tonight."

"I'm not?"

"No," she shakes her head. "You're a partier. A hedonist."

"What does a hedonist do?" I ask naively.

"You start by opening the wine and joining us," she says, pointing to a bottle of white wine on the bedside table.

Us.

The single, one-syllable word ricochets around in my head for several seconds like a silver ball in a pinball machine. Metallic-sounding bells and whistles go off in my mind.

Us.

Even though I know what to expect, I don't manage to grasp who she's referring to because the room appears empty except for the two of us. "Join us" can't possibly mean her and me, can it? That wouldn't make sense. Then, as I light a few additional candles and place them near the bed at her instruction, I notice the rather large and obviously human bulge under the blankets between her legs.

"You remember Ian, right?" Kate asks. The handsome raven-haired man emerges from under the crimson satin comforter on the four-poster bed. He grins—somewhat sheepishly, I think, for a rock star—and then he offers me a slightly sticky hand to shake. I look him over, even more impressed by his almost unreal beauty at close range. He has the dark good looks of a matinee star combined with a dangerous electrifying sexiness that is emphasized now by the fact that he's completely naked. His shoulders are broad and strong. His chest is well-muscled without being obscenely so. I wonder if his appeal is enhanced by the fact that I've made love with his songs playing in the background in the past. There is an aura about him that is nearly mesmerizing, and I am pulled closer to him as if drawn forward magnetically.

"Charmed," he says.

As I shake his hand, my attention shifts for a moment to Kate. I can't help but stare, somewhat awed, at my best friend's naked body. Even though I've seen Kate naked before, now she appears as untouchable as Ian, as if his rock god status has mystically transformed her into some supermodel or sex goddess. How can I possibly join the two of them? Again, Kate apparently senses precisely what I'm thinking.

"Relax," she tells me. "Don't worry so much, Alex. Take a sip of wine and take your time. This whole experience is simple—just friends hanging out. Having fun. Doing what they want to." Sounds good. Sounds promising. The problem I discover right away is that I don't know what I want. Not only have I never been with a man and a woman at the same time, I've never even really fantasized about it. Not in any great detail, anyway. Sure, Justin talked ménage every once in awhile. Doesn't every man have the fantasy of making love to two women at once? And I have found myself aroused by films featuring ménages a trois. Then there's Kate. She's regaled me with sultry multiple-member stories in the past, but I've always been happy to picture her in the starring role of her fabulous X-rated tales. I've never even thought to try myself as the lead in a frisky three-way fantasy.

"She's a novice," Kate explains to Ian, and he gives me another soft smile that again makes me feel my heart flutter rapidly in my chest. What's come over me? It's not as if I've never been close to celebrities. I'm not a fresh arrival to L.A. I've taken plenty of photographs for one of Los Angeles' premier alternative weekly newspapers—even the smallest papers in L.A. are afforded press passes—and those experiences have gotten me right up in the faces of some of today's biggest stars. But now 'biggest' has an entirely different connotation, because as Ian moves to get more comfortable in the bed, I see the stupefying tent he's creating beneath the sheets. Suddenly, I find myself really interested in being a part of this passion play.

"An innocent," Kate continues, glancing over at me when I shoot her daggers with my eyes. So what if it's true? I don't need her sharing all of my secrets. Maybe I'd be more comfortable if Ian thought I was as experienced as the two of them most obviously are. But Ian doesn't seem to mind my naiveté. In fact, he seems to be incredibly interested in learning more about me. Maybe he's turned on at the thought of being my teacher. Maybe he's experienced one too many groupies who want something from him—a notch on their g-strings.

"An innocent," he repeats, looking at me. "We'll have to change that," he says with a coy half-smile.

"You think?" I ask, realizing that the flirting response must be some natural instinct kicking in again after all this time laying dormant.

"Sandwiches can be the sexiest bedtime snacks on the erotic menu," he continues, and I have an instant image of what he's offering—although who will be the filling? I can't tell. Can't think that far ahead. Kate gives me a lazy grin and leans back against the luxuriously full pillows. Her hair is down, spread in a golden shimmering wave over the red velvet of the pillow covers. "Ian's great at going down, Alex. You should let him give you a whirl and a twirl." As she says the words, Ian puts his hand out to me again, beckoning me to come onto the mattress with them.

Every instinct in my body tells me to reach for the camera—how crazy is that? *Hide behind the lens*, my brain screams. *Start clicking!* But I know that it won't go over big with the rock 'n roll king if I pull out my Nikon. He'll think this was a set-up, a way to get pictures to sell to some down-and-dirty gossip magazine. And pictures like that do bring in the big bucks, let me tell you. I know many photographers who would kill for a shot like this one. Still, I need comfort, and that's what my camera brings to me. So I make a suggestion.

"You know," I say, working out my plan in my head, "I take pictures for a living."

Ian's dark eyebrows rise in a curious expression. He waits for me to continue.

"But it's more than that." Now my voice is the hushed whisper of a dirty confession. "I need to take pictures."

"Need?" Ian asks, head titled.

"Need." I repeat. "It's foreplay for me."

Again, I'm rewarded with his dazzling smile. "You dirty little thing," he says. "And you look so shy and sweet on the surface—"

"An illusion," I lie. But this next part is the truth. "Turns me on like nothing else." Taking pictures gives me power. Helps me find my place in the world. As I'm speaking, Kate's shaking her head no, despite the fact that she was the one who suggested I take pictures and upload them onto the Internet. That was only a farce, I see now, for her to get me to consider her proposition.

"Just listen," I say. "Let me snap a few pictures of the two of you—no faces. Only bodies. It will be art. I promise. And then, when I'm ready—"

"How will we know when you're ready?" Ian asks.

"You'll know," I say, giving him my sexiest smirk. "Let me assure you, you'll definitely know."

For some reason, I can tell that Ian's into the idea. Don't all celebrities like to be adored, worshipped by their fans? What is a better sign of worship than to have a photographer witness your every move with a camera? He takes my word that I won't catch his face, and then he starts to slide his body over Kate's, his mouth finding the nape of her neck, licking and kissing her there.

"You okay with this?" I ask Kate, but I should know better. Of course, she is. Kate likes to be a star. Now, she is center stage, being made love to by a member of America's most esteemed rock royalty. Few things could make her any more 'okay' than she is at this moment.

SNAP!

I win myself a beautiful shot right off the bat. I can feel it as my finger presses the trigger. Their bodies are sealed together, and I know that when I develop this picture, a tremor of memory will flare through me, so strong that I'll have to sit down and stare at the shot, mentally reliving every moment. They are too beautiful to deny. I move in closer to the bed—SNAP!—taking a picture now of Kate's full parted lips. Just her lips. She has a beautiful mouth. Open and willing. Her lips are so soft. So inviting. I know in the black and white shot, she will look transformed.

Now, I focus on the rock star. Ian has a striking body. He's lean and long, and his arms and back are corded with muscles. He keeps himself fit, obviously, and I know that even frames of parts of his body will be spectacular. I like the thought of a close shot of his arm around Kate's waist, and I shoot that picture. Then I move down the bed, standing up on the mattress in order to get the view I want. Skin on skin. Where does one stop and the other start? Their bodies are like puzzle pieces, fitting perfectly together. Even while I'm clicking away, they are making love. I can feel their heat, hear the sounds of their sexy arousal, and I find myself getting more turned on. But I don't rush things. I want to make this evening last, so I take another shot of their legs entwined, moving so close that I know viewers won't be able to guess what part of a body they're looking at, or how many players are participating in the shot.

And then Ian maneuvers Kate so that she's fully down on her back and he parts her legs and gets between. Now, I find that I have to set the camera down. This is too much. I'm such a voyeur. That fetish is alive and beating with wings inside my chest. Staring is so sexy I can't believe it, and I watch for as long as I can. Watch Kate's face change as the bliss of being dined upon works through her. Ian is making her feel amazing. I can tell by the glow in her eyes and the way her entire body trembles. I watch until she comes, and that moment is unreal. I've managed to separate my feelings, somehow. Yes, I know that this is my best friend and I'm watching her having sex. That's odd. But I've placed the scenario in a style that I can accept. We're three hungry people here, and now, I'm the hungriest of all.

"Join us," Kate says again, her voice a husky sigh.

I realize suddenly that while they are completely stripped, I'm still dressed. My clothes are suddenly too constricting. I need to be free of them. But with both Ian and Kate watching, I go back into my shy mode once again.

"Take off your clothes, kiddo," Kate urges.

I have on a black turtleneck sweater and a silk gray and white skirt. Beneath, I am wearing peach-colored satin panties. I pull off the sweater and kick my way out of the skirt, but I can't do the rest.

"Come over here," Ian croons. As soon as I approach the bed, Ian turns his attention on me, and in an instant, he has his hands inside my waistband and is pulling those silky underpants down my thighs. I watch Kate lean forward to get a candle. She brings it closer to the action, as if she desperately wants a better look.

"Now, climb onto the mattress and straddle his face," she instructs. That sounds extremely crass, and I give her a sharp look. She grins at me, understanding my expression easily. "We're all in bed together," she says, "nobody will be offended by my choice of language. Not here."

I am not exactly sure how to go about doing this, but Ian helps me. He gets on his back next to Kate and he lifts my hips and positions me until my sex is against his mouth. The sensation of true fluttering pleasure is immediate and almost over-powering. Pleasure, wet pleasure, fills me as his tongue trips along my nether lips. I sigh and close my eyes, but Kate quickly admonishes me.

"Don't go away," she says, "don't lose yourself in some far away place. Nothing you imagine could be as good as where you are right now. So stay here. Keep your eyes open. Watch him, or watch me."

Intrigued by her words, I turn to look at her, staring fixedly as she brings one hand between her thighs and begins to touch herself. For a moment, I see other images in my mind. I see Kate and me together, trying on bathing suits, and I recall her total lack of modesty as she stripped from one to another. I see the two of us in a bar, Kate bantering with the handsome bartender, making wagers. And when she lost, she simply shrugged and then leaned over the counter, locking lips with the handsome blue-eyed man.

Now, I see Kate at her most stripped down. So naked and exposed. Her fingernails are painted a deep, dark blue. I watch in total fascination as she strums just the tips of her fingers against her hot little gem before plunging two fingers up inside herself. I am so turned on by watching her that I almost forget what Ian is doing between my legs. Forget, that is, until he quickly switches our position, pulling his mouth away and sliding underneath my body. I get the concept immediately. He wants me on my back now, and at his gesture, I obey. I am right next to Kate, and I feel her body press to mine as Ian goes back to work between my thighs. But he's playing teasing games now. First, he licks me, then he moves over to lick Kate. Me, then her, then me again.

Kate reaches one slippery hand out and grips onto mine, holding tightly as I feel myself rise up to that first wave of pleasure. She squeezes my fingers even more firmly when I tell her that I am going to come.

"Kiss me," she insists, and I lean toward her, feeling her hands cradling my face, and kiss her as Ian brings me over the edge.

It's crazy how good I feel, and I close my eyes and bask in the bliss of it. Close my eyes and try to convince myself that I'm not dreaming. That I'm not in bed with Justin, fantasizing about living out a Kate-style situation; that I'm not downstairs in my own hotel room, drunk off my butt, making up sexy stories to put myself to sleep. What really happens is that I close my eyes and I fall asleep.

Can't believe it. Wouldn't have thought it would be possible. Not after an experience like that. But it's true. When I wake up, I'm in the room alone. Kate has left a note telling me to meet her at a party in Hollywood, but I don't think I will.

Without a look back, I leave the suite, ride the green-lit elevator down to my floor, and get between my own crisp sheets. Kate has taught me many things over the years of our friendship. But what she taught me tonight was the most important lesson of all.

*****

Hal says, "Are the pictures arranged in a particular order?"

"What do you mean?"

"Put them together correctly and they tell a story.

I like the way that he's thinking. "What does the story say to you?" I ask him. It's fun to turn the tables, to slide into the role of interviewer rather than the one being interrogated.

He shrugs, then spins slowly, looking around the room. "Well," he says finally, "it's a little hard to tell where to start."

"That's always the problem," I agree with him. "Isn't it?"

CHAPTER SEVENTEEN

Breakfast in bed is delivered to me by my beautiful, blonde bombshell of a best friend. As the key in the lock turns and the door opens, I roll over in bed to see who's entering my hotel room. Maid, maybe? Did I forget to leave the 'do not disturb' sign out? That's a big possibility. I wasn't myself last night. But wouldn't I have heard the maids out in the hall, pushing the cart, talking to one another? Yawning, I call out a 'hello.' Nobody answers, and I push myself up on the bed and wait to see who will emerge from around the corner. For some reason, I'm not scared at all—only curious.

When I realize that it's Kate, I smile at her. When I see the room service tray in her hands and I smile even broader. I'm ravenous. But after a moment of silence, I understand that she's not bringing me a fresh plate of food out of the goodness of her heart. I figure that out right away. Because when I see that she's with Ian, I feel my heart start to beat a little faster, and I push myself up quickly, trying to figure out if I look presentable. Do I? Could I possibly after a night like that?

"Hey, sleepyhead," Kate says, "we missed you at the party."

The two of them look fine, as if they thrive on no sleep and lots of sex. In fact, they are both positively aglow. Maybe I am as well. Maybe having a threesome changes the way you feel inside and the way you look outside. There's no time for me to tell, though. No way to excuse myself for a quick peek in the bathroom mirror.

I gaze at the tray Kate has carried with her into the hotel room, a room service dish covered so dramatically by a rounded silver cover. With great aplomb, she removes the bell-shaped cover, revealing ripe, red strawberries, a banana, a crescent of green melon, and a bunch of purple grapes. Ian laughs softly as I stare in wonderment at the meal. Are they here to dine with me? Or *on* me? From the presentation, and the girlish game-show-hostess way that Kate is motioning to each of the treats, I start to feel myself heat up. I squirm to get comfortable beneath the sheets, realizing that I'm naked, and realizing in the same moment, that somehow that's okay.

"You hungry?" Ian asks.

I nod, then I look at Kate's shining eyes. She has plans. I can tell. I know her. In general, I've heard about her escapades after they take place—like the one with the nameless rooftop stud and the man on the road crew. I am not totally sure about how I feel about having a staring role in her real world relationships.

No, that's a blatant lie. I know exactly how I feel. Thrilled and excited and honored. And, if I may say it, a bit like a slut. But that's an entirely new sensation for me, so I just go for it. There's nothing wrong with being a slut-in-training, is there?

"Hungry?" Kate says, repeating Ian's question as she keeps on grinning at me.

"A little," I answer, honestly. Who wouldn't be hungry after all of the energetic activities of the night?

"Ready?" Ian asks, and that's a different question entirely.

Isn't it? Ready for what? To play as we did last night, perhaps. To partake in all of the delights that three willing people have to offer—maybe. But then something surprising happens. Kate gives us both her most professional smile, and she says that she has to get back to work. And then she leaves. Leaves me with the rock star women fantasize about the most, as duly reported in the latest issue of Kate's favorite ladies magazine. Leaves me alone with a man so amazingly handsome I have a difficult time not staring at him, my mouth open, jaw dropped like some starstruck groupie.

A part of me—a sane part, however small it is—reminds me that I just left my boyfriend, less than a day ago, and that I have a healthy, growing crush on a new man, Connor, specifically. So why am I doing this? I find that question amazingly easy to answer: Because when will I ever have the opportunity again?

Ian stops all similar thoughts by climbing into bed with me, stripping off his navy blue shirt and deliciously faded jeans to show that he's entirely naked beneath. I like the fact that he had no boxers or briefs under his denim. For a moment, I am in awe of his form.

As I observe Ian in his naked splendor, I wonder whether things like this happen to other people all the time. Yeah, they happen to Kate, but what about other people? Had my life with Justin, my attitude while dating him, shielded me from experiencing pleasures such as this? Does everyone else walk around in a state of perpetual horniness? And what has happened to change me in the past day so that I now seem to send out a welcoming signal for any sultry situation?

Again, Ian erases my thoughts with his actions. With extreme casualness, he lifts the banana and peels it. Watching him move is like watching a porn show, live, happening in real time on the foot of my bed. Ian discards the skin and then strokes the supple fruit between my legs. Upward, back and forth, then jumping it to move along my belly, ignoring the space between my thighs. Not quite yet ripe, the fruit makes the ideal sex toy, thick and hard.

But what is he going to do with this?

Oh—the answer is almost unbelievable. I feel the fruit inch along the split of my body and then Ian thrusts it gently inside me.

I can't believe how it feels. Cool, moist, firm. What's happening to me? I am actually letting a near stranger make love to me with a piece of fruit. And it's turning me on. Ian pulls out the banana, licks off my juices, and then slides it back inside me, a little further. Oh, God, does this feel good. Who would have guessed it? I realize with a sudden blush that I will never make it through the produce aisle again without turning as red-faced as one of the tomatoes. Then I think about Connor, about the fact that he works with fruit all day, and I wonder whether he has ever played like this. He must have, I decide. I read an article recently in which famous people were asked about the sexiest scenarios they could think of. All of these different celebrity chefs named dirty deeds done with foods: fruit, vegetables, and (most often named) virgin olive oil. At the time, I thought the concept was silly. Now, I can start to understand the appeal.

But the thing of it is, I'm not a chef. I'm just a photographer.

Does that matter? Can I just roll with the program this morning? If the program appears to be playing with food, can't I just enjoy it?

Never will I be able to heft a bunch of bananas without thinking of this moment, of what Ian did to me, of how much I liked it. Because I do like it. My body contracts on the yellow tubular fruit, searching for purchase.

To calm myself, I grab hold of one of the down-filled pillows and hold it to my chest, needing support. Ian plays with the fruit for a few more seconds, before discarding it in favor of a sliver of honeydew melon. What is he going to do with that? I learn the answer right away. More of the same, but this is a different feeling entirely. The melon is already cut into a crescent, the rind removed, forming a sort of pale green, watery spear. Ian holds my nether lips open with one hand and slides the length of the melon into me. It is colder than the banana, and its own juices seem to bring forth a flood of mine, mingling together until I can actually feel them seeping to coat my inner thighs.

"You're so wet," Ian sighs, observing for a moment before bending, licking my skin, pulling out the melon with his mouth and taking one bite after another until it is all gone. I feel empty without it in me and I hope that Ian will have something else to fill me with.

And quickly.

From fruit virgin to fruit tart in seconds. Who would ever have thought?

Instead, of fulfilling my fantasy of being filled—or really, *refilled*—he leans over the bed and plucks a strawberry from the white porcelain plate. Where he is going with the berry, I can only wonder. But luckily for my libido, I don't have to wonder for long.

As I watch, Ian uses his famous fingers to squeeze juice from the ripe berry. He does this over my concave belly, and I feel the thick, red juices as they rain in heavy droplets onto my bare skin. As soon as I feel the cold drops on me, Ian bends to lick away the liquid. Then he squeezes more, licks more, until I can feel the climax building again inside me—powerful and unstoppable.

Ian pulps the berry with his fingers until it's a sticky mess and he spreads this along my body, painting me with the thick sweet liquid, marking me with different designs. Then he licks me clean once more. I close my eyes and grip into the pillow, trying so hard not to come. I know that there is more waiting for me. From last night, I know all about Ian's stamina. I don't want to let him down, don't want to let myself down. Know there are other fruits on the plate and wonder what uses they could possibly have. How slow have I been in the past? Are there cookbooks filled with erotic suggestions such as this? The Aphrodisiac Arts for Beginners?

Then I have to stop wondering about anything as Ian slips his tongue inside me and begins to tickle me on the inside. This is too good, too much, and I moan and grind my hips upward against his mouth. Hard. Who is this wild untamed woman in my bed? Is it really me? I can hardly process how this feels. All I hope is that he won't stop.

But, of course, he does. Are all men like Justin? Turned on by denial, by withholding? To my great relief, Ian doesn't leave me for long. He moves away only long enough to pull his secret toy out from under the crisp white napkin on the room service tray. Then he holds it up so that I can see: a red-and-white can of whipped cream. Ian starts slowly, pressing the nozzle on the can of cold cream and shooting a river of it the sweet white fluff in a line over my flat belly.

My breath catches in a half-sob, half-sigh. It feels so damn dirty to have him doing that to me, and knowing that he is going to lick me clean again has my body tensed tightly in a wound-up state of anticipation. Again and again, Ian brings the white corrugated nozzle to my body, sprays the whipped topping on me, and then licks it away with his warm, flat tongue. This is what whipped cream was made for.

But just when I think I might come from this alone, Ian ups the intensity of the encounter. Now he has me position myself on all fours. As I am doing so, he removes one more hidden item from the second plate, not letting me see it, but letting me hear as he undoes the cap. Whatever it is comes in a jar with a screw-on metal lid. I hear the jar unsealing, and then I feel it. Disbelief floods through me. Kate works at this hotel. What was she thinking when she arranged the tray for us? Ruining the sheets, destroying hotel property—

Once again, Ian sidetracks my serious thoughts by continuing to pour the honey—yes, honey—along the split of my body, letting me feel the sensuous stream of the sweet liquid coat my nether lips, slip down my thighs, so sticky. He tops it with more spritzes of the whipped cream, brings the banana back into play, and goes to work on me with his mouth.

I've become a dessert, a fantasy confection. When I say this aloud, Ian responds immediately. "Desserts are my favorite part of the meal," he says. "Any meal." He truly savors me, licking slowly at the honey that has spread to my inner thighs, lapping his way like a hungry cat up to my sex and getting his face wet and creamy with the mixture of sauces that include my own. I come when his tongue touches that little gem between my legs—just touches it. I come again as he slides the banana inside me while slurping the rest of the honey away.

And when it's over, when we are both dripping with fruit juices, and the juices of our own making, I roll over in bed and look at him.

"What are you thinking?" Ian asks dreamily, running the tips of his toes up the back of my calf.

Not anything. That's the truth. Not about Justin. Not about Judith. Not about Kate or Connor or anything.

"You're thinking about your camera," Ian says, with a low chuckle. Am I such an easy read? "Go on and get it, baby. I'll take your picture."

*****

"Self portrait by rock star," Hal says. "I don't get it."

"No," I say nodding. "No, you don't. You couldn't."

"So explain it to me."

But I can't.

"And that one?" Hal asks.

"The apartment."

"Yeah. Tell me about that picture. It's different from some of your others, isn't it? No models. Just a light up in that one window."

"My best friend lives there."

"Tell me about the light."

The picture shows Kate's apartment building at dawn. The sky is a ribbon of silver. Her home became a haven. I hope that shows through in the photo. To me, it's easy to tell. But maybe other people only see a building.

CHAPTER EIGHTEEN

Justin comes to see me after I've moved my stuff into Kate's apartment. At least, after I've moved the small amount of stuff that I took when I left. It's funny how you find out what you really need at the end of the day. We surround ourselves with all sorts of belongings, and we get attached to them. But when it all comes down to necessities, what do we really need?

I can't speak for everyone. I can only speak for myself. I just need my camera. Truly, that's it. What I brought was a few of my favorite pieces of clothing—but I hardly am aware that I end up wearing nearly the same things every day.

"You're staying here? I thought for sure you'd be at your darkroom."

That would have been too lonely. The space is small, but we've made it work, with me taking over the tiny dining room as my bedroom.

"You've got to be kidding," Justin says when he looks around.

"You've got to be kidding," is what I say to him. "Judith?"

"It's not what you think."

"What do you think I think?"

"Are you just going to repeat me now?"

I shake my head. "No. But I'm curious. Why do you think I left if I'm mistaken? Why has it taken you this long to come explain the real situation to me."

"I tried," he says. "I called. You wouldn't answer your cell. And Kate—she's like a guard dog. She wouldn't put me through."

"She's looking out for me."

"Seems to me as if you were the one looking. Spying, even."

"You and Judith. Together at her apartment."

"Doesn't mean anything," he says. "She was congratulating me."

"On—"

"There's this audition," he says, and I know he means the one that will take him to Europe for several months. France, in particular. "It's down to one other actor and me."

"And she was congratulating you with her body?"

"Peeping," he says, "who would have thought you had it in you?" And he actually smiles when he says it. "Sure, she kissed me. But that was it. I didn't go forward."

"The other pictures," I say. "Of the blonde."

He looks confused, but he's a good actor. I know that from our years together. "My old camera," I tell him. "I used it and developed the roll, and there were pictures on it. Pictures I didn't take. Twice." But he doesn't admit anything. He shakes his head and tells me I must have forgotten the roll. "Doesn't really matter, though," he says. "You want out. I can tell. So let's do this. Let's give us a break for a bit. What do you say? If it sticks, it sticks. If we're meant to be together, we'll work it out."

And I'm dizzy with questions and guilt from being with Ian, and I don't know what else to say except yes. But as soon as he leaves, I miss him. How crazy is that? I just miss him. Without seeing him face-to-face, I could just be angry. Now, I think that maybe I'm the one who was wrong. Could they really have been innocent in there? Could I have mistaken what I thought I saw? I should go and develop the pictures to be sure, but I don't have the heart.

Kate's gone tonight. Working late. Without her, there's nothing for me to do but sit in the living room, in front of her stereo, as close to the speaker as I can get without morphing into it. Kate and I don't share the same taste in music for the most part, but we both like the Stones. 'Like' is a mild word for it. We're fanatical. I get out her copy of Some Girls and I play my favorite part on repeat. As I listen, I think about everything that's taken me to this point. How crazy and mixed up sex can get. Can you love someone and like someone else? Could Justin be with Judith but want to be with me?

Nobody ever said relationships were easy. I know that. But nobody told me that emotions could be this inexplicable. I was at ease when Justin and I first were together. I got used to his flaws and learned to overlook them. When did everything become so complicated? How did I get to the point where I am at my best friend's apartment, in her living room, getting drunk to old music?

I know how Kate lives her life. Without the confusion and heartbreak of growing too attached. But I also know that most people can't pull that off. I can't. Desperation whirs through me. So I do the only thing I know how. I drink and I bow my head as if in silent meditation and listen to Jagger's dark whiskey moan. The cover is by my side, the colorful print of the women in their different wigs, all going for a look, a glamorous shot, a new way out. I sip from a nearby bottle, my hand sliding around the cool neck of it, and I let Mick's voice steal over me, let him wrap me in the sweet satin strands and strangle me.

If Kate were here, she'd talk sense to me. Or she'd take me out and get me properly drunk and happy at our favorite bar. But I haven't given her all the facts, have I? I haven't let her in so that she can actually help. I've just glossed over the main picture, without showing her the black-and-white photographs. That concept makes me sad.

The music makes me sadder still.

When the night is finally over and I can make my way through the empty apartment to take a shower, I click off the repeat button and let the song play one last time. Thank God Kate's working a party at the hotel. What would she do with me if she saw me in this state? She'd find some guy to have sex with me. That's her cure for everything, isn't it? A good, old-fashioned romp on a firm mattress. To Kate, that's the sanest answer in the world.

But I miss Justin. And although I'm not sure that I've done the right thing, I know that I can't go back. Not now. Not after Ian Langer. Post ice-cold shower, draped in a towel with my hair wrapped tightly, I wander into my bedroom and open my suitcase. I don't even look at the still-made bed. No sense trying to sleep. No sense climbing beneath the sheets.

No sense at all.

I dress myself carefully, keeping in mind what Justin would like to see me in if we were to run into each other. Keeping in mind that Justin likes me in jeans—tight jeans—and a white cotton T-shirt that's been washed many times and has a soft sheen to it. Then I walk back to Kate's bathroom and turn on the light. I stare at myself without really seeing my reflection. Instead, I see Ian on the bed, looking at me. And then I blink and I see Connor telling me secrets over a shot glass of tequila. Finally, I see Justin, and my stomach starts to hurt.

The mirror shows me what I look like. The T-shirt is slightly oversized, but when I move, when I turn my head, the fabric pulls taught over my breasts and shows off their curves, lays flat at my smooth belly, rides slightly out of my jeans to give a quick glimpse of the slim, pale line of my back. The Levis manage to conceal my long legs, the subtle roundness of my hips, but only barely, as if a strong wind might blow the ruined fabric to bits and leave me naked and free.

Quickly to the door, before the fear can work on me to hold me home. My keys are in my pocket, my sunglasses shielding me from the light. A few steps to the car, and I am safe again, ready to cruise, blocking out the words that form in my head and bat against my skull like thick, neoprene bubbles.

Not gonna see him, that voice says.

And he doesn't want to see you anyway, it continues as I drive slowly through the neighborhood on my way to Judith's house just to check, just to see if his Harley is parked outside.

It's not.

I know that all of this is something an unstable person would do, and I also know that my eyes have a haunted look to them—the eyes of someone who was about to say something, but has forgotten what, something that's right on the tip, right there, (I can almost taste it), right on the tip of my tongue, but it's gone. Because he's gone— it's over. God, and I'm the one who ended it. Why I am feeling this lost?

It's all a mess in my head. I know that I slept with Ian, and that sealed the deal. Even if I wanted to make-up with Justin, to come clean about following him and insist that he come clean with me, I couldn't. Is that why I agreed to the ménage in the first place? To make it impossible for me to go back home?

Back at home, hours later, I undress myself carefully— still keeping in mind what he would like to see me in if we were to run into each other. Keeping in mind that he likes me smooth at night, and fragrant from a cool, midnight bath. Cool skin, powdered dry, warm mouth on his, warm lips on his, my hands roaming over his body, fitting together with his in the jumble of our sheets, in the twisting and turning of a night no longer lonely.

Oh, how I miss him.

I keep the tip of my tongue poised against my teeth to say his name as he moves against me, slides against me, drives his body hard against mine. Keep the tip of my tongue poised to say his name the way he likes me to say it, a low moan, a sigh, a silent mouthing of his name with my head thrown back, exposing the vulnerable whiteness of my throat, exposing—

I am quiet and still on my makeshift bed, wearing nothing but the smell of my body, the smell of my skin and my freshly washed hair and the heat that steals from me that he used to replace. But now I'm alone, and I think that every small sound is his knock on the door, a soft rapping of his knuckles to let me know that he's there. That he's waiting, and my body readies itself for him—as if it has nothing to do with my brain—it readies itself and my hips shift so slightly and my heart beats so fast, and if he were to walk in and tear down the sheet he could fill me and turn, turn, and open, and then it would end.

But the truth is that he's gone.

And I don't think he's coming back.

*****

"No," Kate says immediately when I confess my longing after a week's gone by. "No, he's not coming back. That's what a break-up is all about, Alex. The 'not coming back' part is the crucial part." She emphasizes these words, and she looks me over and I can tell that she's not impressed with what she sees.

"You're the one who initiated this," she reminds me.

"Not sure I made the right decision."

"Judith," she says.

"He denied it."

"He would," Kate insists. "And regardless, there were problems. Larger problems than a pretty agent named Judith."

I don't tell her everything. I don't tell her about listening to the Stones on endless repeat. About dressing with his tastes in mind, or drinking with my own tastes in mind. I just say, "Maybe I really could crash here for awhile, not hurry to find my own space right away," and her eyes light up, because she's sick to death of living alone in her apartment, and she's always reminiscing of the fun days we had when we were two bachelor girls hanging out in L.A. doing the club scene, and the party scene, and the having fun scene rather than moping around alone scene—which isn't really a scene at all. It's just misery.

But living with Kate comes with all of her Kate-ness—her inability not to solve a problem that shows itself to her. Kate always has answers. And her first answer on the agenda of solving my problems is to set me up on a date.

"Going out again will completely change your attitude," she promises me. Turns out, she's right. I go immediately from bad to worse. Yet Kate insists on a post-mortem for every date. And date one goes like this—

*****

"It swung to the left."

"It what?"

"Swung to the left."

"What did?"

"It."

"Is that bad?"

"He couldn't get it in."

"Oh, my."

Date two is just as depressingly strange:

"He paid in nickels."

"Were you at an arcade?" Kate asks. "I just read how 'in' those are again. You get to relive your junior high days. And the cool thing is, you can drink beer while you play Asteroids. Of course, the more you drink, the lower your score on the machine. But probably the more likely you are to score in an entirely different way, if you catch my drift—"

"We were at a real restaurant," I interrupt her knowing that she could go on and on for hours.

Kate looks perplexed. "Well, why would he do that? Is he

another starving artist? You've got a thing for guys who can't pay the bills, don't you?"

"Justin could pay the bills."

"Now," she says, "but at first, he was leeching off of you."

"This guy was a banker. He said, 'I really like nickels.' Then he took out eighteen rolls and placed them on the tray for the waitress. You should have seen her face."

"Eighteen..." Kate says, trying to figure it out.

"Thirty-six dollars."

"The man broke his piggy bank for you," Kate smiles, looking, as always, for the positive spin.

Date three makes me reconsider dating and start taking classes at a convent:

"I forgot his name. That's how little of an impression he made on me. I couldn't for the life of me remember what it was."

"Really?" Kate asks. "Did you try to get a look at his license or something?"

"Doug...Dirk...Daniel.... Something with a 'D.'"

"Maybe you've been going out too much."

"You said the best way to get over a break-up was to plunge back into the dating pool."

"Or drink tequila until you pass out."

"I already did that. I'm onto something else now."

"Why didn't you just call him 'sweetie' or 'darling'?"

"We ran into an artist I know. I had to make introductions, aside from 'Molly Monroe, I'd like you to meet Sweetie Honey-Pie.'"

Kate giggles, picturing it.

"You would have been proud of me," I tell her. "I recovered nicely. We even joked about it. He had a good sense of humor, until I started laughing at his..."

"You didn't," Kate interrupts.

"That had a name, too."

"Uh oh."

"When he said he wanted me to meet 'Hairy Larry,' I thought he was talking about a dog."

"Did you meet...him?"

I shake my head. "Is this what dating is usually like, Kate?"

"They don't all have names," she promises.

"Tell me something to make me feel better."

"Like a bedtime story?"

"You know what I mean, Kate," I insist.

She does, of course, and her eyes taken on a heated glow to them, as if a light has just flickered to life in the very center of her pupils. "I've been wanting to," she says, "but you've been so down."

"Holding out, have you?" I tease, and for the first time in weeks, I really sound like myself.

"Not so much holding out," she says, "but savoring."

"So spill."

"Started like this," she says. "Me and Maggie, finishing up the day, when I got an important call buzzed through from reception. I answered in my most professional tone, 'Kate Derrick, you know?"

I nod.

"And this voice says, 'You wearing panties, baby?'"

I gesture to Molly that I want some privacy, and immediately she hurries from the room and closes the door behind her.

"Who was on the phone?" I want to know.

"At this point, I'm not sure. Could be any number of people."

"You're my hero, Kate," I tell her, but she waves away my compliment. "So I say, 'That's privileged information.'" 'I get it,' he says. 'Only a select few get to know?' 'Right,' I tell him. 'You give me the code word, and I'll let you know.' There's this dark chuckle on the line, and now I've narrowed him down to one of three possibles. Then he says, 'Code word: crimson,' and immediately I know that it's Ed."

"Ah," I say, remembering. "Ed."

Ed is one of Kate's favorite sex-buddies. But the thing about him is that he always seems to call her when she has her 'monthly visitor.' That's his schtick. It's as if he knows her schedule by heart. Now was no different. He came to the hotel, and Kate took him to a vacated room that hadn't yet been cleaned. It's one of her favorite things to do on a date. She could get in trouble, definitely, if she ever got caught. But nobody thinks to question her. She and Ed climbed onto the bed and made love all night long—the night she didn't come home. The night Justin was here.

"Do you like it, too?" I ask her, curious. "I mean, does it turn you on the way it turns him on?"

"First," Kate says, "I get turned on by how excited he is. And second, yeah. I'm always extra-sensitive during that time of the month. When you're with someone who is really free about it, the sex can be amazing. And you know I'm not the only one who likes it. The Chili Peppers even have a song about it."

"Purple Stain," I say, remembering. I like that song.

"But does he ever talk about what he likes?" I want to know. "Does he ever say, 'I'll call you in a month,' or something like that?"

Kate shakes her head. "It was amazing, Alex," she says. "So base. So primal. We tore the place up. If I didn't work at the hotel, I'd hate guests like me."

It's something so Kate that I have to smile.

CHAPTER NINETEEN

You know that song 'looking for love in all the wrong places'? Well, I'm pretty sure the singer was talking about L.A. Because out here in La-La Land, in a glittering city where everyone is beautiful and almost anything goes, love seems to be the last taboo, the one four-letter word you're not allowed to use with anyone. Make the mistake of letting it slip too soon, and watch your partner flee into the night.

And the thing of it is, I'm not even one of those sappy romantic women. I don't go to chick flicks. I don't expect a man to pay the tab or hold the door. Maybe my problem is I listen to too many oldies on the radio. But deep down, I do want someone to love.

Kate's always assured me that it's going to happen. But maybe Kate's got more faith in me than I have. And right when I start to lose faith, she suggests Connor.

*****

"Smile."

Connor poses without question, one arm against my doorframe, chin forward. God, is he handsome. The way he smiles at me makes my heart triple-beat. Luckily, the camera gives me something to do with my hands, something to think about so that I won't simply drag him into the apartment and make love to him on the hardwood floor of Kate's foyer.

Instead, I take the picture, replace the cap quickly, and follow him out the door. I've been wanting to go out with him for so long now, but I postponed it at the start. Wasn't ready. Not for something big. And I get the feeling that this could be something big.

At first it's strange, though, to hang out with him without the safety net of our customer/client situation. Yet Connor doesn't seem to mind, or notice. In fact, he's the same old Connor as always. Doesn't ask too many questions about Justin. Doesn't ask any at all, actually.

When we get to his truck, he pulls out a disposable camera and turns to me. "Smile," he says. I do it automatically, tossing my dark hair out of my eyes and grinning for the lens. Sometimes it's nice to be taken off-guard.

"Where do you want to go?" he asks next.

I choose the Observatory, which turns out to be a mistake. Tour buses fill the roundabout. Crowds of people crush at the balcony, staring at the city as if it holds the answer to every question. We decide to drive in search of the Hollywood sign instead, but get lost, circling around and around through the winding roads of the Hollywood Hills.

"That's where Brad Pitt lives," he says, pointing. "And that's the hotel where Belushi died. There's the place where they shot *Sunset Boulevard*."

"How do you know all these things?"

"I sold star maps one summer," he says, and for some reason, I like him a little bit more. From the car, we each take pictures of the different places, like tourists, and after the date, I can't wait to develop my roll of film.

We have dinner at one of the coolest old dives in Hollywood, and we giggle together as we make quiet fun of the rest of the patrons. Most of the people here are older than the two of us put together and they look as if they've gotten dressed in a different era. I like how at ease we are, and when he asks me, quietly, if I'd like to go somewhere else, I know that he's being sweet with me. Sweeter than he might be with another girl. I know this, because I know he likes me.

"Sure," I say. "Kate's working tonight. Let's go back to the apartment."

But Connor has other ideas.

*****

Connor drives the same type of insanely sexy vintage truck that my high school boyfriend did way back in the late 80s. I'm no hot-rod chick—you won't find me drooling in front of the shiny four-color car magazines at the newsstand—but you don't have to be a machine-head to appreciate this type of vehicle. It's one of those classic old Fords, with the seductive curves, the high bench-style seat, and the perfumed aroma of well-worn leather. I know of few scents more arousing than that. Oh man, I remember that smell. And smells are important. They can take you back with one single whiff to a whole different time and place.

The summer before I left for college, my boyfriend and I spent hours in his truck, spread out on the front seat, his body on mine, and the butter-soft leather beneath me. I remember everything about that truck. At this point, almost more than I remember about the guy. Now, he's been long reduced to a hazy blur in my memory. A good blur—blond and handsome, rugged and young. But his truck remains bold and clear in my head, and whenever I see another truck like it, I find my heart racing all over again.

I can tell the truck holds the same appeal for Connor. When he steps out of the cab, he always runs his hand gently along the door, as if he's petting the metal, caressing the body. If trucks could talk,

Connor's would purr. Yet I've got the feeling that his identity isn't wrapped up with his vehicle. Some guys are all about the cars they drive, but I can tell from the way that Connor moves, that he knows how to hold his own. This is just a core feeling I have. He doesn't need to hide behind something else to make himself appear cool. His coolness comes from within him. The knowledge that someday people will take him seriously for his artistic achievements, not demean him for the fact that he has to work two jobs. That he is a bartender and a grocer, not a movie star or a musician.

Connor likes the truck for what it represents, but it doesn't define him.

Still, in Hollywood, everything's about what you wear, not who you are. What you drive, not what you think. So I appreciate that old truck of Connor's, and the way he holds the door open for me and waits for me to get inside before shutting it carefully. Then I wait in the darkness of the cab until he opens the driver's side. And in those few moments, I breathe in the smell, that vintage truck smell, and it takes me back in time. Once again, my heart goes screaming in my chest, and I find myself desperately aware of the fact that my panties are already dripping.

Forget the drive, I think. Forget it all. Just spread me out here, take me right here.

But then in a wave of self-preservation, I remember exactly where "here" is—on the busy street of Santa Monica Boulevard, speared by the lights of every passing car, by the observant glances of any nosy pedestrian heading toward the clubs lined up in a row. And although exhibitionism has its time and place, I know that this is neither. So I sigh and try to keep myself contained as Connor starts the car and heads down the gleaming black strip of asphalt.

I think I know where he's going. If I have him pegged correctly, then he'll be taking a right and heading us back up toward the Hollywood Hills, to Griffith Observatory. We tried to go there together in the light of day. Things should be different at night.

I smile when I see that yes, I've nailed his plans, and I stare out the window as he reaches for my hand again. For a moment, I think he's going to be sweet and old-fashioned and squeeze my fingertips. Or else he might make a play for a little preview taste of what's to come and run his hand along my body. Instead, Connor surprises me and takes my hand and sets it high up on his thigh. I feel the warm, worn denim, and I run my fingers up and down, up and down, dying to inch them over, to feel his hardness beneath the button-fly.

There is no denying how much I want Connor. How, if we were in a movie, I'd take control of the wheel and turn us, tires screeching, down the next side street, sliding the truck into whatever space I could find and hiking up my dress to let Connor know what I wanted him to do. But we're in real life here, where crazy behavior like that is not always rewarded, so I take a deep breath and draw my fingers in lazy spirals high up on his thigh. I feel the hardness of his muscles beneath the denim, and I imagine what it will feel like when my naked skin meets his. It's an image I've visualized often since I first caught sight of Connor. I've got the idea that this preview will pale in comparison to the feature presentation.

The truck handles the curves of the road with ease, as if the vehicle has transformed into a fast-paced sports car, as if it's not an old dinosaur chugging up the road. Soon enough we're there, in a spot held perfectly in time. And we can see the view, and the world around us, with the inky dark sky and the golden lights twinkling. Rather than get out Connor reaches for me, and now my fantasies unfold, merging and blending with reality.

The scent of the car wafts around me. Below it is the scent of the two of us—clean and fresh, perfumed and oiled, and below that our skin. Just skin. I lean up on Connor, push my arms on the seat behind him, and feel exactly how turned-on he is when his body meets mine. We are still clothed, and I like that. Like the taking-our-time moments before the real fun starts.

I press myself to Connor, sealing myself to him, and it's as if our bodies are kissing, interlocking even through the barrier of our outerwear. We press together like that for a minute, taking our time. Then Connor slips his hand into my panties, reaching there between my lips to feel the wetness, and when he nods his head I know he wants me to take my panties off. I squirm out of his embrace to do so, slipping those silky underthings down my lean thighs and watching as Connor splits the button fly of his jeans.

I'm back on top of him in a heartbeat, and then I'm doing the work, riding him. Driving him the way that he drives his truck. I take charge, working up and down on my thighs, in total control. We both know that I'm in the driver's seat, and that's fine with him. I can tell from the look in his eyes that he's perfectly happy letting me set the pace. I like the fact that my mind has a double-vision of this action. Yesterday and today—long ago and right now. And even though I've been there before, and I've done this before, with Connor it's all new. The way I feel when he brings his strong, warm hands to my breasts and rubs his slightly calloused thumbs along my nipples, still hidden away under my dress and bra. The way I sigh when Connor reaches to pull me even closer so that he can kiss me while we make love.

His mouth is hot on mine, and he works so slowly, nibbling at me, even while we move against one another in a quick, necessary motion. I like that. Like how in control he is, even as I'm on top. I sigh as Connor keeps kissing me, now turning my head so that he can lick against my neck. He draws his hands through my hair, cradling me as he brings my lips against his one more time.

I squeeze tightly each time Connor kisses me. Maybe he already understands my rhythms. Maybe he and I are so in tune that he's figured out how to make me go slower or faster, rougher or more gently just by the way he kisses me. And then I get it. He's the one driving, maneuvering those dangerous curves, steering along the dangerous precipice. Connor knows all about handling a fine ride—

and that's what I've willingly become. He turns me on and takes me for the sweetest spin ever. Up I buck on his body, and then down I slide. Connor has his hands around my waist now, helping, urging me on. His thumb flicks over that most perfect place, finding just the spot that I need him to touch. I shiver as he works me, and I come when Connor kisses me again.

The night is alive with the traffic melody of Hollywood, with the silver celluloid memories of screen stars and movie magic. But we're here together, alone together, taking a little piece of pleasure and making it our own.

*****

Kate says, "So how was the night with Connor? Worth the wait?"

I nod, happily.

"Good short-term replacement," she says. "Good fling material."

I nod again, but I don't agree with her assessment. I see more than that where Connor is concerned. I see endless possibilities. I keep my mouth shut, though. And I go to my darkroom to develop the pictures, reveling in the way he looks in each shot.

*****

For a week, after that, I'm excited about being with Connor. I'm thrilled, really. I was right about everything. How easy it would be with him. How sweet everything felt when we were together. And then I'm surprised, because at first he doesn't call, and then he doesn't call me back. I can't make myself go to the store to see him or go to the bar and stare into his eyes, to see if I can read what went wrong.

Kate puts one arm around me and says, "It's good, Alexandra. You liked him. You'll like others."

I look at the picture of Connor standing next to the Hollywood sign, after we'd finally found it. His pose is casual, with his head back, one hand in his hip pocket. He stares directly at me from the picture in my hand.

Everybody's looking for something in Hollywood. All I'm looking for is love.

CHAPTER TWENTY

Kate says that she knows what she's doing. Setting me up with her friends and friends of friends, with anyone who calls himself a man. It's more than trial by fire. She is positively throwing me into the barbecue pit. All these different men want me, she insists. That should be doing something positive for my ego.

"They want sex," I tell her.

But she just smiles at that. "So do you," she reminds me, and I have no answer for that. I have made it my job to get over Connor now as well as Justin. Throw myself into the sizzling flames? Fine. I can give it my all. But sometimes even that's not enough. When Kate asks what I mean, I just give her the low-down on the latest and greatest date disaster. Why do things like this happen to me and not to Kate? I can't answer that one.

"He didn't shower."

"What do you mean?"

"I mean he didn't shower. As in, he arrived for the date without showering."

"Did he give you an explanation?"

"Like, 'I smell bad because I didn't shower'?"

"Like, 'I didn't shower because my water heater broke. So sorry.'"

"Nope. I don't think he realized he stunk. I did. The other people at Hamburger Hamlet did."

"Stunk," Kate repeats. "I don't think that's the right word."

"It's the right word, all right. Believe me, this man stunk."

Kate bites her bottom lip, thinking. "No, it's stank, Stink, stank, stunk." She moves toward her beloved dictionary, but stops as I lower my head in that time-honored, soap opera *'What am I going to do?'* gesture.

"Relax, Alexandra," Kate says, off her teacher's podium. "You dated a lot of guys before you fell in love with Justin, right?"

Instead of answering, I take out my camera and start to load my film. The simple motion of it puts me instantly at ease. If my camera were a man, I'd be all set.

*****

By date six, I have developed a sense of humor. It's as if being off the market for four years made me forget what dating was like in L.A. But now, it's all coming back to me. Loud, clear, and furry—

"He brought his what?"

"His rat."

"Did you say 'rat'?"

"Yes. He brought his rat with him on the date. It was on a red leash with a little rhinestone studded-collar. He let it scratch on the door until I opened up."

"Euuuuuuuw!"

*****

"It's a date," Kate insists. "He called you up. He asked you out. That's what a date is. If you look up the word in a dictionary, that's what it will say."

"You're sexist," I tell her. "Why does the guy have to call the girl?"

Instead of answering, she inspects my outfit, shaking her head in disapproval at my faded jeans, white tank top, and beat-up Doc Martins. Kate prefers a more feminine look. But I don't care. I'm not getting fancy for my ex.

"It isn't a date," I say, making a face at the blue-and-white sundress she's holding out for me as a loaner. "We broke up. It's an..." I pause, searching for the word, "...encounter. A getting-together-to-see-how-each-one-of-us-is-doing type of thing."

"You did that already when he stopped by to drop off more of your stuff. You were both doing jolly well. This time it's a date. He said he missed you on the answering machine. I heard it myself." She sprays me with perfume before I can duck.

*****

The Insomnia Café is six blocks from our apartment. I walk slowly from where I park my car, not wanting to beat him to our old hangout. We both play this game, and for once, I win because he's already there, seated in our spot. I take his picture through the window when he's not looking. Then I put away my Nikon, stroll through the front door, and grab a seat at Justin's side, kicking my Docs up on the chair across the way. At least I won the clothing battle with Kate, even if I didn't win the perfume one.

Justin looks at me, pushes his shades on top of his sun-streaked hair, and smiles. "I wanted to say 'goodbye,'" he says, and I lower my feet and pull my chair closer to the table. Maybe he's going to win this round after all.

"Goodbye?"

"I'm going to France."

"You got the part," I guess, stating the obvious. Smiling again, he says, "You're looking great, Alexandra, you know it?"

He wants to have sex, for old time's sake. I can't. It would hurt too much. He's leaving for four months, and I don't need to have one last rumble as my final memory.

"You took my picture, didn't you?"

I nod as he reaches for my camera bag, pulls out the Nikon, aims and shoots. I won't have to develop that photograph. I already know what I look like when I'm sad.

*****

Back home I ask Kate, "If the guy wants to do it, is it a date?"

"Unless you're a prostitute. Then it's a job."

"What if you don't end up doing it?"

"I don't believe you."

"What if you did end up doing it, but you wish you hadn't?"

"You went over to your old place after you met at the cafe," she says. Now she's the one stating the obvious.

"So?"

"How do you get yourself into these things, Alexandra?"

"He's leaving," I tell her, and I hope I'm not going to start crying.

She says, "That's perfect."

"What are you talking about?"

"You're with the same guy for ages, you both need some 'away time' before you can commit for real. Just breaking up wasn't enough for either of you. It wasn't final."

"I've gone out with six guys since we split," I say. "That's pretty final."

"You slept with Justin again, Alexandra. You'd keep on falling into each other's beds if he stayed in town. Now that he's leaving the country, you have the chance to keep seeing other people. Have a fling or two. Find out what it is you like."

"I had a fling and I got flung. I liked Connor. It didn't work. I liked Justin," I say, even though I know it sounds pathetic. "And usually it did work with him."

"Usually," Kate repeats. "Until it started working out with him and Judith.

I conveniently forget that for the moment. "I haven't had much success with men recently."

"You'll like some of the others," she assures me.

I start to empty my film bag, and she looks at the rolls in my hand.

"How many pictures did you take, anyway?" Kate asks.

"Six rolls."

"What in the world were you guys doing?"

"Saying goodbye.

That's the truth. Doesn't make it easier to bear. Saying goodbye with our bodies when our voices had left us. Justin held me up over him, his muscles tight as he positioned me exactly how he wanted me. The SNAP! of the camera didn't interrupt us at all; it was a background beat that we worked to. Justin made love to me so that I felt it deep within my body. He screwed me so that I'd remember his taste and his smell, the way his skin felt beneath my fingertips. The way his eyes looked when he gazed at me.

He brought everything up to the surface again, and the pleasure of each of the many orgasms we shared was tainted with the knowledge that we were both liars. We both had secrets. We might be together in the future, but things would never be the same between us again.

Photographs don't lie, but people do.

Is that why my camera is my true best friend?

*****

Kate's tired of me moping. I'm not too tired of it, yet. Moping is a new sensation for me.

"I hate to see you like this," Kate says. "You were doing so well before you met with Justin."

"Nice euphemism," I tell her. "'Met with.'"

"You were a little whirlwind," Kate insists. "Going out every weekend."

"I guess I thought that if he were still in town, we might get back together."

"Nobody knows the future," Kate says, "except those nice people at the Psychic Friends' Network. And I'm hoping that you won't get so down that you start calling them for advice. So why don't you go out with Aaron? He's totally cute."

*****

She's right. He is totally cute. "Smile," I tell him, when I open the door. I have my Nikon up and ready.

He's confused, but he grins anyway. As a male model, he's used to posing. I take the picture of him, framed in my doorway. Then I set down the camera and grab my leather jacket.

"What was that for?" he wants to know as I lock the door behind us.

"Posterity. If you ever get famous, I can sell it to *The Star*."

I'm joking, of course, but he looks deeply flattered.

After parking on the street, we walk down Beverly Boulevard to El Coyote. There's a list for people who want the patio, so we add our names and wait in the bar. It's still early and sunlight gleams through the circular stained glass windows.

Next to us, a young couple discusses their plans for the evening. I wait for Aaron to talk to me, to ask about my work or my hobbies. He doesn't. Instead, he tilts his head to listen to the people at the next table. He looks like the dog on the RCA label: His Master's Voice.

"*Last Tango* is playing at the New Beverly," the woman says.

"I've seen it twice."

"There's a De Niro retrospective at the Nuart."

The man shakes his head. "How about the new Bruce Willis flick?"

Aaron clears his throat, apparently unable to wait any longer. "I couldn't help overhearing," he says, leaning over their table, "that you're talking about the movies."

The couple nods together, before they can ask themselves why this person is talking to them. Strangers don't chat in L.A. We're not like New Yorkers, after all.

"You really ought to see *L'Air du Femme*," he continues, "It's French, and it's fabulous."

They're silent, staring at him.

"I'm in the business," Aaron smiles winningly, as if he's being featured in a tooth paste commercial. All of his teeth show in two neat rows. "I know an awful lot about movies." Then he sits back in his chair, looking happy to have done his good, Hollywood, star-studded deed for the day.

The couple thanks him, politely, then stand and walk to the door, as if they're checking with the hostess to see where they are on the list, but obviously to get away from the lunatic who has butted into their private conversation. Who does that sort of thing outside of the movies?

I wonder if Aaron honestly thinks two local advertisements make him an expert on cinema. Before I can ask, he says, "Sorry about that, Alexandra, but people stop me everywhere I go." He has a way of saying my name that I truly despise. He hits every single syllable evenly. Al-ex-an-dra.

Now, I wait for him to crack a grin, to show that me he's joking. He doesn't. Instead, he pauses before adding, "And Alexandra, if that picture comes out, do you think I could get a copy?"

*****

Hal likes that shot. "Stud in a doorway," he grins.

I move him on to the next one. Justin's is only a few feet behind us now. I wonder if he's going to say something to me, and I hope that I'll be coherent if he does. "This is one of my favorites," I tell Hal, hurrying him on.

CHAPTER TWENTY-ONE

"My other car is a Porsche," Byron says, leading me to the gold convertible Jaguar waiting in the driveway. He doesn't seem aware that he's actually quoting a bumper sticker. Holding the door open for me, he continues, "I have a summer house in Paris and a second home in Palm Springs."

He takes me to Patina, a very expensive restaurant on Melrose, where he speaks flawed French to the waiter, who shoots me several sympathetic stares throughout the dinner. Poor you, he seems to be saying. Stuck with that. How can you possibly eat? I think my date orders me a plate of bone marrow, but I'm not entirely sure. The conversation drones on, but all I do is nod, eyes glazed, dreaming of a peanut-butter-and-jelly sandwich and the remote control.

At home, afterward, I replay the conversation for Kate.

"I have a time-share. I have a mink coat. I have a swimming pool. I have an itty-bitty-teeny-weeny..."

"Did he?"

I nod.

"How tiny?"

"Um, thimble," I say. "Is this what dating is usually like?" I ask again.

"I know you're new to the scene, Alexandra, but you don't actually have to mess around with them on the first date."

"Postpone it. That's what you're telling me. Learn the disastrous news later on, when I'm already attached."

But she just shrugs. Things that work for Kate don't always seem to work for me.

*****

The adorable valet parking attendant across from the gallery hosting my next exhibition finally gets up the nerve to ask me out.

"I see you almost every day," he says. "Do you want to get a coffee with me on Friday night?"

This is one of the first dates I've created myself, and I'm pleased. That is, until after we go on the actual date. I don't tell Kate until after the fact, because I think she'll disapprove. I'm right.

Kate's nonplussed with the news. "Valet?" She asks, sniffing.

"Better than out-of-work model," I reply, not actually wanting to tell her all the details of the date.

"Two local commercials is not exactly out of work."

"He bangs on the drums in one, stands in line in the other."

"Tell me about the valet guy," she interrupts. "What happened?"

"He picked me up and took me to Hollywood." I move past Kate to hang up my red velvet coat, acting busy. "We went to this crowded place and had some coffee." Now, I walk toward the kitchen, as if that's that. Kate follows me.

"How crowded?"

"Packed, actually. I even saw some movie stars."

Kate likes movie stars. "Who?"

"I'm not supposed to say."

"Secret service recruiting valet attendants now?" She has a suspicious look on her face. Kate can always sniff out the truth. She's like a detective—or a beagle.

I sigh. "It's not that..."

"Then what is it?"

"He introduced me around and we all talked. End of story."

"Twenty questions," Kate says suddenly. "Was this at a café?"

"A lodge, sort of."

"Introduced you how?"

"Haven't you ever introduced someone before?" I ask, but Kate knows I'm stalling.

"How?" she demands.

I shrug. "I don't know. Something like, 'My name is Gabriel, and I'm an alcoholic. This is my friend Alexandra...'" I concede.

"He took you to an AA meeting on your first date?"

"He's seen the two of us having wine at that restaurant near the gallery. He was worried."

"Me?" Kate's nearly hysterical with disbelief.

"Well, we do go there a lot..."

"I'm not an alcoholic!"

"Denial's a major sign..." I tell her, rifling through the fridge for a beer.

*****

"I see many famous patients," the doctor tells me over dinner at a ritzy nightspot in Westwood. He's a specialist at UCLA Medical Center, and has asked me to meet him here at the end of his day. I wouldn't usually date someone so much older, but he was extremely suave when we met. He saw me in the lobby of the hospital, talking to the director about a gallery installation, and he said something witty about displaying my picture instead of the pandering crap they have on the walls now.

"You wouldn't believe how many people have OCD," he tells me now.

"What exactly is it?"

"Obsessive Compulsive Disorder," the doctor says, rubbing the tines of his fork six times against his napkin. He doesn't seem to notice that I'm watching him closely.

"I've heard of that. It's like a need to keep washing your hands over and over. Is that right?"

"That's one type," he says, arranging his plate so that the petite peas don't touch the parsley potatoes or steak. When a little crimson rivulet of meat juice threatens the sanctity of his potatoes, he creates a small watercress barrier between the two. "I have a patient who is actually afraid of telephones," he says.

"Of telemarketers? Or creditors?" I can understand that.

"Not the callers, the actual phones themselves."

"How is that OCD?"

"It's a symptom of a symptom. The dark truth is that she's afraid that she might call someone up and scream obscenities over the line. She feels she'd have no way to stop herself from doing such an act. Losing control is the root of the issue. This fear manifests itself as a fear of phones." He takes a bite of steak and pushes it to the left side of his mouth. I watch him chew precisely six times before he slides the bite over to the right side, chews six times, and swallows. "She also has a fear of pens and papers, for the same reason. What if she went crazy one day and scribbled down hateful notes to people before she could stop herself? The inner rage is intense. Yet if you met her, you'd think she was the sweetest little lady imaginable." He takes another bite, which he begins chewing on the opposite side of his mouth. Then switches over. One. Two. Three. Four. Five. Six. Swallow.

"Maybe she should just write down all the bad words she can think of and get it over with," I suggest.

"Do you have any fears?" He picks up his peas one at a time, spearing them with the center tine of his fork.

Oh, yes. Now that he asks, I realize that I do. I have a very specific fear, a fear that this date is never going to end. I decide not to share this fear with him, but I scoop up a medley of my peas with a spoon and I watch him grimace as I bite down hard.

*****

"His name was Chico," I tell Kate after my next round with a loser.

"He wore a diamond," she sings, moving her shoulders gracefully to the imaginary beat of that old 1970s tune. "But that was thirty years ago, when they used to have a show. Now it's a disco, but not for Chico..."

"He didn't have a diamond," I tell her. "It was a three-inch long shark's tooth embedded in his curly black chest hair."

Kate makes a face. She doesn't like overly hairy men. Her most recent boyfriend, George, was an amateur swimmer, who actually shaved his legs daily in order to keep his time down. Kate thought that was spectacular.

"Where'd you go?"

"Magic Mountain. He led me around all day by the elbow instead of the hand, as if I might escape. The truth was, I'd have liked to escape. Maybe he was right to hold me like that."

"But by the elbow?"

I shrug.

"That sounds like square-dancing time at school, doesn't it?" Kate asks. "Remember how the boys were all so frightened of getting cooties that they didn't want to touch the girls at all. They held onto the girls' sleeves instead of their hands. 'Course that changed when they hit puberty and then we were in charge—"

"It was just like that," I tell her. "Cooties and everything."

As Kate starts humming again, I pack up my stuff. I'm going to take a retreat to my darkroom where I'm actually looking forward to seeing Chico again, in photo form. This evening, Kate is dateless, and she wants to come with me.

*****

"I deserve a break," I call out to Kate while the pictures are drying. "I don't know if I'm ever going out again."

"But you're doing so well. Why not keep it up?"

"I've said 'yes' to everyone who's asked over the past two months. Ninety-percent have failed my ten-minute rule." I come out of the darkroom and collapse on the floor looking up at her.

"What rule?"

"They don't ask me a single question about myself within the first ten minutes of the date. Aside from wanting to know why the f— I'm taking their picture, all they talk about is themselves. How much money they make, how many groupies they've slept with, how messed up their patients are. How many drinks they used to consume in a single evening. How chanting got them everything they've ever wanted."

"You're too picky," Kate says, "You should stay with one of the dates for awhile, not bounce around so often."

"Which one would you choose?" I ask her. "The guy who took me to the grocery store so that we could suck the gas from the tops of whipped cream containers? Or the stud-muffin who brought me to an AA meeting because he'd seen the two of us at a bar?"

"Neither," she concedes, shaking her head.

"What if there's no chemistry?" I ask, next. "What if I'm out with someone totally normal, and I just want to kill him because we don't have anything to say to each other?"

"You never give anyone a second chance," Kate argues, "and that's just not fair. It took two months for George to grow on me."

"You make him sound like mold."

She gives me a look.

"Don't get me wrong. Mold is great. It's what makes blue cheese so yummy, right?" I pause. "I mean, for people who like blue cheese."

"Stop it," Kate says.

"And his teeth were sort of green...besides," I remind her. "You and George have been over for a year. And now you're more of a dating slut than I am. Far more—"

"Call Connor. He was cool." She's right, but then he didn't call again. Something went wrong, and I never knew what. But maybe I should give him another chance. Maybe—

When we get back to her place, I rummage around in my date book. But before I can find Connor's number, the phone rings. It's Rat Boy, wanting another date. To appease Kate, I accept for next weekend. She looks horrified. I guess she didn't expect him to be the one I'd choose for a second go-round.

"What are we going to do now?" she asks after I hang up.

I bring out the manila folder of my date photos. I've got a wide array—guys standing in the doorway, smiling at me, a picture of Rat Boy and his furry, little friend. Now I add several shots of Chico at the amusement park, his capped teeth glinting in the light. Kate follows me to the red Formica kitchen table. Here, I spread out all of the guys except for Justin and hand over a pair of scissors.

"Take your best shot."

"What?"

"Make the perfect man," I tell her, picking up the photo of Chico and detaching his shark's tooth from his hairy chest. His chest is actually pretty nice without the silly accoutrement.

"Do you have one of your itty-bitty beau?"

I point to him.

"My god, Alexandra, he's gorgeous."

I shrug, cutting off his head and adding it to Rat Boy's body.

"Do you have a picture of his...thing?"

"I'm not a pervert, Kate, I'm a photographer."

"How am I supposed to make the perfect man if I don't have a thing?"

I give her a copy of one of my still lifes, a photo of a bowl filled with vegetables, and we spend the rest of the evening creating collages. Kate's ideal man is made of three different dates and a cucumber. Mine is still Justin, but I don't dare admit it because in Kate's eyes I know that it would be wrong. Instead, I cut apart Aaron the Actor and Mr. Nickles and put them together like a jigsaw puzzle.

Of course, I know it's not the looks that matter. The L.A. frame of mind hasn't tainted me yet. But there's no way for me to cross the inner circuitry, to pull one guy's sense of humor and another guy's shy charm. To dispose of an over-inflated ego and a need to start every sentence with the word 'I.'

When we're finished cutting and pasting, we post the pictures on thick cardboard and spray them with clear laminate sealer. We'll hang them in the hallway, a shrine to the elusive Mr. Right.

CHAPTER TWENTY-TWO

On our second date, Rat Boy leaves the rat at home. But while we're sitting in the Chinese Theater watching an action flick, I feel something small and furry on my arm. It's a mouse—a tiny, red-eyed, white-furred mouse. I stifle a scream, and Rat Boy laughs. Then he tucks his little friend into his pocket and buttons it closed. Just the nose and whiskers poke out, sniffing around. It's actually sort of cute.

At Rae's in Santa Monica, eating pie after the movie, he says, "Haven't you ever had a pet, Alexandra?"

"A cat," I say. "Zippy."

"What did he look like?"

"Orange and white. Four-legged. With a tail." I think I know where he's going with this, and I beat him to it. "My mother's maiden name was Reiter. So my stripping name would be Zippy Reiter. I've played that game before."

He doesn't seem to understand what I'm talking about.

"You know," I say. "You take your first pet's name and your

mom's maiden name. Put them together and that would be your stripper name for a girl or your porn star name for a guy. Usually, it's like Fifi Levine. Or Fluffy Chapel. And for guys it's more like Spike Laney. And Bowser Lipman."

Rat boy looks horrified. "Back to Zippy," he says. "Were you close?"

I look at him, suspiciously.

"I mean, did you like him?"

"Sure," I nod. "He was a great cat."

"You know, you were probably lovers in a former life."

"Former life?" I ask, but maybe that's the wrong question. I probably should have said, "Lovers?"

"You know," he says, emphatically, leaning toward me across the table, "reincarnation." He has light brown eyes and arched brows. His gold-spiky hair falls over his forehead and he tosses his head back impatiently. "My mouse and I were definitely man and wife in our previous lives."

The date ends here, before I can ask which one was man and which one was wife. Before I can ask if he was having an affair with the rat.

Damn Kate for telling me I was too picky.

*****

"What are you wearing?" Allan asks me on the phone. For a moment, I find myself getting excited, thinking it's phone sex. I like phone sex.

"You mean, am I dressed?" I ask as seductively as possible. I look at myself in the mirror across the room, but I think about him. He's a model I met at a gallery opening where he spent the evening staring at me instead of the art.

"No," he says, "What are you going to wear tonight?"

"Something casual," I tell him. We're just going to a club on Pico to hear a new band. Kate's newest beau is playing, and he got us tickets.

"All right," Allan says and hangs up the phone.

It rings a minute later.

"Are jeans okay, Alexandra?"

"Yeah."

"What kind?"

"What do you mean?"

"Shredded or whole?"

I'm momentarily stunned. "Either," I say. "It's only a club."

He hangs up. This time, I stand by the phone, waiting. When it rings again, I just say, "Yes?"

"But what are *you* wearing?"

I sigh, staring at my image in the mirror. "A dress," I tell him. Part of me hopes that he'll show up in one, too. I have my camera at the ready, just in case.

*****

Shredded Jeans calls twice before our second date.

"Are we going dressy or casual?"

"Casual."

"Which city will we dine in: Beverly Hills or West Hollywood?"

"West Hollywood."

"Strange," Kate says, listening in. "He's overly preoccupied with his attire, isn't he?"

"He wants to look good for me," I insist.

Kate shakes her head. "The only men I know who are that interested in their clothes aren't interested in women." Interested is in italics. I can tell by the way she enunciates the word. So is *business*, and I tell her to mind her own.

*****

Allan rings the bell at five after six, on time without appearing either anxious or anal, although the phone calls would lead one to believe that he's safely ensconced in the second category.

Still, I wait a few seconds, for the same reasons, and then open the door.

This time, he's wearing khakis, and a blue denim shirt open to reveal the top of a white tank top. He looks absolutely and totally normal. Relief floods through me.

On the stroll to the restaurant, he takes off his shirt, then puts it back on, takes it off, puts it on again. I notice a large, colorful Grateful Dead tattoo on his forearm. As I've mentioned, I do like tattoos, but I'm not a Deadhead. Nor would I ever get a band logo etched onto my body. Turns you immediately into a walking advertisement, doesn't it? Without ever getting paid for the billboard space of your skin.

While we wait for our drinks, Allan puts his shirt on again. When the food arrives, he takes his shirt off and ties it around his waist. During our appetizers he does his shirt thing twice more.

"Nice tattoo," I finally say, since he really seems to want me to notice it.

"Yeah," he agrees. "Since we were going to be in West Hollywood, I thought it would be appropriate."

Now I stare at him, not sure whether he's joking or not. I hope so, but somehow, as he fiddles with his denim shirt again, I don't think he is. Did he get a tattoo to go with dinner?

"Faux," he says, softly, now that his secret out.

When he leaves to use the restroom, the waitress walks up to me. She watches Allan's fine ass move under those tight jeans, then lowers her voice to ask, "How on Earth can you go out with someone so good-looking?"

"Gee, thanks."

"I mean," she amends, still oblivious to the fact that she's offended me, "he's stunning."

I think of the phone calls ahead of time, the planning that goes into making Allan stunning, and I shrug. "It's easier than you'd think."

*****

"Walter wouldn't wash his woke up."

"What?"

"Walter wouldn't wash his wok up."

"Is that a new tongue-twister?" Kate asks.

"You could say that."

"Make sense, Alexandra."

I think for a second. "Walter wished to whip up wonders, but he wouldn't wash his wok up."

"Say that five times fast," challenges Kate.

"I would, but I've had a wittle whiskey."

Kate grins at me. She's enjoying this. "So the wok was dirty?"

"Had never been cleaned."

"What do you mean?" Kate asks, but from the wrinkle in her brow, I think she knows.

"It had bits of every other meal he'd ever cooked in it, sealed to the metal with grease."

Kate doesn't want to believe me. It's obvious from her expression. I manage to convince her. In great detail--"Eggs. Onions. Sardines..."--until she begs me to stop. We spend the rest of the evening writing our own truly twisted tongue-twisters.

*****

"He failed the ten-minute rule."

"Remind me what that is again..."

"He didn't ask me a single question in the first ten minutes."

"How long did it take?"

"Two-and-a-half hours."

"What did he ask you?"

I hesitate, while she stares at me, waiting.

"If I preferred ribbed for my pleasure.'"

"What did you tell him?"

I give her a sheepish grin, "Yeah."

She looks me over. She sees my camera.

"Which one was he again?"

"Artist. The one from the gallery."

"And how was it?"

I bring Kate to my darkroom and I develop the pictures while she watches. This is like porn come to life. She gets to see the different images emerge one by one, and she learns the story of what we did together. Funny, isn't it? Kate uses words and I use pictures. Together we could create quite a sexy compilation.

"Tell me," she says, pointing to a picture in which Dameron has his back to camera. He's poised over me, pushing up. "Was it good?"

"Can't you tell?"

"Sure," she nods, "but I don't ever get to see things like this. Not with the guys I'm with. We don't do photo essays of our encounters."

Her words give me a sexy idea. "I could take pictures," I tell her. "Like with Ian, but different."

"Hide out," you mean. "But wouldn't the click of the camera give you away?"

She's right, of course. Yet the image intrigues me, and I think about ways we could work it out. Maybe she could find someone who'd be willing to be photographed. Not just the body shots, close-ups like I did with Ian, but whole portraits, full sex portraits of two pretty people. It would different for me than the ones I take of myself. Kate promises to think about it.

CHAPTER TWENTY-THREE

Dameron and I plan to meet at a men's store, where he wants me to see a suit he's thinking of buying. "Your artistic opinion," he says dramatically on the phone, "is important to me."

"Artistic opinion," snorts my roommate Kate when I tell her the plan. "He wants to do you at the store."

I shake my head. She's wrong. It's me who wants to do Dameron.

In the men's department at Macy's, we surreptitiously sneak into the extra-large fitting room at the back. I sit on the plush, padded bench while Dameron unbuttons his faded blue work shirt and peels off the white T-shirt beneath it. I watch, hungrily, as he undoes the fly on his jeans. They're paint-splattered, stiff where the pigment has been ground into the denim.

"It's important," he says, trying to make me understand that he's asked me here under pure circumstances. "I've got a big interview tomorrow."

I'm listening to him, but now we're down to his crimson silk boxers and I can hardly contain my lust. I stand and lean against the cold glass of the mirror, watching as he slides into the gabardine slacks, buttons up the crisp blue shirt, adds a tie and the well-cut jacket.

"Perfect," I tell him, and then, from his expression, I decide that Kate was wrong. He *really* did want my opinion. Embarrassed, I grab my purse and pull out a lipstick, just to be doing something, anything, with my hands. My cheeks are flushed, my eyes have that glossy look to them that I get whenever I'm really turned on. As I stare at my reflection with my lips partway open, I see in the mirror that he's watching me with a strange expression. Yearning.

"You look pretty when you do that."

The compliment makes me smile.

"Let me try," he says next, and I hold my breath as I hand over the lipstick. Carefully, he colors my bottom lip, taking his time as he uses his thumb to catch a smear of the rose-colored hue. Then he stands back, inspecting his work. "Perfect," he says, mimicking me. "But I'd like to see it a little bit different."

"How?"

"Smeared across my—"

He's interrupted by the salesman asking, "Everything okay, Sir?"

"Perfect," Dameron calls out, and I try not to giggle. Then, softer, to me, he says, "I had this fantasy the other day of you surrounded by mirrors. It's why I asked you to meet me here." As he talks, he slowly unbuttons my lavender shirt. I help him because it's not going fast enough. Reaching down to untie my worn black docs and kick them off. Slithering out of my shiny black pants.

He takes me against the mirror. My palms are flat on it and his body is behind mine. His hands steady me, holding onto my waist, pulling me back against him. I feel him, steely hard and warm inside me, and I hold him tight within me, squeezing like the motion of a hand clenching and releasing. And soon we forget where we are or that we ought to be quiet. Forget that there are other people in rooms nearby, trying on clothes like good little boys.

Dameron takes control of the rhythm, speeding up, then slowing way down, and I lower my head as I feel the climax build inside me. My midnight-colored hair falls forward over my face, hiding me.

"Look at yourself," Dameron whispers. "Stare into the mirror when you come."

It's difficult, but I manage to do as he says. I bite my bottom lip to stop myself from saying his name, from crying out. He leans forward, pressing his lips to my ear, whispering where he'd like to see my lipstick kisses—decorating his chest, and then working down lower, lower. My mouth is finally around him.

"Every so often you'd lift your head and I'd redo your lipstick," he whispers to me, "shiny and thick, and you'd paint me with it again."

All you need is an artist to have the same filthy ideas as yourself.

*****

When I get home, Kate looks me over. My clothes are wrinkled, my shirt unbuttoned at the bottom. I look as unkempt as I feel, as out of control.

"I know what you're doing," Kate says.

"At least one of us does."

She gives me her sternest look. "You're experimenting," she says. "I mean, how many guys were you with before Justin?"

"Before?"

She nods.

I act like I'm thinking hard, but she nudges me, so I have to say, "One."

"One plus Justin?"

"No, one including Justin."

"You were a virgin when the two of you got together?"

"I messed around before, but I never went all the way."

Kate is most obviously shocked.

I don't know why she can't believe it, so I just ask, "How about you?" I wait, but she doesn't chime in with her list.

"Come on, Kate."

She says, "Shhh. I'm counting."

"Wow. You have to think about it?"

Finally, she shrugs. "Numbers are just numbers. Not really that important unless you give them extra weight."

"So you don't think it's too odd that I keep getting myself into these sorts of ...situations?"

"You're looking for love and finding sex."

I shrug. "Maybe if I look for sex, I'll find love."

"No," Kate says, "You'll just get arrested...."

*****

The next morning, she comes in with coffee and perches on the edge of my bedroll. "You know, if you don't want to sleep with someone right away, I have some tricks," Kate says. This is surprising news from Kate.

"You're saying this?" I ask her.

"I know," she nods. "Crazy, huh? But you and I are different. You're not as easy-going as I am."

"Oh, thanks."

"I'm trying to look out for you," she says. "I know I told you to get back in the game, but you get attached more quickly than I do."

"So tell me your tricks," I repeat lecherously, grinning.

"Methods," she continues, as if I haven't interrupted her. "Ways to postpone it."

"I'm horny," I tell her. Justin and I fooled around a lot. I mean, almost every day."

"Did he make you come?" she leans forward, genuinely interested.

"Sure," I say. "Usually."

"Just through intercourse?"

I shrug, but she wants more information. "Occasionally," I admit.

"And the rest of the time?"

"I took care of it."

"So take care of it now," she says, lowering her voice even though it's only the two of us alone in our apartment. In case I don't know what she means, she adds, "Masturbate."

"That's your trick?" I'm not impressed at all.

"All right, so don't do your toenails."

"If I didn't have sex because my nails were chipped, Justin would have been a very bitter man."

"If you won't try my 'no pedicure' idea, then don't clean your room."

"You know I never bring them back here. And I wouldn't care, anyway. Messy can be good. There are some crazy things you can do with feather dusters."

She comes closer, as if this secret, this one way, could fix the world population problem in a jiffy. "Don't shave."

"Don't shave what?"

"Your..." she lowers her voice. "Your muff."

"My muff," I say, liking the word. "All right. I'll give it a try."

*****

When I get home from my date with Dameron, Kate raises her eyebrows, asking me silently how it went. She seems to have a sense about these things. Maybe she knows that when I don't meet her gaze, I have something to hide.

"Alexandra...?" she asks now.

I shrug.

"You didn't."

"It's all your fault."

"What do you mean?"

"Turns out that he was into shaving."

*****

"Dr. Doolittle called again," Kate says when I get home from my date.

"The itty-bitty guy?"

She smiles. "No, Rat Boy."

"We should choose one nickname and stick with it."

"Are you going out with him again?"

I consider it. "I don't think I can date someone who believes his rat was his ex-wife."

"Former wife," Kate says. "He doesn't think he divorced her, he thinks he and she were married in a previous life. And it was the mouse, not the rat."

"Does it matter whether he believes in reincarnation or bestiality?" I ask Kate. "He's a nut case."

"Where'd you meet him in the first place, Alexandra?"

I blush. She always knows which questions will cause me the most embarrassment. "The pet store. I was buying goldfish for the bowl at the gallery."

"And he was?"

"Talking to some bunnies in the window. I thought it was cute."

"You should have known better."

"That's right," I tell her. "It's all me."

*****

"You were right," I tell Kate. "Shredded Jeans is gay."

"Happy?" she asks hopefully.

I shake my head.

"Festive? Celebratory? Filled with joy?"

"Gay."

"Why on earth would he ask you out?" She continues before I can answer, "Wasn't this your third date?"

"He wanted to see what it would be like."

"It?" she asks, and I nod and open my eyes wide waiting for her to catch on. Finally, she does.

"What was it like?" she asks cautiously.

"We had hideous sex at his place, and immediately afterward he hopped around the room shouting, "I'm okay, I'm okay!"

"That must have been pretty exciting."

"Afterward, he took me to Cafe Figaro in West Hollywood and spent the rest of the evening talking loudly about the pretty young boys in the bar. Angelic. Perfect. Boys."

"So he wasn't okay after all."

"No, he was fine. Gay, but fine. He just wanted to make sure that the other men in the restaurant wouldn't think he was interested in me in a romantic way.

"Did it work?"

"I guess so. Our waiter asked for his number."

"Maybe you should take a break."

I look at her, surprised.

"You've been out every weekend for the past three months."

"I thought that was the game plan."

"Take a break," she says. I promise to think about it.

But then Dameron calls again.

"Who's Dameron again?"

"An artist from the gallery," I say, and from my blush Kate knows to ask more questions.

"Which artist?"

"The one I dated a few weeks ago."

"Which date?" Kate wants to know.

"The one who liked shaving," I remind her.

Kate sighs.

"He brought in some paintings last week. All were nudes. Mostly artistic. But this one was totally erotic. A woman surrounded by mirrors. I can't describe it."

"Try," Kate says.

I take a breath and picture it in my mind. "There were all these angles, and you could see that the mirrors showed different views, different sides of her personality. Not true reflections in glass."

*****

"Where is he?" Kate asks.

I shrug.

Kate checks the clock over the mantel. "He's forty-five minutes late."

"You act as if you were the one going out."

"Aren't you upset? I mean, you sleep with him and then he blows you off."

I shrug again.

"Aren't you even going to call him?"

When I shrug for the third time, she says, "That's not an actual answer, Alexandra."

I remain silent.

"If it happened to me, I'd be upset," Kate says righteously.

"Then be upset," I tell her, "I'd rather be something else."

But that's it. No more, I decide. No more.

*****

Justin is eying me. I can tell that he wants to say something, but he's unwilling to interrupt Hal and me. That's fine. I feel safe as long as the interview continues. Strange that Justin has decided to come to this opening, when he would act in pain when I asked him to attend others in the past.

"We need to talk," he mouths at me when I look in his direction.

I don't want to, but I excuse myself from Hal and make my way over to where Justin is standing, all alone in the corner.

CHAPTER TWENTY-FOUR

"We'll have a party," Kate announces.

"Why?"

"If you refuse to go out, I'll bring the men to you."

"Doesn't that make you a pimp?"

"I think it's 'Madam.'"

"Whatever," I tell her. "I thought you wanted me to take a break."

"But you look so miserable," she says, sitting by my side on the couch.

"I thought he liked me."

"He obviously liked you," Kate says.

"Then why did he blow me off...?"

She shakes her head. "Men are impossible to figure out. You need to get Dameron out of your head and move on. A party will take care of that. I promise. And you know that I throw the best parties." I think about what she's suggesting. Kate's right. She's known for hosting fabulous fiestas. Still, I'm not sure it's such a great idea. But when Kate says we can have a painting theme, I agree.

*****

After work, I go to the paint store to get supplies.

"What if nobody comes?" I ask Kate that night.

"If you have a party, they will come. Trust me. It's the way the world works."

I prepare for the event by moving the furniture into the bedrooms and spreading newspaper on the living room floor. I set up the spray cans on every ledge, and then wait. Kate comes in with candles, which I veto. "You don't want to be lighting matches in a room with thirty cans of spray paint."

Kate looked confused. "*Spray paint?*"

"We're going to graffiti the place," I tell her. "Didn't you read the invite?"

The bell rings before Kate can argue, and she runs to open the door. It's a group of several artists from the gallery, thrilled to be let loose on canvases as big as the four living room walls. They go straight for the cans.

"Any rules?" Josh asks.

"No obscenities," Kate says immediately. When I look at her, she shrugs. "My parents stop by every now and then."

"F—n' awesome," Josh says, opening the can of red. "This is my space." He draws a box on the wall next to the fireplace. "All Mine." Then he labels it with his name and the date. "F—n' awesome," he repeats, moving closer to the wall and placing one hand on it, as if feeling for a heartbeat.

James takes the other side of the fireplace. Valerie settles herself directly in front of it and begins spraying fake flames onto the white plaster.

"You're really fine with all this?" I ask.

"My dream come true," she says.

"What do you mean?"

"When this is done, we'll have to hire a real painter to redo the walls. I've been wanting an update for months." I smile at her, then I open a beer and sit in the corner to watch. More people arrive from Kate's work and she takes over the role of entertainer, choosing music, offering liquor, pointing out blank wall space that could be put to good use.

An hour into the evening, our apartment is filled with eligible men, extreme amounts of alcohol, and extensive fumes. I sit on our drop cloth covered sofa and watch as one of the partiers glues dried cat kibble to the wall.

"That's not exactly painting," Kate points out to me.

I don't answer. I just get my camera and start documenting the event. Art in motion. I feel happier than I have in months. Maybe that's why I accept the next offer of a date.

*****

"He brought a girl with him."

"What do you mean?"

"He brought a girl with him," I repeat.

"Another date?"

I nod.

"I don't get it." She waits patiently for me to explain, as if I have the answers to all of her questions.

"Neither did we."

"He brought a date to your date?" Kate asks, carefully enunciating each word in case she's missed something.

I nod again.

"Was it a scheduling mix-up? He forgot he asked you both out, so he doubled up. Made it seem as if he wanted to have a little party."

"He wanted to have a party, all right," I tell her.

"Seriously, Alex."

"Seriously. He just wanted to be out with two girls."

"You don't mind that," Kate teases me. Then she says one word. "Ian." And I blush.

"This man was no Ian Langer."

"So what did you do?"

"We all watched the movie together, and then we went out to eat."

"You didn't sleep with him, did you, Alexandra? I mean, not after that."

I shake my head.

"Did you sleep with her...?"

Kate always knows the questions to ask. And me without an answer to give her.

*****

"No more. No more dates."

"What happened?"

"I hate men. I'm never going out again."

"Come on, Alexandra."

"Really. We'll be old maids together. We'll sit around the card table playing canasta."

"I don't know how to play canasta."

"Bridge. Crazy eights. Pinochle. I don't care. You name the game, I'll bring the cards."

"What happened?"

"He left me for the cigarette girl." I sit down on the couch and let her put an arm around me. "I liked him, Kate." I try not to sound pathetic, but I fail.

She pets my hair. "I know you did. Tell me what happened? Where were you?"

"That club on Sunset...The Coconut Teaser."

"And?" She keeps stroking my hair. It starts to make me feel a little bit better.

"This little blonde fluffy thing came up and with her tiny outfit and her tray of toys and he asked her if she had a light. She said yes, pushing her boobs in his face. He followed her off down the hallway somewhere, and I didn't see him again."

"How long did you wait?"

"Half hour. The bartender told me this girl does it all the time. Goes off with men and then reappears, rejuvenated, an hour later. I don't know why they don't fire her."

"She's obviously keeping customers coming back," Kate says in her managerial role. "Who was driving?"

"He was."

"How'd you get home? Did you cab?"

I find it in myself to smile.

"What?"

"I had the valet ticket in my purse."

"Uh oh," Kate says, shaking her head. She stands to see if his car is parked out front of our building, but I stop her.

"I drove his Spyder down the hill and parked by the police station..."

She knows me well enough to wait.

"...In front of a hydrant. Then I walked to Pavilion's and called a taxi."

"You're bad, Alexandra."

"Smoking is bad," I tell her innocently. "Smoking will get you into trouble every time."

*****

"Look, we have to talk," Justin says.

"Why?"

"We just do."

"Here?"

He nods. I see Kate watching us and there is a fierce expression on her face. She's sending me warning signs. Don't get involved.

Don't make that mess again.

"So talk," I say. "But quickly. Hal's waiting."

"You were right," Justin says.

"Judith?"

He shakes his head. "The pictures."

CHAPTER TWENTY-FIVE

Connor calls me again. It's been three months since our first date and a week-and-a-half since my moratorium on going out. Kate comes at me with the cordless phone, mouthing "Connor." When I wave her away angrily, she hisses, "What are you doing? You like him. Give him another chance, Alexandra. Let him explain." She hands me the phone with a look my mother used when I was a kid to stop me from talking back.

"I'm sorry," he says, when I pick up the receiver, "I wasn't totally honest with you last time we went out."

Kate is hovering too close to me. I walk down the hall and into the dining room, shutting the door on her. I can hear her pacing back and forth.

"What do you mean?" I ask, looking at the picture of him in front of the Hollywood sign. It's tacked up on my bulletin board. I play with the edges, straightening the pins as I listen.

"Can we get together for coffee? I'd rather explain in person."

Don't be gay, I think. Don't be gay, don't be gay, don't be gay.

I couldn't handle that again. Out loud, I say, "Where?" and he suggests that we meet at Insomnia. Apparently, it's the best place for revelations. This time, I don't wear jeans and Docs. At Kate's insistence, I put on a dress and a pair of strappy sandals. Still, it feels odd to be there with someone besides Justin. At least we don't sit in "our" spot.

"I had a girlfriend," he says, "the last time we went out."

I think about the girl who sometimes came to meet him at the bar, the pretty blonde with the pixie haircut.

"And now?" I ask.

"I don't."

"Did you break up because of me?"

He shakes his head. "I asked you out because you captivated me. I broke up with her because it was over. It had been over for a long time. In fact, we'd broken up and gotten back together several times. Just too lazy to make it stick, I guess." He takes a sip of coffee. "I suppose I was just clinging to a bad relationship rather than seeing what it would be like to be on my own. Does that make sense?"

I nod. It makes a lot of sense.

On the walls of the cafe are awful paintings, extremely awful paintings. Connor looks at them, then looks at me. "Scary, huh?" he asks. I'm not sure if he means the art, or the concept of being alone. Both are pretty frightening when you think about it.

"How about you?" he asks me. "What's going on with you? Can you talk about it now? Can you talk about Justin?"

"He's gone," I tell him. "He's in France. It's really over." I smile at him and hope he believes me.

Then I wonder whether or not I believe myself.

*****

"You know," Connor says at our next meeting, "I saw you one night."

"Which night?"

"You really don't know?"

I wait, realizing that he's playing with me.

"At the grocery store."

I squint, as if it will somehow aid my memory.

"You were with this geek," he says, and he starts to smile. "And he was sucking the gas out of whipped cream containers."

"Oh, damn," I say, "You were there? You saw that?"

"Yeah," he smiles broader.

"And you still wanted to go out with me after that?"

"I mean if you were going out with someone of that caliber, I was pretty sure I had a chance."

*****

"Who's your favorite artist?" Connor asks on our next date. I suddenly realize he's the first guy to ask me this question. I also realize that on all of our dates he's beat my ten-minute rule with time to spare.

"Man Ray," I say without having to consider it.

"Which picture?" he asks, "the one with the tears? The woman as a violin? The lady and the mask?"

"It's not famous."

"Try me."

"The one of the dandelions."

He smiles. "There's a photography exhibit going on that I think has one or two of his."

We drive together in his truck, but this time we don't have sex. We arrive at the museum and buy our tickets. Then we walk hand in hand through the museum. I find something insanely sexual about sharing the experience of looking at a picture. Two people can stand in front of the same piece of art, both absorbing it, both bringing something of their own to it, and taking something separate away. It forms a bond. Sharing art can actually be more intimate than sex.

When I come back home, Kate says, "So how was it?"

"I'll let you know after I develop him."

She watches me gather my supplies. Then I'm off to my darkroom, to relive the night.

*****

"Smile."

"Again?"

"Just smile." I hold up my Nikon.

"I thought you got that out of your system last time," Connor says. He gives me a purposefully confused look, which I consider capturing on film forever. Then he tilts his head and smiles, and something about his grin makes my heart beat a little bit faster. I take the picture, set down the camera, and come into his arms.

"Can I use that later?" he asks me.

"When?"

"Later," he says, teasing, "you know, later." He stretches out that word and I easily visualize him standing over me in bed, camera cradled in his hands, zooming in close on my face, on my breasts, on my belly. I have the tripod. We could set up the timer. We could play all the dirty bed games that I know.

I shake my head.

"Come on," he says, and I think about Justin, and our six-roll finale. I have the pictures locked in the bottom drawer of my file cabinet. I haven't attacked them with the scissors. Can I give over the camera to someone else?

I shake my head again. Not yet.

"I'll trade you," he says, "a photo for a song."

I start to reconsider.

"Think about it tonight," he says, driving up to the Hollywood Bowl. "Just think about it."

So I think about it. And after the concert, I tell him, fine, but I need to get some supplies. In the camera store, I walk through the aisles in search for different items that I want to take home with us. I'm on a mission, and I don't pay attention to my surroundings. This is why Connor is able to take my picture with a disposable camera without me being aware.

I look up, into the wall of mirrors, as the camera clicks. I can see from where I'm standing that he's set up the shot correctly. He'll get both of us in the reflection without a flare from a flash.

He comes to stand behind me, to look over my shoulder at the pewter frame in my hand. Then he checks out the rolls of film in my basket.

"Planning a party?"

I shake my head.

"You've got ten rolls of film, and you like to take pictures of your dates..." he's pondering this in a very Agatha Christie way. He even strokes his chin as if that will help him think. Now, he reconsiders. "An orgy?"

Another head shake.

He lifts one of the rolls and looks it over. "Twenty-four exposure. Meant for indoor lighting. Tell me you're not planning something wild."

"You know me and film," I finally admit.

"Why not get thirty-sixes?" he says softly, "And add one of these to the fray." He drops a red filter into the basket.

"Talk to me about apertures, baby," I say, just as quietly, trying not to laugh.

Back at my studio, we go wild. We take pictures of each other, and I find myself letting my guard down once again. I know that I might get hurt, but somehow that doesn't matter to me right now. All that matters is that I like Connor, and I like the way he looks at me as he aims the camera. And I like the way he looks when he sets the camera down and takes mine from my hands. There is no awkward moment with him. We are two people, coming together tightly, his hands on my body, his lips on my own. He kisses perfectly. His lips are so light at first, just gently pressed against mine. Then he parts my lips with his tongue and we are quickly on one another. Ravenous. Unstoppable. Yet still I hear the camera clicking in my head. Even though we aren't using a tripod, haven't set one up. I hear the SNAP! and imagine each picture, each frame to go with each action: me naked and bent over; Connor taking me from behind, the force of him the raw heat of him against me. Then it's Connor with his back against the wall, and me in his arms, almost climbing his body as if he were an obstacle course. Getting myself as close to him as I possibly can. Forcing myself up on him by locking my feet behind his calves and pushing.

Connor lets me go, lets me set the pace. And then he moves me once again, over to my sofa, where we sprawl out Missionary-style. Looking into his eyes I see everything. I see how much he likes me, and I know the look is echoed back. As he slides back and forth, slippery wet in my juices, he slips one hand between our bodies and touches me there. Right where I need him to be. He makes sure that we come together. I hear explosions around us. I feel heat as if I fire has consumed us. I close my eyes and slide into the depth of it, as pleasure rises all around.

*****

"The pictures," I repeat to Justin. "The ones of the girl. You said you didn't know what I was talking about. You said I was crazy."

He shrugs.

"Why would you use my camera? Did you want to get caught?"

"It was her idea. I was going to take the film out the first time, but I forgot. We did it again, and I could tell things were ending between you and me. I mean, I could just tell. You'd gone cold somehow, even when other things were so hot. So I just didn't bother."

"Her idea," I say, and I feel Kate's eyes burning into me. "Which her?"

But even as I ask the question, I know. Didn't I always know?

BOOK THREE

Pop!

CHAPTER TWENTY-SIX

"How did it go again?" I moan to Kate.

"Liquor then wine, you'll always be fine. Wine and then liquor, never sicker."

"Oh, man," I sigh, leaning my head on the nice, sweet, heavenly, cool tile floor of our bathroom. The black-and-white squares are peaceful. I'm thinking of moving into the bathroom, living here full time. "I guess I had it wrong."

"What did you think it was?" Kate asks. I look up at her from my fetal position near the toilet. She is healthy and pink-cheeked, sitting on the edge of our white porcelain tub.

"Liquor then wine is for the swine. Wine and then liquor, you'll get drunk quicker."

"You're making that up."

I shrug as best I can without moving any muscles. Basically, I shrug with my eyelids. I don't think any room has spun this much since the last time I went on the round-about ride at the Santa Monica beach.

"Why did you get drunk, anyway, Alexandra?"

"Why?" I repeat, as if it's the most confusing question I've ever been asked.

"What were you thinking?"

"He said I'd get drunk, but not sick."

"He who?"

"He my date. We had a beer. Then we had a shot. Then we had another beer. And another shot. And another beer..." Kate cuts me off, sensing where this is going. She's good at seeing the patterns in other people's behaviors.

"What was the point?"

I give another no-muscle shrug. "What's the point of it ever?"

"Something to prove?" she asks.

I mumble under my breath and she leans down to hear, then gets a whiff of me and sits back on the edge of the tub.

"Justin's coming home," I repeat, slightly louder. "He left a message on the machine." I take a breath. "In French."

*****

"Je manque," Justin says.

My high school French trickles slowly into my brain. "You eat me?" I ask, hoping I don't sound too excited.

"That's mange," he corrects me, stepping into the apartment and holding his arms open. "Manque is missed. I missed you." It's been five months. I take a photo of him like this, arms outstretched, serious look on his handsome face. He's grown a beard. It's slightly darker than the hair on his head, which is more sun-streaked than ever.

Justin is home for vacation for one week. We don't talk about the women he's dating in France, or the men I'm seeing in L.A. I don't mean to have sex with him, but I do.

He says, "Smile," holding the camera in front of the two of us. He loves taking pictures in bed, digs around in my closet for the tripod and sets it up, even better with the timer than I am. Apparently, it's still his favorite frisky hobby, getting the sheets in the background, or a jumble of pillows. He thinks it's sexy, and since I have my own darkroom, there's never a problem about who's going to develop the pictures.

*****

"You didn't," Kate says when she visits me at the studio and sees the many rolls of film lined up on the mantle. One for each month he was away. "Oh, Alexandra, you promised you wouldn't sleep with him. He's leaving on Monday. Now, it's all going to start over again. You're at ground zero."

I walk into my darkroom and flick on the red light. It's the easiest way to shut her out. When I get to the final picture of Justin at the doorway, his back to the camera, I develop it and then sit on my stool and stare while it dries. But Kate doesn't leave me alone even though I want her to.

"So what are you going to do now?" Kate wants to know.

"About what?"

"Connor."

"Nothing."

"You mean you aren't going out with him anymore?"

"No. I mean that I'm not telling him about Justin. We're not exclusive. There's no reason to share."

"He'll know," she tells me. "He'll sense it."

*****

I meet Connor at the market a little before his shift ends. I'm early, but it's been over a week since I last saw him. It's difficult for me to believe how much I missed him in his absence.

"Ten minutes," he says, winking at me.

"Where should I meet you?"

He gives me a look that I can't immediately decipher, then nods toward the freight elevator. "Upstairs."

"What's upstairs?"

"Me in ten minutes," he says, leading me to the elevator and pushing the button.

I ride up in silence, aware of the smell of peaches and strawberries, the coldness seeping in from the refrigeration room. The ride ends on the second floor and I get out and sit on a crate, waiting for him. He's not long at all.

"I had this idea," he says, and from the lecherous look in his eyes I can't help but smile.

"Tell me."

"I'd rather show you."

I watch as he pulls a wheeled cart with a flat top over to me. Then I let him lift me up and bend me over it, feel his hands undoing my slacks and sliding them down my thighs.

"Won't you get in trouble?"

"Shhhh," he whispers, and I feel his warm skin pressing into mine. He makes love to me against the wheeled cart, with his motions pushing us forward. I am weightless, my feet on the lower rack, moving each time he thrusts inside me. The smell of fruit is all around us, and our own scent of sex and sweat and heat mingles with the pure fragrance of ripe peaches and honeydews.

Connor pulls out before he finishes, and moves away from me. I look over my shoulder and he shakes his head and tells me to hush, to close my eyes, to trust him.

I lower my head on the cool metal of the cart and wait. Soon, I feel something else inside me. Not Connor at all, but something hard and cool, stroking me gently, filling me up. As I start to come, Connor enters me again, finishing the job with warm flesh instead of cool cucumber.

"So which was better?" he asks me, as I try to regain my composure. I look up at him, breathless, my hair in my eyes, my face flushed.

"Do you mean you or the vegetable?"

"I mean the vegetable or your ex?"

"Oh," I say, embarrassed. "How'd you know?"

He smiles at me. "You don't remember much about your drinking binge, do you?"

"I told you?"

He nods. "You said he was in town, that you weren't sure what you were going to do. And I figured you saw him, since it took a week for you to get back to me."

I start to put my clothes back on, feeling suddenly too naked.

"I'm not upset," he says. "We didn't make any deals. I just like to know what's going on."

"He's gone," I say, realizing as I say it that I've said it to Connor before, these very same words.

"And it's over?"

I nod.

"For real this time?"

I nod again.

"So which was better?" he wants to know. But we both start laughing before I can think of an answer.

CHAPTER TWENTY-SEVEN

"I'm not sure how to tell you this," Kate says.

I stare up at her from my sprawled position on the couch. It's been two days since I changed clothes, and I have a feeling I know what Kate is going to say. She surprises me.

"I just saw Connor at the grocery store."

"And?"

"He wasn't alone."

"Why would he be alone if he was at the grocery store?"

"He was holding this blonde girl," Kate says, and I know instantly which blonde girl she's referring to.

"We don't have any commitment," I tell her. "Just look at me and Justin and our little week-long fling."

"But you like him," she says.

And she's right. And I don't have anything to say to that. So I say nothing. But when another guy asks me out the next evening, I agree. When will the roundabout stop? I don't know. I'm too dizzy to consider. Too dizzy to even know when it's time to get off.

*****

"I could do that," Eric says loudly, looking at the pictures on the gallery wall.

"What do you mean?" I ask, against better judgment.

"That picture. That's not art. Why would anyone pay for something like that?"

I look at the canvas. It's what Kate calls "hyper modern," a creation by a new artist. The guy has talent in my opinion. And, actually, not just in my opinion, in other people's opinions, as well. Two collectors have already shown interest. I don't know how deep into this conversation I should get with Eric.

"At least you take pictures," he says. "Photographs. Those look like what they're supposed to look like."

I remember a painting I saw at the San Francisco Museum of Modern Art, a very realistic portrait of a station wagon. I wonder if Eric would consider that art. "These are just doodles," he says.

"If it doesn't look like something specific or something recognizable to you, then it's not art?" I ask.

"If I could do it, it's not art."

I really should not go further, I tell myself, but I can't help it. When people are this closed minded to a new topic, it's generally better to move on. Yet, I have nothing to lose. And I'm tired of playing quiet all the time, of listening while people voice opinions that I don't buy.

"You don't think the idea is worth something? I mean, you could copy this, but you didn't think it up yourself."

"Squiggles on a page," he says, dismissively, lifting another glass of champagne from a passing waiter.

"What does it make you think of?"

"Is this a test?"

I shake my head. I suddenly wish I were with Connor because even if Connor didn't like the art, he'd be willing to have an adult conversation about it. He wouldn't dismiss the image with a shrug.

"Come on," I say, trying to forge something from nothing. "Doesn't it make you think of anything? How would you describe it to someone who'd never seen it?"

"It looks like green spaghetti," he says.

"But that's cool, isn't it?" I ask. "You weren't thinking of that before, were you? The idea of emerald pasta had never entered your mind."

"There's better stuff in the coffee shop on the corner," he snorts. "This stuff sucks."

And here's what I think: If two people bring something to a piece of art, they can take something away together. Eric's not bringing anything to it, and he's leaving all the fun behind. But maybe it's not his fault. You can't recreate an experience with someone new. He just wasn't the right person to bring to the exhibit.

"The champagne's okay, though," Eric says, as if that counts for something. I don't even take my camera out of the bag tonight. All my interest in taking pictures fades with the look on Eric's face.

*****

"Ed called today," Kate tells me.

"And...?" I look at her, waiting for the punch line.

"I got my period this morning."

Now, I nod. We've been here before.

"How come he only calls when I'm on the rag?"

"Some guys are wired funny."

"What do you mean?"

My eyes gleam. I don't often get to tease Kate like this. Usually, she's the one with all the knowledge. "Vampire sex."

"You're gross."

"I'm not the one calling you when your monthly visitor arrives."

I watch suspiciously as she balls up her sheets and gets ready to do the laundry.

"Kate," I say, playing mom for once, "What am I going to do with you?"

She shrugs, then grabs the bleach and heads to the laundry room.

*****

He picks me up on a Harley and we drive to a fish spot on Pacific Coast Highway. His bike joins the line in front of the restaurant. Women in leather halters and cut-off shorts bring men their beers.

"As it should be," my date says, then continues to rant about his work in contract law. When he finally asks a question about me, I note that he's failed my ten-minute test by an hour and thirty-two minutes.

"So you work in a gallery?" he says, picking bits of shrimp out of his teeth.

"That's just a cover," I say.

He waits.

"I'm really a call girl. You knew that, didn't you?"

His face goes a little bit whiter than snow.

"A thousand dollars a night." I pause, as if I just don't understand the confusion.

He shakes his head. He looks ill.

"Didn't you talk to a woman when you booked me?"

He shakes his head again. "I thought I was talking to you."

"No, that was Kate. She handles my appointments. But she's new," I say, as if that explains it. I wait for him to come up with something, anything. I see dollar signs flashing in his eyes. When he fails to speak, I borrow his cell phone and call Kate, telling her where to pick me up. Then I go outside and chat with the real bikers. At least they have something interesting to say.

*****

"He wanted me to call him Daddy."

"Really?" Kate asks looking half-horrified, half-interested.

"I couldn't do it."

"Not even for fun?"

I shake my head.

"What did you do instead?"

"We played a different game."

She looks more interested, less horrified. "Spill it."

"I called him Santa."

"That's my girl," Kate grins. "Somehow, I'm guessing you weren't on his nice list.

"You know me," I tell her. "Naughty all the way."

"Well," Kate says judiciously, " "Tis the season."

*****

I manage to meet Todd when I'm out with Tony.

"How do you do that?" Kate wants to know. She's not upset, she's simply curious. Really curious. Because even though it's an endeavor she might work out, she can't imagine me doing something like this. I'm too much of a novice to juggle two men—especially in one single evening.

"Which part?"

"How do you get another guy's number when you're out on a date?"

"Tony was flirting with the cocktail waitress. I didn't see anything wrong with accepting Todd's number. I'm sure even Miss Manners would take my side."

"Maybe," Kate agrees, "But she'd tell you not to move so fast."

"How fast is too fast?" I ask Kate, and when she pauses, I realize that she's trying to think of rules for me that are different from her rules for herself.

"No way," I say. "You tell me what's too fast in your world.

Don't give me a handicap because I'm not all tough and rough-edged like you. I'm learning."

Kate smiles at me. "Yeah," she says. "You are—" I smile back, before I realize she's not finished. "You're learning to be cold-hearted and jaded, just like me. Is that where you want to go?"

"Works for you."

"You know why I'm here."

*****

Todd moves in for a week. The sex is incredible. He gets Kate's cat stoned. Then he gets us stoned. We do topsy-turvy upside down acrobatics on my futon. We stay up all night and take pictures of the sunrise together. We play word association games and both of us win.

"Baby," he says.

"Oil," I say.

He grins and heads to the bathroom, and I can see him down the hall, looking through our medicine cabinet. Back in bed, with the baby oil bottle open, the slick liquid lubing up his hands, he says, "Pose."

"Madonna."

"We're not playing that game any more."

"Oh. You mean you actually want me to pose."

He nods.

I play statue, and he motions for me to disrobe. I break the pose, undress, and hold still again. He oils me up, my face, my limbs, my body. I start to shake. His hands on me feel so good. I start to think that maybe I can learn from Kate. Maybe if you don't love anybody, if you don't take care of anyone but yourself, you can not only survive, but enjoy life because this feels amazing.

Todd rubs his hands over my breasts, cradling them. Lifting them. I feel so glistening-glossy, so ripe and ready, that when he moves his hands down lower, to part my nether lips and get me oily there, I let out a deep, husky moan, surprising both of us. Usually, I'm more contained than that. But maybe Kate was right. Maybe, with flings and one-time romantic partners, you can get crazy. You can do things you wouldn't do with a true love. Don't have to worry so much about long-time memories, or about embarrassing yourself.

Todd returns to the bathroom for more supplies, returns with hair gel and slicks my heavy hair back from my face.

When he sets up the camera to take pictures, I start to smile.

*****

"What's going on?" Kate wants to know when Todd walks into the kitchen wearing only a towel. "Is this going to happen often?" she murmurs as he roots through our refrigerator.

I shrug. "He's crashing here for a few days," I tell her, and he does until our food disappears and he makes no effort to replace it. Until Kate gets the phone bill and there are calls to Guam. Until I shake my head at him when he asks if he can stay another week.

Todd moves back out. The only thing he leaves behind are traffic tickets. Many traffic tickets. Scattered around the bottom of my closet. And they're all in some other girl's name.

So maybe it's good for Kate—these flings. These ripe and raunchy one-offs, as she calls them. But I'm not so easy with them. I have to force myself from paying the traffic tickets. Keep myself from calling him, from calling Justin.

"Leave it alone," Kate says finally. "Just leave it alone—"

"And he'll come home?" I ask. "Wagging his tail behind him."

CHAPTER TWENTY-EIGHT

"I have to tell you something," Connor says.

"We've been here before."

"I know Kate saw me that day. And I was embarrassed. But nothing happened. Nothing really. I promise you that."

"Fine," I say. That's all I have to say. "Fine."

"But it's not fine," he tells me. "This isn't the way it's supposed to be. Not with us. Come see me. I'm working tonight."

It's strange that I believe him, right? It's strange that all of a sudden, I no longer care.

I head immediately to the bar, but I'm not interested in alcohol. My nerves are rattled and jangling. Connor sees me, and he instantly knows what I need. I can tell that he knows. He brings me a coffee, black in a porcelain cup. I take the first sip right away, then savor it, drinking slowly, feeling an intense rush from my toes to the back of my neck. The soft hairs on my arms raise up as if I'm frightened instead of aroused. Connor stands behind the counter, greeting customers with a casual nod as they walk through the door, his eyes always returning to me. I drink a long sip, then flick my tongue over my lips, and that's all it takes. Calling excuses to his Van, Connor hurries me out of the bar and to his car in the downstairs garage. We don't say a word. Opening the door, we slide into the back seat and fall into each other.

We're in a blur of motion, but I register every single touch—his warm body, strong hands on mine. This is right. It must be right. To feel this good, it has to be right. His hands are on me, lifting my dress, pulling it up and over my head.

Windows steam up from our heat as his mouth opens on mine, then moves down my neck, lips sliding on my skin, mouth open, tongue in a line, down my body. *Oh yes, I think, do that, that bad thing, pull them down. Pull my panties down and take them off. Now, yes, now.*

He spreads me open, parts my lips, and licks away the cream that awaits him.

*****

"Come on, Alex," Justin says. "We've had our differences. I know that. I know all about it. And I know just how messy everything got. How totally confusing and f—ed up. But I can't leave things like this. Don't make me say it out loud. Don't make me tell you what you already know."

CHAPTER TWENTY-NINE

Kate says, "Well, my rooftop Romeo came back."

"When?" I ask, leaning back in the chair across from her desk and settling myself in to listen. I haven't told her about Connor yet, but I can save the news. Kate is raring and ready to go. She's difficult to stop when she has a story.

"Yesterday morning. I can't wait to tell you."

I nod, indicating that I'm dying to hear, leaning back on Kate's lip-shaped sofa. Bright red velvet, it's cut to look a bit like the logo from the Rolling Stones. In front of me is her Zen garden, a coffee table contraption covered with sand and pebbles, meant to soothe the soul.

"It all started with an innocent pair of bedroom slippers," Kate says. She opens a Frederick's of Hollywood catalog that just happens to be on her desk and points to the shoes. "I bought them last week, ordered them through the mail. I had gone down to sign for them just when my rooftop neighbor pulled up in front of the building in a taxi. He got out and came directly over to me.

'I've been out of town,' he said, 'working a show back east, and I forgot to bring your number.' Then he looked at the box in my hand. The label read 'Frederick's' in bold letters, and he got this devious smile on his face when he saw it. 'Open the box,' he said. I wouldn't do it on the street, so we walked up the stairs to my apartment. He had his suitcase with him, didn't seem to mind that he was coming to my house before going to his.

"I kicked off my heels, pulled off my black stockings, and slid into the marabou mules. The white bit of fluff on the toes made the shoes look like some sort of pastry, a fantasy confection created just for feet. My red toenails peeked through the opening. It was lucky," Kate says, "I'd just had a pedicure," she winks at me.

"He just loved them. I mean loved them. With me entirely naked, wearing only those sinful slippers, he spread me out on the bed and had his way with me. I was lucky you weren't home. If you had been, you'd definitely have heard us."

I just smile at her.

"I came so hard, and he rubbed the toe of the slipper against my dripping muff. He got my come all over those naughty feathers, matting the feathers into a sticky mess. They were disposable shoes, I guess. I'll never wear them again."

Even after my eye-opening evening, Kate's still my hero.

"That's amazing."

"It was," Kate agrees. Now that she's divulged her news, she turns her attention to me. And I tell her. I tell her that I want Connor.

While I watch, Kate stands up from her desk and comes to sit at my side on the sofa. She begins to play with her Zen garden, dragging the rake back and forth in the sand. She doesn't have anything to say, which is unusual for her. Or maybe she has too much to say, but she doesn't know where to start. Finally, she asks, "How do you know?"

"What do you mean?"

Kate's designs in the sand are circles within circles. She puts the rake down and lifts a few of the smooth gray pebbles, placing them in and around the spiraling creations.

"He works at a store," Kate says slowly.

I stare at her. Really, I glare at her.

"A *grocery* store," she adds emphatically, as if I didn't know that important tidbit of information, or as if it means something deeper than a simple factual statement of where Connor works.

"I work at a store, too," I remind her.

"Occasionally you temp at an art gallery. There's a difference."

"You're right," I say, nodding, aware that I'm going to say something hard-edged before the words are out of my mouth. I'm not upset with Kate, so why am I taking my mood out on her? "It's just a store filled with high-brow art that's so expensive no normal person can possibly afford it."

"It's not the same thing," she insists.

"How?" I'm forcing her say the things that I don't want to hear. And I can tell from the way she's staring at me that she doesn't want to say the things any more than I want to hear them.

"You're an artist," she says slowly, "and you want to date someone who stacks fruit for a living? Someone who's job it is to announce the correct price of cucumbers over the loudspeaker?"

I think about cucumbers and Connor and start to blush. "When did you turn into a snob?" I ask, hoping Kate doesn't notice my flushed cheeks, doesn't guess what they might mean. "And why haven't you said anything about the rest of my winners: valet parking attendant, cemetery care-taker, waiter, actor, dog-walker, felon..."

"I said something about the felon."

"You understand what I'm getting at."

"I guess I thought you'd flush the dating thing out of your system and wind up happily ever after with Justin."

"What's so great about Justin?"

"He's talented."

I stare at her, waiting. There has to be more to it than this.

"He's got ambitions, too," she announces grandly, as if that makes everything perfect. "Just like you. You guys were made for each other. I always thought you were, anyway."

I shrug.

"All this time, after every bad date, you've talked about missing him, despite his flaws, or because of them. I don't know. He's your whole life," she says.

"Was," I remind her. "He left."

"He's back."

"He left me for Judith."

"You know that's not true. You were tailing him. He was getting back at you. Served you right, didn't it? So give him another chance. The guy at the grocery store can wait."

I don't like the way she says 'the guy,' especially since she knows his name perfectly well, but I don't call her on it. She says, "Think about it, Alex."

I pick up the rake, and begin to draw my own designs. Kate watches as I draw a series of hearts. She seems to be waiting for me to tell her more, to tell her something else. "Did your rooftop Romeo stay over afterward?"

"No, he had to go back home and get ready for work. But we're getting together tomorrow night. He's taking me to a play at his theater."

I stay quiet for a moment, and then I look at her. "So the real question, the twenty-thousand-dollar question is this: You don't know his name yet, do you, Kate?"

My best friend blushes becomingly and shakes her head.

*****

"I have to tell you something," I say to Connor.

"I've heard this before," he says.

"I'm serious."

He waits, looking at me.

"I wasn't all together honest with you before either. Not as honest as I should have been, anyway."

He continues staring at me. He's waiting to hear what I have to say, but I don't really want to say it.

"I didn't lie," I say, defending my honor out of habit more than anything else. Why can't I be completely honest? With anyone? With myself.

"Tell me," he says. "Just spill it."

"My ex really was gone, but I might not have been totally over him."

"And you're telling me that now because..."

"Because he's back."

"And you want to see him?"

I lower my head. Will he understand? Sure he will. We're alike, Connor and me. We don't have to spell things out for each other.

"You did see him," Connor says, putting it all together. He takes my silence for what it is—pathetic affirmative.

"We don't have any commitment," Connor says, the words taking on a different meaning since the last time he said them.

"No," I say.

Connor's hand reaches out and holds mine. His skin is warm. His touch sends a shiver through me. "Do you love him?"

Now I look at him, meet his gaze. It's a fair question. "I don't think so."

Clearly, it's not the answer he wants to hear. Connor stands up. He pulls his heavy black leather jacket from the back of the chair. He stares at my camera bag for a moment with a look that is so menacing I almost reach out to protect it. He'd crush the Nikon to pieces if he could, wouldn't he? Grind it into dust with the heel of his heavy work boots.

Then he bends down to me and kisses me once on the lips. Lightly, not lingering, but reminding me of what it is like to be with him.

"Call me when you know for sure," he says. He amends it. "Or, if you don't call me, then I guess I'll know for sure."

I watch him leave.

Then I close my eyes.

*****

Justin arrives with a six-pack in one hand and a single red rose in the other. This peace offering should make me feel something, right? Instead, I wonder whether he stole the rose from someone's garden. Who brings a solitary flower to a girlfriend's house?

"I'm painting," I tell him.

"I know. I'll help."

He helps by sitting himself on my drop cloth and opening the first beer. I ignore him and continue to paint my skyscraper. The buildings are already outlined in black. I shake the red can and begin to fill in one of the outlines.

"The fumes are massive," Justin says, waving a hand in front of his face.

"I told you I was painting," I remind him.

"That's right," he says, drinking the beer in several gulps and cracking open the second. "You did."

I continue with the red until that building is done. Then I reach for the blue. A long time ago, my best friend in high school and I discovered that blue spray paint does something weird to the insides of your nose. If you sneeze after you've used it, you sneeze blue. The residue lasts for days, and it can be very disconcerting if you forget what's going on. Suddenly, your tissues are cobalt and you think you've developed some rare autoimmune disease, and then it all floods back to you. But I don't care. I want a blue building next to the red one.

Such is the suffering for art.

When the phone rings, I hear Kate tell the person on the other end of the line that I'm busy. Justin doesn't even look up.

Apparently, he doesn't think the phone could either be for me, or be from someone important. He simply drinks in silence for another beer and a half. Then he lines up the three empty bottles and attempts to bowl them over with an orange. He does this until I think I may have to kill him. Barely controlling myself, I say, "You know what? I'm just not really in the mood for company tonight."

Justin pouts. "You could have told me that before I drove over here from Venice."

"Didn't I?"

I stare at him, wondering if he can see the blue up my nose. He pouts for another moment, then reaches forward, to tickle me. That used to work. A long time ago, back when we were different people. But nothing's the same anymore.

Was he doing Judith? *Wasn't* he?

Was I crazy for following him? *Wasn't* I?

Suddenly, I wonder if Kate was playing devil's advocate again. She likes Connor, and she called him 'the guy.' Was she testing me? Am I so lame that I really need testing?

I pick up a can of spray paint and he backs off. I instantly picture him sprayed gold all over, like the dead girl in *Goldfinger*. Maybe something in my eyes shows him what I'm thinking. He collects his remaining two beers and leaves, not saying that he'll call or that he'll see me.

But I don't care.

I test myself. I think about it.

Really, I don't care at all.

✳✳✳✳✳

Hal interrupts before I can figure out exactly what Justin wants me to say. "Excuse me," Hal says. "I know this is you." He looks at Justin. "Can you tell me something about the picture. I'd like to include other people's words about Alex's work."

"Which picture?" Justin asks.

"That photo?" the journalist wants to know. He's trying to get us to paint a deeper picture for him--to set a place and a time and give the photo a real meaning.

I tilt my head as I stare at it. Picture of Justin, sunglasses down, head leaning forward. A picture of a kiss about to happen. Last kiss. I wait to hear what Justin will say, but he looks down at the ground, unwilling to speak.

"Hard to describe," I say, and when he looks at me and nods, I know that we can leave it at that.

Hal moves off again, and it's Justin and me. And Kate in the corner watching.

"You didn't," I say.

He shakes his head.

"But I don't understand. Why would she?"

"You know Kate," he says, and I swallow hard and try to think of something to say to that. I see her shaking her head as she makes her way out the door of the gallery. Yeah, I guess I do know Kate. I guess so. Always out for the next conquest. But there are still things that I don't understand. Why did she move me in with her? Did she want to turn me into someone like her?

Before I can ask him any questions, Justin leaves, too, one beat behind her.

Kate and Justin? Why would she have wanted me to stay with him, then? Why would she have tried so hard to be my friend? Strictly out of a guilty conscience? Too many whys and not enough answers. I go over to Hal and tell him it's time to finish the story, because at least now I understand the ending.

CHAPTER THIRTY

At midnight, I go to the grocery store. Connor is still hard at work, stacking perfectly round cantaloupes into green-tinted pyramids. I imagine taking a photograph, a close-up of the melons, and I think that when I someday do capture the image, the picture will be deeply erotic. The roundness of the melons. The rough texture of their skin. Two sensations like that together are what I look for. The two intentionally opposing textures melding in one single way. But for now I turn off the artist in my head, focusing instead on Connor.

When Connor sees me, he doesn't say a word. He simply pulls out a sharp red-handled pocketknife and cuts open one ripe melon, slicing a wedge of the dripping fruit and holding it out to me. I eat the sweet melon flesh from his hand, like a tame animal, and then lick my lips and stare directly into his eyes. They're gold-flecked. Under the fluorescent light, they shine.

"Thought you had a date tonight," he says, looking down at me. "That's what Kate said anyway."

So that's who called, I think, and I find myself warming up inside. *He called me.* All I do is shake my head. "She got it wrong." I bite my lip, reconsidering the statement. It wasn't Kate who messed up. This isn't her life. "Or *I* got it wrong," I say, taking the blame, as it's deserved. "But I think that I have it right now."

"So you're free?"

I nod. So free.

"Got your camera?"

"Yeah." I pat my black bag and nod again.

"Let me go punch out and I'll be right with you."

I sit outside on the edge of the concrete wall, waiting for him. The full moon fills the parking lot with a white dreamy light, making the ribbons of pearly paint between parking spaces seem to glow.

As soon as Connor steps through the automatic doors, I snap his picture. The bars of fluorescent lights behind him turn the shot into a silhouette. He is a dark figure moving gently through a halo of light.

Connor comes toward me, takes the camera out of my hands and kisses me. He kisses me hard, until my lips feel bruised. Kissing like that has my body alive and humming in a second. I want him to spread me out right where we are, in the center of the city, in the midst of a parking lot. Connor keeps kissing me until I forget who I am and what my name is.

"Alexandra," he says, reminding me. "I missed you. God, you know it? I missed you. I called, even though I said I wouldn't. I drove by and saw his Harley outside, and I almost came up there after you. Crazy, isn't it? That's not the type of guy I am. But you know—" He lowers his head, and his hair falls into his eyes, and I brush his hair away as I finish the statement for him.

"I had to come to the realization myself," I say. "I had to be sure."

Smiling, he nods to my camera, which is friend now rather than foe. He grins at me, as I reach my arm out in front of us and shoot a picture of the two of us together, cheek-to-cheek.

*****

"That's your boyfriend?" the man from the Times wants to know. I think Hal's pointing to the photo. In fact, I'm sure of it. Until I see Connor walking through the doors, that familiar smile on his chiseled face, and I sigh and set down my glass of champagne and I go into his arms.

"Picture?" the photographer for the Times wants to know. She's got her camera up, and I gaze at Connor as he nods. But then I reach into my own satchel and I hand her my camera instead.

"Here, use this," I say, and I watch her let her own camera dangle on the strap around her neck. She focuses mine and aims. I know what the photo is going to look like the second she snaps the picture. It's going to be perfect. I'm going to develop that one as soon as I get home. As soon as we get home.

Heck, I might even have it framed.

*****

Then later, on the fire escape, Connor takes me from behind. He has me put my hands on the cool iron railing, has me stare out at the lights of the city, twinkling like a fairy city before us. Yes, it's like my fantasies. But it's better because this is real. Connor lines his body up with mine, not entering me, not kissing me, just letting me feel his warmth against my skin. I couldn't have asked for a better sensation. It makes me more aroused than anything I'd thought of, anything I'd ever done.

Just his body pressed to mine—that's all I need. Because his body tells me stories, makes me promises. If you trust yourself, his body seems to say, then everything you want will come true. If you let yourself go and stop playing games, then I can make magic with you.

My silence is all he needs. No questions, no preparation, no guessing what is to come. Connor runs his hands along my arms and his touch sends a shiver through me. He cradles my breasts in his hands as gently as if he were holding two ripe pieces of fruit, then brushes my nipples with his thumbs. It creates a yearning inside me that is like a fire burning. I can picture it in my mind, flames of orange and gold licking up and down beneath my skin. Still, I keep my tongue, don't beg him, don't tell him what I want. This is Connor's time to teach me, and I play the good pupil and remain silent.

Connor works his fingertips down my sides to my waist, and grips me here. He holds me steady, and he slowly brings his sex against me. Slips it between my thighs and presses forward, working me with just the tip. The sensation is delicious, dreamy, and it makes me realize what I've been missing.

His fingers grip into me, and I like that. His body, his hard chest, presses into my back, and I like that, too. Will there ever be something that he could do that I won't like?

I don't think so.

*****

Stories are supposed to have proper endings. You know you're there when the print on the page runs out. But pictures go on forever. Pictures, like the ones of Kate—and now I know that they were of Kate—they live and live and live.

But I think that I've been too caught up in pictures to enjoy the real world around me. It's time to set my camera aside and figure out what it's like to be in a three dimensional world. What it's like to be with Connor. What it's like to be with me.

Blue Valentine? Or, more realistically, a black-and-white one? I've learned that the world is multicolored. Multi-textured. Things aren't as clear and clean as they seem. So maybe now that I understand all the pieces I can set my camera down for a while now and learn to be comfortable in the frame instead of always hiding behind the lens.